Miss TAVISTOCK'S MISTAKE

The Brides of Mayfair
Book One

LINORE ROSE BURKARD

LILLIPUT PRESS

OHIO

MISS TAVISTOCK'S MISTAKE
Copyright © 2020 by Linore Rose Burkard
Published by LILLIPUT PRESS
OHIO 45068
www.LilliputPressllc.com

Publishers Cataloging-in-Publication Data
Name: Burkard, Linore Rose, author
Title: miss tavistock's mistake / by Linore Rose Burkard
Description: 1st edition
Summary: A young woman's impulsive subterfuge becomes a growing problem for her budding romance in Regency England.

Identifiers: Library of Congress Control Number: 2020907241
ISBN : 978-1-7333111-2-0 (print) / ISBN: 978-1-7333111-4-4 (ebook) /
Subjects: 1. Fiction—Romance, Historical, Regency 2.Fiction—Romance, Comedic

Printed in the United States of America

Back of Book
Special Features

- Background History: The Fête at Carlton House

- Excerpt, *Miss Fanshawe's Fortune*, Book Two of The Brides of Mayfair

- Other books by Linore Rose Burkard

- Reader's Regency Glossary

Truth be veiled, but still it burneth;
Love repulsed—but it returneth.
Percy Bysshe Shelley

What Readers Are Saying

"Burkard, the author of *Forever, Lately* (2019) offers a humorous romp about misunderstanding and forgiveness amid the blindness of love….A delightful and comedic story that will certainly please historical fiction aficionados and those who enjoy wholesome, romantic stories."
KIRKUS REVIEWS

"Light, witty regency romance..an uproarious case of mistaken identity..endearing characterization…Readers will gleefully follow the heroine as her hilarious subterfuge gets her in deepening trouble while she finds herself unexpectedly falling in love."
BOOKLIFE PRIZE

"A witty, swoony Regency romp!...I was laughing out loud in places."
JILL HART, ReedsyDiscovery, VINE VOICE

"What a fun story! I couldn't put it down!"
MARYLU TYNDALL, Award-winning Author, *The Reckoning*

"I was pleasantly surprised by this novel…I was expecting intro→sex→sex→interlude→more sex. However, this was pure romance, with an understandable and even reasonable plot!"
SAMANTHA ETTINGER, SamIAmReadingandReviewing Blog

"For clean Regency romance, you cannot go wrong with a Linore Burkard book."
LAURA DAVIS, InterviewsandReviews.com

"A Deceptively Pure Delight!"
BECKY LEWIS, VINE VOICE

"A joy to read! Linore's superior command of Regency vernacular and the period are just exhilarating! She had fun writing this and it shows."
L.K. SIMONDS, Author, *All In*

"Jane Austen herself would likely enjoy this clean romance!"
KATHLEEN ROUSER, *The Great Lakes Lighthouse Brides Collection*

"A lot of research has gone into the period detail in this novel which I found fascinating…naval battles and life at sea, the wonderful variety of food and the colourful slang words and expressions."
ROSIE AMBER'S BOOK REVIEW TEAM (Sandra)

"I'm a big fan of Georgette Heyer's Regency romances, and this stands up nicely alongside them…I would give this ten stars if I could!"
JULIANA DEERING, Author, *The Drew Fathering Mysteries*

"The Jane-esque language in this novel is exquisite…(and) like a runaway horse, the plot picks up speed, hurtling along!"
JANICE L. DICK, Author, *The Road to Happenstance*

Burkard has a deft way of helping the reader immerse themselves in the genre's conventions…Almacks, balls, and curricle rides.The scenes are also fairly fast paced and entertaining, and there is some intrigue and villainy to keep the plot moving forward.
REGENCY READER BLOG, Regrom.com.

"Delightful Regency romance…a la Georgette Heyer!"
MARLENE HENTSCHEL, GoodReads Reviewer

PROLOGUE

1801, Yorkshire

Numerous gentlemen stood about the vast parlour at Toadingham, the Duke of Trent's ancient seat in Blythewold of the Yorkshire dales, speaking in muted but jovial tones. Only two of those present seemed sensible of the recent tragedy which had occasioned the gathering. One was the duke, for his sister and her husband had died in a coaching accident. The other, Miss Feodora Margaret Tavistock, "Feenie,"only nine years old and fresh from America, was sitting on a bench on the side of the room: frowning, lonely, clutching a frozen-eyed porcelain doll, and trying not to cry. The dead were her parents, though it was her father's loss only that she grieved, the father who had reconciled across an ocean with his estranged wife only to die right along with her a mere three days after arriving by ship with Feodora.

She had two living relations in England who might care for her, two uncles, the brothers of her mother. But only one, the duke, volunteered to do so. In his late forties, a quiet, perpetually uncomfortable looking man, he seemed as bewildered as the young orphan.

Chatting solicitors, looking important in their grey topcoats, nondescript pantaloons, and voluminous cravats, helped themselves to snuff from little porcelain or gilded cases whipped from waistcoats and returned in practiced gestures that took mere seconds. Feodora noticed this not, as her entire attention was directed inwards, where tears were suppressed but fighting to come forth. She'd been scolded by her uncle's servants enough to know better than to let them out. Even now, a grim-faced housekeeper by name of Mrs. Pudding—a name which might have made Feenie laugh under other circumstances—kept a sharp eye upon her, standing silently against the far wall.

Feodora huddled with her arms tightly about her little doll. The world had come to an end. With Papa gone, how could life continue? The memory of the carriage overturning, and the sight of him, so still and lifeless, haunted her. The sight of her mother was disturbing too, but she'd only just been reacquainted with that lady. Her father had taken her off to America when she was a mere infant for reasons unknown to her. But now he was gone. She would never, ever recover. She would never laugh or be happy. She wanted to die and join Papa in heaven. He must be in heaven, of course. She wished to be there, too, not in England, not in her uncle's home. Much better if she could return to America and live with her old nurse, Persippany, who had cried buckets at her leaving. That world was lost to her now.

After the carriage had overturned the previous night, only miles from the duke's residence, the next thing Feenie remembered was being handled roughly. Grim countenances of unfamiliar faces staring hard at her...the housekeeper's stern, frightening expression. She'd grabbed hold of Feodora and carted her kicking and screaming, to a small room, where she was told to stop her hysterics or she'd sleep there alone in the dark. The memory shook a fresh small sob from deep within her.

Mrs. Pudding was there in a moment and whisked Feenie in one stout arm against her side as she scurried from the room with her. "I might have known it!" she huffed, setting the girl on her feet after progressing down a carpeted hall for some distance. She opened a door and roughly pushed the girl in before closing it behind them. Swiftly she crossed the room, grabbed a switch from near the fireplace and came menacingly toward Feodora, who sobbed louder. Papa had never given her the switch! Mrs. Pudding wore a sour expression, and came at her with an arm raised. "Shush your 'owling this instant!" She bent over as if to strike, but at just that moment the door opened.

A young man's face, filled with consternation, peered inside and was followed in an instant by the rest of him; a tall, well-dressed frame, with an elegant cravat and a bearing equal to the station of an earl's second son. Glaring at Mrs. Pudding, who instantly straightened and hid the switch behind an ample posterior, he stepped in and came toward Feenie and stood between her and the servant. His expression of righteous indignation, coupled with blazing eyes, surely conveyed to that lady the distinct impression that her penal actions had best cease.

She frowned at him. The Hon. Mr.Rempeare was only a lad, not more than fourteen or fifteen; a boy of the quality and a nephew of her master's but still a lad. She put her hands on her hips, inadvertently revealing the switch.

The young man grabbed it and shook it in the servant's face. "Leave this room!" he ordered, "or I'll teach you how it feels at the end of this." He spoke as one who held no doubt that he would be obeyed. Mrs. Pudding opened her mouth—she would argue—but his presence, young as he was, impressed her, and she said only, "But sir, she must keep silent in company!"

"I heard nothing from her," he said, imperiously. "And has she not suffered the loss of her parents? Only last night? Young as she is?"

The housekeeper nodded stiffly. "Aye." Quickly she added this torrent: "But it don't make it right that she should scream like kingdom come and all bedlam loose, like she done last night!"

"Perhaps, in her mind, it is," he answered, and turning, opened the door while eying her in such a way that she exited with a great frown. Feodora was left with the tall lad who turned and surveyed her. He smiled and bowed. "We are cousins, my dear," he said brightly. "Gabriel Rempeare, at your service." She regarded him, blinking. Her tears ceased. He pulled a handkerchief from his waistcoat pocket and said, "There, now. The old battleax shan't harm you. I'll see to that." She took the handkerchief and blew her nose and looked up at him with instant and ardent adoration.

Young Master Rempeare looked over his little American cousin. She had an abundance of curly orange locks...a liberal sprinkling of freckles...was painfully skinny. Hysterics did nothing to improve matters, for her nose and cheeks were bright red. Looking rather miserable, she clung to a porcelain doll with a ferocity that made him examine it as if to determine whether it was bejewelled. While she sniffed and stared, he wondered vaguely how to proceed. He should give her time to settle herself, no doubt.

While considering this, he paced about the room with one hand on his chin. He took a few lunges with the switch to fight off an imaginary Frenchie, but then returned his attention to the forlorn little girl. His compassionate eyes must have made an impression, because when he went toward her with an outstretched hand, she took it easily. He gently led her to a sofa. To his shock, when he sat down beside her, she climbed onto his lap, put her little bony arms around his neck and lay her head on his shoulder. In moments, she was asleep.

Gabriel held his new charge with a dazed expression. He had hoped to come to her aid somehow, but never had he dreamed of it being like this. He decided right then and there that he would champion this new little cousin. Indeed, his dear departed mama had told him about his American cousin, and that when she was of age, he must marry her. Her looks were hardly inspiring, but he was little concerned about that. He was soon to enter His Majesty's Navy and his mind was filled with images of ships and ocean swells and sword fighting and honour.

His father, the fifth Earl Stafford, had remonstrated all the way to Toadingham that his brother the duke was a fool to take the child. Looking down at the homely drawn little face, Gabriel was glad he had. He would let her sleep for as long as she liked. For as long as they were left alone in peace.

CHAPTER ONE

Ten years later
1811, Yorkshire

"Mrs. Filbert! Only guess what I have learned from my uncle!" Miss Tavistock, the nineteen-year-old orphaned ward of the Duke of Trent, rushed across the great library at Toadingham to where her companion, Mrs. Filbert, lay settled upon a settee amongst layers of pillows and blankets near the fire, sniffling and sneezing. Mrs. Filbert was laid up in the library where her ague bothered no one else in the household but where she could take comfort in books during her affliction.

Margaret—for Miss Tavistock detested the name Feodora and went by her second name now—held a letter in her slim hands as she arrived before the companion, her strawberry-blonde curls bouncing and her gown still swishing against legs that had moved far more quickly than was usual for a genteel young lady. Her cheeks, bright with excitement, were outshone only by the shimmering sea green of her eyes. She hovered, breathless, before the settee with its profusion of blankets, uncertain where the boundaries of the middle-aged Mrs. Filbert ended.

"Here, dear," the comfortably plump personage said, patting a spot on the blankets. "Only do not stay close, lest this dreadful ague passes to you! *Achoo!*"

"Bless you," said Miss Tavistock absently, depositing herself upon the designated seat. Mrs. Filbert noted the rosy glow upon her face with pleasure. She disapproved of the girl's daily horseback riding, but had to concede that the country air surrounding Toadingham christened her cherubic countenance with an almost absurd vitality and youthful beauty.

"I must tell you!" the cherub exclaimed, settling herself more comfortably while peering at Mrs. Filbert. "Or shall you guess it?"

"Indeed, I am sure I may not, my dear!"

"Very well." Margaret tried in vain to hold back an irrepressible smile. "'Tis regarding my cousin, Captain Rempeare!"

"Indeed!" said the lady appreciatively. Word of the captain, who was betrothed to Margaret by the particular wish of both their now deceased parents, was exceedingly scarce at Toadingham. It was so scarce that Margaret had vowed, on more than one occasion, to break off the nuptials, though it would disappoint the duke and go against the wish of the dearly departed.

"The captain's injury is not as bad as we feared," she said now. "But his ship is beyond repair and has been decommissioned! He is ashore and says he will call upon me!" Margaret's red lips, full and scandalously voluptuous, smiled, her green eyes sparkling.

"Decommissioned?" asked the older lady. "We must thank Providence his injury wasn't worse, if the ship fared so badly." They had learned of the battle and the captain's injury from *The Times* and *The Morning Chronicle*, where Margaret got most all her news of the war against Napoleon and of London's upper class. She clipped and saved every mention of her elusive cousin and his skirmishes at sea. During the Battle at Lissa, the captain valiantly held off and routed a much greater French and Spanish force than what he commanded. Despite the victory, there were casualties and wounded. The captain's sword arm had taken a nasty hit. He was blessed, his letter to the duke said, that he hadn't lost the limb.

"Isn't it wonderful?" Margaret held the letter against her bosom and stared out at the room smiling, appreciating the wonder. She hadn't seen the captain in near a decade, almost since before he entered His Majesty's Navy. But she prayed for him faithfully each night and was mindful of the marriage arrangement, her private journal even littered with the words, "Captain and Mrs. Gabriel Rempeare." She adored the sound of it, and thought it wise to grow accustomed to her future name.

"I dare say he must dislike it," said Mrs. Filbert.

The smile on the rapturous face vanished. "Dislike it?" she asked. "After ten years at sea? I should think he'd be pleased!"

Mrs. Filbert hated to crush excitement in her charge, there was so little in her life, but she said, "It all depends, my love—oh, *achoo!*—excuse me, dearest. This wretched chill!"

"Bless you," responded the girl despondently. "Why do you say it depends—on what?"

"On why he ran off to sea in the first place. Men have a penchant for getting it in their blood, and some never wish for a regular life on land again. The sea takes hold of a man in strange ways, you know."

"Pooh!" said the young miss unromantically. "He went to sea to escape his overbearing father, or so says the duke. A father who is no longer with us. And if my cousin wished to remain at sea, then he would not have got himself injured and his ship decommissioned."

"Why, my love! How can you say so! When he was fighting a war!"

"Well, perhaps he had enough of war. *I* certainly have!" Miss Tavistock looked at the ceiling in an injured fashion as if she herself had suffered hardships from the French blockade.

"But, my dear, how fortunate we are here in Yorkshire, situated near the coast where smugglers' ships get through aplenty. We never lack sugar, tea, French silks, or lace. In London, such contraband costs a pretty penny!"

Margaret nodded, looking unconvinced. Smoothing the fold of her gown, trimmed at the bust along the front centre skirt with prohibited French lace, she said, "I own I want for nothing. My uncle is too generous by halves!"

Mrs. Filbert nodded. "The cross you bear is a want of happy society. What should be part and parcel of the life of a duke's ward is sadly absent in this wild country! If His Grace were not *such* a recluse—"

"He doesn't snivel at surrounding me with servants, the best dancing master, or pianoforte instructors!" interrupted Margaret, hoping to cut off the remonstrances against her uncle that she knew from long acquaintance with her companion, were about to erupt.

"I dare say you've seen little in the way of company *except* for governesses and servants."

"Do not forget Sir Thomas—"

"Who is now departed, God rest him, and whose two sons were ever seldom in residence! I never met a man more determined to avoid his own offspring! What you wanted all along was female acquaintance."

"But his amiable wife, Lady Frances—"

"Another recluse!" broke in the elder lady.

Margaret looked bereft. "They say Sir Thomas kept her almost under lock and key. But on the occasion we met, she never uttered a complaint against him."

"A baronet's wife—under lock and key? I cannot credit it." Mrs. Filbert further pressed her point by nodding severely at Margaret. "I hate to speak against my betters, you know 'tis true, but she is no doubt that simpering sort of woman, a church mouse, not at all the thing for good conversation or company." She pointed a finger. "And she supplied no daughters for your acquaintance."

"A grave failing, indeed," said Margaret, suppressing a smile, and with a sideways glance at Mrs. Filbert. Playfully, she added, "But my uncle has been only magnanimous: why, the moment I thought to ask for a companion, he gave me *you!*"

Mrs. Filbert smiled, but her company was not at all the same as being in polite society. Little wonder Margaret had accepted Mrs. Filbert for a companion when a more worldly-wise young miss might have insisted on one closer to her own age. Mrs. Filbert was five years widowed and just approaching her fiftieth year when she arrived from London in answer to the advertisement. To her concern, she'd been taken straight to the duke himself, when usually a housekeeper conducted interviews. But His Grace, a bespectacled, mild-spoken grey-haired man not much older than herself, had approved her for the situation faster than she thought possible, almost faster than she thought respectable.

There were questions that hadn't been asked. She knew next to nothing about the girl she was to provide chaperonage for, and usually, the much-pampered young woman would come and inspect her and finally give her reluctant agreement—if Mrs. Filbert was lucky—or whimper that she was too old (in her very presence) and send her off. Miss Tavistock had shown neither hide nor hair, yet Mrs. Filbert had been escorted by a footman to a bedchamber, which had apparently been designated for her by that young woman previous to her arrival.

Mrs. Filbert was positively suspicious. Did the young miss have a terrible deficiency? Was she mentally impaired? Ugly and awkward? There had to be some reason why the young lady had not required an interview, and her mind could furnish only those which seemed macabre.

All her fears were laid to rest when Miss Tavistock, unbidden, came to bestow a curious welcome to the new addition to the household. A firm rap on the door. "May I come in?" said a clear voice. "It is Miss Tavistock." The door opened to reveal a slim young woman who crossed the portal and swept into the room with pointed elegance. Mrs. Filbert's heart sank, for such a poised beauty would never desire an old widow for a companion, she was sure. At a loss for words, and finding herself under the scrutiny of a pair of wide-open, sea-green eyes, she uttered hastily, "Your uncle sent you, no doubt?"

"The duke?" she asked, smiling prettily. "No, indeed! I heard from the servants you'd arrived." Only later would Mrs. Filbert discover that His Grace rarely spoke a word that wasn't strictly necessary, which explained the hasty interview.

Miss Tavistock sat upon the bed, still looking curiously at Mrs. Filbert. Her lovely reddish blonde hair, more blonde than red, fell in tight little ringlets about her head, and her dress was of the latest fashion. Mrs. Filbert was to learn that all of Miss Tavistock's stylishness came from a steady subscription to fashion magazines and journals. And that the poor child had never in her life attended a ball or concert outside of the small village beyond the Hall, except once, at the estate of the captain's father, her other uncle.

"I was hoping," the young woman said quietly, not lowering her eyes, "that you would be younger." Quickly she added, "I beg you'll pardon my saying so. I can be frightfully rude, I'm afraid, for I speak my mind."

"Not at all, my dear," Mrs. Filbert said warmly. Unlike the spoiled young chits who criticised her as if she weren't present, this lovely girl had apologised for an honest appraisal. "I should think you *would* want a younger companion," she added sympathetically. She was careful not to show her disappointment; for only two minutes in this young lady's presence had made her feel certain she would have liked to stay. But she couldn't blame Miss Tavistock for wanting younger blood for company.

"But that's that!" her new charge exclaimed, surprising her not a little. "I'm sure we'll get on famously."

The older woman blinked in surprise. "Do you mean you don't wish for me to leave?"

"Leave?" she asked innocently. "*Fire and brimstone*, pray do not!" The cry was heartfelt. The young miss looked thoughtfully at Mrs. Filbert's much-worn apparel, adding, "I dare say you need this appointment." Her frank eyes rose to meet Mrs. Filbert's. "And I am in need of company. All the gentry in these parts have gone off to London: the Season, you know." She swallowed and looked suddenly sad.

"Have you had a debut—" Mrs. Filbert started to ask. Margaret said, "I couldn't bear to ask the duke; he wouldn't abide setting up an establishment in London. He loathes society, you must know."

Mrs. Filbert nodded, for the duke was a famous recluse. "But surely there are other ways. He needn't go himself."

Miss Tavistock eyed her hopefully. "Do you indeed think so? We must discuss this further!" But she had the good breeding to check her curiosity, saying, "After you've settled in and rested. You've obviously travelled from some distance." The young eyes had appraised the signs of a weary traveller correctly. "From where?" she enquired. "You look to have been on the road for days."

Mrs. Filbert could not feel reproachful at this description for it was true. "From London," she said, and was instantly glad to have come from that place, for the young lady's eyes lit up.

"London? Famous! You will tell me about it?"

"Of course, my dear, whatever I can." The eagerness in her new charge's eyes eloquently bespoke the years of loneliness the girl had suffered. The young woman rose.

"Dinner is served at six—early by London standards, is it not?"

"Yes, eight or nine is customary there."

Margaret's eyes glittered for having known this much of London styles, and Mrs. Filbert's heart warmed again.

All that was nearly two years ago, now. Since then, a great affection had sprung up between the two. Mrs. Filbert was grateful for being treated nearly as an equal (though she made sure never to forget she was a hired companion) and the motherless Margaret was blessed by the company and care of an older woman who had witnessed much of life and London.

The duke kept largely to himself. If he felt badly for not providing the girl with society, he made up for it by giving her all the niceties and fripperies any female could want. The only thing he denied his niece was the thing he could not countenance for himself—society. Margaret had bloomed beneath his lackadaisical care; but was lonely.

She felt sure the captain would have called upon them during shore leaves if only His Grace wasn't averse to company. When she enquired about her cousin's absence, the duke said that seamen often preferred to take their leave on foreign soils where adventure and excitement lay. Margaret tried hard not to believe that exotic women went along with that excitement. She might have succeeded, too, if not for Roderick.

The Honourable Roderick Rempeare, eternal student at Cambridge, was the captain's younger brother. He did not come often to

Toadingham—usually only for Michaelmas term break and Christmas—but when there, he had nothing good to say of the captain. With his perpetually disdainful eye, he would say things like, "My brother ever did lack common sentiment such as would encourage him to write you, Feodora. You should scarcely be surprised at it. I wonder you haven't called off the arrangement: don't want to enter the parson's mousetrap to regret it, eh?"

"Fire and brimstone, Roddy! Have I not asked you for this age to please call me Margaret?" As usual he ignored this plea, merely looking down his Cambridge nose at her. Roderick claimed to be a poet. Or so he said this year, though last year he had been intent upon mastering the study of anatomy, and the year before, it was antiquities and archaeology that fascinated him. Margaret had long admired his scholarship, except her whole conception of Roderick had changed at Christmas when he recited his most recent creation, a poem entitled "Poetical."

I've no sense o' the highly poetical
But if I may be theoretical
For only a minute—
I'll put a rhyme in it—
And end with a good parenthetical.

She'd been doubtful of his talent ever since.

"Does his letter say when he will call upon you?" asked Mrs. Filbert, dragging her mind back to the present.

Margaret had no need to scan the note. "In exactly a fortnight." She shook her head to assure herself it was all quite real. Her future husband—coming at last! Her eyes grew far away. "I remember him quite well, you know. He had striking eyes, dark curly hair, and was very tall. He seemed quite elegant," she said with a giggle. But her look turned more serious. "He rescued me once."

"Rescued you?" Mrs. Filbert was faintly amazed, never having heard of this rescue. She pictured a damsel in distress, the captain valiantly drawing a sword to defend her....

"From Mrs. Pudding," Margaret added. "Who was housekeeper. She's long gone now, of course."

Mrs. Filbert wiped her brow.

Margaret continued, "I was a child then, but he seemed a proper hero to me, I assure you." She smiled. "He was only a boy, I suppose, but so tall and...and I thought, manly, at the time. And those eyes."

"You said they were striking?" asked Mrs. Filbert.

"Upon my word, yes. I even bestowed on them a space in my diary, describing them thus"—and here she stood and struck a pose like that of an actor reciting lines—"a pair of iridescent opals, only darker." She curtseyed to an imaginary audience and resumed her seat.

"We shall see if his eyes are still iridescent opals," said Mrs. Filbert with a fond smile.

"Say nothing of that description, if you please," Margaret said quickly, blushing. "I dare say a decade in His Majesty's Navy must change a man."

Mrs. Filbert was about to opine that seafaring men might change in many aspects, indeed, but that eye colour was not likely to be one of them. But Margaret let out a heartfelt sigh. "I am sure when he comes he will explain why he wrote so seldom," she said in a tone that conveyed she was anything but sure.

Mrs. Filbert made a clucking sound with her tongue. "I should say! Hardly a letter per annum! For a near decade!"

Margaret coloured but said, "Not all men take well to the pen, you know."

"Only those with half a brain," murmured the lady.

"You are determined to dislike him."

"You are determined to protect him."

Margaret paused and gave an impish smile. "I am determined only to *marry* him," she said with a happy sigh. "It was my parents' wish; it was his mother's wish, and I have no other prospect, as you well know."

"You could have enormous prospects if you allow me to chaperon you in London." All of Mrs. Filbert's encouragement had so far failed to move Margaret to approach the duke for permission for a Season.

"But the marriage is arranged, recollect. And in any case, the captain will end my days of solitude. You'll see."

Margaret bustled about, glowing with the added responsibility of getting the ancient house sparklingly in order. For herself, visits to the mantua maker, urgent orders to London merchants, and a thorough examination of the latest styles as put forth in *La Belle Assemblée* and other fashion magazines, were all necessary before she felt herself ready to receive her guest.

The morning of the arrival dawned. The house shone at its best.

A disconcerting notice in the morning *Times* gave the ladies pause, for it said in the society column that Captain Rempeare, though new to Town and already sought after as a war hero, was busy setting up an establishment in a townhouse in Mayfair. Margaret maintained it wouldn't postpone his visit. And then the letter arrived, not even a letter, but so brief as to have been a dictated message

"Visit postponed indefinitely. Deepest regrets. Captain Rempeare."

"Insufferable!" said Margaret of her cousin's abrupt change of plan. Holding out the message in one slim hand, injury in her eyes, she cried, "He fails even to furnish a reason for such rudeness! Nor is the letter sealed with his signet; he no doubt employed a footman to write and post it!"

Even Mrs. Filbert could not think why a gentleman could not take the time to send a polite apology, especially when it was he who had extended the invitation to himself, in effect, to begin with. Over the next few days, the morning papers enlightened them. That the captain had remained in London was clear. That he was an admired and popular dinner guest was equally clear. That he had sent nothing further in the way of excuse or apology, was unforgivable. After reading the most prominent news and reports in the *Times*, Margaret turned blithely to the morning *Herald,* scanned its contents—and froze. With an agonised look at Mrs. Filbert, she returned her gaze to the paper, horrified.

"My dear!" cried the companion. "Is it the captain?"

Margaret wordlessly passed the newspaper to Mrs. Filbert. "In the left column," she said, woodenly. Mrs. Filbert scanned the place on the page to where it said:

From a reliable source: the reclusive Duke of T. is said to have a liaison, a beautiful and mysterious "Lady X." The pair are said to meet secretly at Toadingham. This coincides with another report which may interest our readers, of the duke's nephew, our own newly famous war hero, one Captain R., who has been seen with an avowed lightskirt; reportedly he also may have suffered a fatal loss at the gaming table. The captain is just returned from the

Adriatic where he faced fierce warfare and must be forgiven. But his uncle? We think the duke must be in his dotage to dally with a demi-monde dame.

She placed a hand upon her heart. "My word," and then passed the paper back to Margaret, who stared at the guilty lines, rolled the periodical and then stood and cast it into the fire. A footman cleared his throat. "The duke 'asn't seen it, mum. Shall I run t'town and get 'nother one?"

"You'll do no such thing," Margaret said severely. "The duke has the *Times*, which is enough. Please go, now." To Mrs. Filbert she gave a face that meant she wished to speak to her privately. When the servant closed the door behind him and they were quite alone she cried, "My uncle must never get a whisper of this horrid rumour!"

"Tell the servants to keep the *Herald* from him," agreed Mrs. Filbert. "But the captain, too!" she cried. "Both smeared at once!"

Margaret stared at her. "I have no doubt that 'tis no fustian concerning the captain!" She gave her companion an earnest look. "He is no longer to be considered, Mrs. Filbert. I will free my heart of every thought of him. He is a *wastrel*. As for my uncle—" She cast troubled eyes at the lady. "How could such a thing occur? Who would invent such a flam? And why? The duke is the dearest man in the world and quite harmless. I can think of no enemies… Oh, *why*?" She clasped her hands together and paced the room.

The next day, Roderick surprised them with a visit. Though he did not share the striking eyes or dark good looks of his brother, Margaret thought he meant to look sharp in *Costume Parisien* of striped trousers and delicate-laced pointed shoes. One hand dangled carelessly from a pocket as he entered the room, but his shoes looked faintly baptised in soil, and a scarlet-striped waistcoat peeked out from the lapels of a buff-green jacket showing signs of wear. A voluminous bow on a high cravat, and a tall beaver with a wide rim which he carried in his other hand, completed the outfit. A quizzing glass hung from a fob, somehow looking untidy. There was often something or other hanging about Roderick, Margaret realised, as if defying one to think he took care at the toilette—as though *that* were a danger.

Roderick had last called upon them for Twelfth Night, when he'd stayed a full week. She and Mrs. Filbert sat at cards with him every evening though he protested he played only as a concession to his poor cousin, for he did not expect she could share his more literary pursuits. But if Margaret tried to converse with him upon poetry, her favourite literary pursuit, he would only yawn and smile at her condescendingly. When she reminded him of the duke's prodigious library, filled with all manner of bookish treasures—for His Grace's nod to the outside world was to read voraciously—he feigned a yawn, saying, "I *live* in libraries, coz; you must allow my holiday."

Nevertheless, bereft for months at a time with precious few visitors, Roderick's were always welcome. As she greeted him in the drawing room, hoping to hear he might intend on a long stay, she was assailed by a sudden dread: What if Roddy had seen that dratted newspaper? She waited in mortification lest he mention it, yet she yearned for word of the captain, though he no longer deserved the least notice.

After initial pleasantries, her fear was realised.

"So what of this Lady X?" he asked, as if it were proper conversation for a drawing room.

"Please, sir!" moaned Margaret. "Must I hear that name spoken? You cannot mean to give credence to that monstrous falsehood. It's all fustian, a Banbury tale, I assure you."

"Has the duke made that claim?" he asked, peering with curious eyes over a pair of spectacles which he had recently begun wearing for effect. He felt sure he looked more studious in them.

Margaret gaped at him. "The duke? I would hardly bring that...that nonsensical story to his attention! He would find it utterly mortifying!"

Roderick shrugged, took a snuffbox from a pocket with a studied air and took a pinch. He went into an immediate paroxysm of coughing during which Margaret sat transfixed with consternation, wondering whether she was about to witness the demise of her cousin—due to snuff. She wondered if anyone had ever died taking it and scolded herself for having such a frivolous thought while Roderick choked. When he recovered his colour (for he had turned bright red) she felt vastly relieved.

The young man busily straightened his clothing, his eyes anywhere but on his cousin.

To change the subject and ease his embarrassment, she asked tightly, though she had vowed not to speak of him, "And how is the captain?"

"My brother," said the young man, pulling himself together and then carelessly lounging back on the settee, "since coming ashore finds dissolution to his liking, I'm afraid. The navy did nothing to refine his character," he added, stretching his neck. With closed eyes, leaning back tiredly, he said, "I think, cousin, you must concede that my siblings are utter wastrels." The current Earl Stafford was the eldest Rempeare male and the duke's heir. He was indeed known so well for dissolute living that his presence at Toadingham was long ago prohibited. His Grace, though indulgent in some ways, was not disposed to allow the earl a chance to debauch his "dear gel." The earl therefore was as much a stranger to Margaret as the captain.

Roderick sat up abruptly and stared hard at Margaret. "Consider yourself warned, coz. You saw it in the paper. He's started in the petticoat line."

Mrs. Filbert cleared her throat warningly, for she felt such talk was not fit for properly bred young ladies. Margaret was only too aware of it. "First Lady X and now this. More talk of *demireps*! Can this family be done with mistresses?" she cried, pursing her lips in annoyance.

Roderick merely smiled.

He stayed the night and was off the next day after achieving a private audience with His Grace, a necessary meeting since Roderick was low in the pocket, and everyone knew the duke was swimming in lard. He'd never been snivelling toward his nephews. Mounting the board to a small gig, Roddy turned and delivered these last words to Margaret before rumbling away.

"Remember what I told you about the captain, fair coz! You must find a nice watering hole—Bath, perhaps, or better yet, Brighton—and make a conquest; stop pining in the country for him to come and rescue you."

Margaret stared long at the retreating equipage, her face slowly flushing pink. It hadn't occurred to her, but Roddy was right. She'd been pining and waiting to be rescued. By a man who was finding dissolution to his liking and who had "started in the petticoat line!" It was not to be borne.

"I was *mad* to anticipate the captain's visit with such expectations," she declared to Mrs. Filbert that night as they sat in the evening at their respective needles. They were sewing childbed linen for the parish box, who gave such things to the poor.

"I dare say the captain must be as cold and unfeeling as...as his uncle," said the woman in rallying tones.

"Mrs. Filbert!" Margaret looked across at her companion, deeply shocked.

The green eyes were large, the cheeks perfectly rosy, and Mrs. Filbert thought for the thousandth time that the masterful Mr. Reynolds could capture her just right, if only the duke would think of it. Less attractive girls had their portraits plastered on some great wall; why shouldn't Margaret, a real beauty, not have a grand portrait?

The real beauty was puzzled. "My uncle is not unfeeling; not at heart. Surely, you know that by now."

Mrs. Filbert returned her gaze doubtfully. "If you say so, then I must be mistaken," she murmured, not having the heart to say what she really thought about the duke. That he was shamefully remiss not to have given Margaret a social life, a debut, even a ball in her honour. The youthful face watching hers was so genuine, so emphatic, however, that she held her tongue.

"My dear Mrs. Filbert," Margaret said, as she returned to her sewing. "You cannot bamboozle me. Come, come speak your mind. I shan't be cross, I promise."

The grey-haired woman took her needle, and jabbing it forcefully into the linen, said, "'Tis the way he abandons you to solitude that I cannot countenance. For myself, I could stay happily beside you at Toadingham forever, dearest; believe me." She stopped her work and cast a soulful look at the young miss. "But a coming out is what you need. A Season! After all these years cloistered away in the middle of nowhere!"

Margaret resumed her work with a serious expression. She couldn't help but agree with Mrs. Filbert. She let out a deep sigh. "I suppose my uncle is aware that most females my age do have a Season." Mrs. Filbert did not agree, and Margaret looked up, worriedly. "But he is not like most...men."

"No, indeed!"

"Well, I only mean, he—he is not in touch with—"

"Anything!"

"Anything?" There was a plaintive note in the question.

"I should say not. Holed up in his study like a hare in its den, or disappearing on the estate for hours hunting to hounds, or overseeing his breed horses, or—nobody *knows* to where! He is not thinking of your needs, my love."

"Why, anything I need, anything at all, he has never once denied me."

"Except company. Society. Music. Conversation." Each word landed with the weight of a thousand years' agony to Margaret, who dropped her needle abruptly, jumped up from her little workstation and moved in agitation toward the window. She stood, looking out at the dark night. The moon was just beginning to rise over the fields in the distance, peeking between two small downs.

In a soft tone, she said, "He doesn't deny me these things out of coldness, or lack of feeling." She turned and faced her companion. "'Tis that...he does not wish for society himself and forgets that others may feel differently."

"To be sure!" Mrs. Filbert should not have pressed her point so hard, only she had long thought the duke to be lacking in this respect. The weight of time had hardened her antipathies.

"I maintain you are too strong against him, Mrs. Filbert. I have not approached him about having a coming out."

"Do you deny that you should, above all else, enjoy the Season in London?"

Margaret swirled around to face the window again. Staring out but seeing nothing except her own unhappy face in the dark glass, she said, "I should so enjoy a Season!" She strode back and stood in front of the older woman. "Roddy said just this morning that I should go to Bath, or some such popular place, and stop pining for the captain to rescue me."

Mrs. Filbert smiled. "Did he? I never took that young man to be the brightest thing on two legs—I thought him chuckleheaded—but I think he's hit upon it! A splendid idea!"

Slowly, a light rose in Margaret's eyes. "Do you think, really, 'tis splendid?"

"Above time! You will adore it," said her companion. "But I think London is far superior to Bath for a coming out. Only think—the opera, concerts, Drury Lane, Vauxhall Gardens! *All* the sights!"

Margaret's eyes had come alight with an inner fire. "Yes, all the sights!" she repeated, enraptured at the thought. She sighed. "But surely the Season is half over by now."

Mrs. Filbert surveyed her fondly. "Which means you will be just the thing to raise excitement, for now everyone has grown used to everyone else. A new, unmarried young woman when the Season is half over, I dare say, is better than one at the start, when there are dozens of you."

Margaret bit her lip, smiling. "Do you mean, people will be eager to make my acquaintance?"

"No doubt!"

Margaret's eyes glittered with hope and joy. "Think of it, Mrs. Filbert! Me, in a ballroom amongst acquaintances!" She did a spin on the floor right then and there, and began practising the steps of a popular country reel.

Mrs. Filbert cooed, "You are positively aching to be out, and unless you insist upon breaking my heart, you must promise to inform the duke that you mean to have your debut."

Margaret's face puckered in thought. She stopped dancing and was suddenly blinking back tears. In a near whisper she cried, "I always hoped...for ever so long...that when *he* came back..." She couldn't finish her sentence.

Mrs. Filbert was in the dark for only a moment. "The captain!" she gasped. Her arms were outstretched instantly, and Margaret moved into them, receiving a very maternal hug.

"There, there," the companion said to the slim figure in her arms. "Only why did you think you must wait for your cousin to introduce you to society?"

"He gave his word that he would when I last saw him! It was so long ago, he's probably quite forgotten. But during his last visit, he was a junior lieutenant then, he said that someday, when I was quite grown up, he should take me to London on his arm, and show me the sights and dance with me at every ball and assembly. I've lived upon those words," she said now, blinking back tears. Here the distressed figure blew her nose. Sniffling, she said, "He called me Feenie after hearing my uncle use the term." Shooting a dark glance at Mrs. Filbert she added, "Another reason I detest that name, 'Feodora!'"

Mrs. Filbert nodded understandingly.

"Imagine, if you will, Mrs. Filbert, what it's like to be burdened with such a name!"

"But your second name is very sensible," the companion said heartily.

Margaret stared at her. "Just so! To my endless remorse! To have an outlandish burdensome name, followed by an utterly sensible one—how droll and unromantic it is!"

"Nonsense!" Mrs. Filbert returned to her sewing needle. "Margaret sounds perfectly pretty, and perhaps, even romantic."

Margaret resumed her seat and took up her needle. "I hardly dare to believe that, but Mrs. Filbert, you are a comfort to me."

"I pray that I am, dear."

"Do you think, truly, that we could make a go of it in London? That we could get on? Without a sponsor?"

Strong nods of affirmation were given here so that Mrs. Filbert's head bobbed. "All you need is a proper chaperon, and that, my dear—is me. A companion is the very thing for a chaperon."

"Mightn't people think it ill-advised of me if I were to set up my own establishment?" Margaret continued, with a concerned look on her face.

"A duke's ward? I should say not!"

This comment earned Mrs. Filbert a gratified smile, although she never saw it, being focused on an untidy knot in her work. She never was very good with needlework.

"I grant, however, that you may need to pose that question to your uncle. After all," the companion added gently, "he is the one with the purse strings."

"Yes," Margaret agreed. "But he never denies me. I'm afraid he spoils me, do you not think so?" Mrs. Filbert silently agreed, recalling her own ample wardrobe acquired since coming to Toadingham. The gown she was sporting at the moment, in fact, a fashionable fresh muslin crepe, had been purchased only weeks ago by Margaret. From almost the moment of her arrival, Margaret had insisted upon refurbishing her wardrobe, much to Mrs. Filbert's astonishment. But it was useless to protest. The young woman delighted in outfitting her companion as much as she enjoyed bespeaking her own wardrobe. More than once, Mrs. Filbert had felt like a doll being dressed by a child, but so be it. If she must be the doll, she would be the doll happily. And the duke never gave so much as a murmur of disapproval.

Margaret said, "I'm afraid it will be a shock. To learn I'm interested in a London coming out."

"Nothing he cannot overcome, my dear," said Mrs. Filbert, in what she hoped was a rallying tone.

"I suppose," she said, "we need not contact my cousin on the matter."

Mrs. Filbert's head rose, and she studied her charge. "'Tis the proper thing to do. Certainly any *gentleman* could do no less than help you get settled, and introduce you in society." There was no need to state that whether or not the captain was a gentleman was, in fact, in question. His precipitate failure to appear was still fresh in their thoughts, as were the dual black charges of dissoluteness and consorting with *impures*.

"Speaking of Town, we must have a means of getting about," said the city-wise Mrs. Filbert. "Do you intend to bring your own horses? And what equipage?"

"I warrant London has horses enough to hire," exclaimed the younger. "I shouldn't like to subject mine to the city." There was an amiable silence for a moment, both women's thoughts wandering where they would. Margaret's had not strayed far. "Did you hear about Midnight?"

"Your uncle's newest stallion?"

"He's been a terrible disappointment, I'm afraid."

"Indeed? Why is that?"

"Mr. McCluskey states emphatically that he'll *never sire*."

"Why is that?"

Margaret glanced at her companion. "Impotence," she said sagely.

Mrs. Filbert nearly dropped her sewing. "Do you mean to say your uncle discusses such matters with you?"

Miss Tavistock's laugh was fluid and clear. "I should say not! Mr. McCluskey did."

"Of all the bad taste! I shall speak a word to that man."

Another giggle escaped Margaret as she added, "Not at all. It was only natural that I should be curious. The duke always puts his best males to stud, and we've had him for a year now to no effect."

"Has it been a full year? Well! I pray you not to speak of such a thing in London, my dear." Mrs. Filbert decided a change of subject was in order. "When shall you speak to your uncle about the Season?"

This quieted Margaret considerably. "Tomorrow," was her sober answer. "In fact, I'm quite done up with the thought of it," she added, piling her thread and needle neatly atop the linen. She rose.

"Won't you have tea, my love?" The tea board was due any moment. It was a ritual neither lady missed often.

"I shan't, if you don't mind, Mrs. Filbert," she said. She looked so tired that her companion instantly insisted she get off to bed.

The next day was cold but gloriously sunny. A leisurely morning ride before breakfast struck Margaret as just the thing to start such a day. It would give her time, she reasoned, as she slipped from a simple shift into a clean cotton one and then a pale olive riding habit, to decide precisely what she would say to the duke later. With a beehive hat of cottage straw, and kid half-boots to complete her ensemble, she reached the stables, grabbed a fine whip, and waited while a stable boy prepared Fairweather for her.

She'd ridden him only once before, but he'd been pronounced safe by Mr. McCluskey, and Margaret meant to make him her own. The stable boy rode a mount behind her as usual. She started slowly in a walk, heading for the long drive that led to the road. She often followed the drive before moving into fields and then woods, for she could veer off to visit a tenant if she wished, as the road wound directly past a number of small cottages on the property.

She slapped Fairweather's reins lightly to move into a trot. Before long, cold frosted her face and seeped through her habit, though it was sturdy Georgian cloth. She slowed to a stop and lowered the veil of white lace that twisted around the rim of her hat and then took off again, with a light kick of her heels. Fairweather fairly flew into a canter. She reined the animal in. She hadn't meant to gallop, but he whinnied and picked up more speed.

Margaret cried out, pulling sharply on the reins. Fairweather slowed, but then whinnied, bucked in protest, and reared. The stable boy hastened to come astride and leaning over, grabbed the head lead while uttering a sharp rebuke. With a pounding heart, and at the boy's insistence, Margaret dismounted. The servant offered her his horse, but she refused. "Take them back; I shan't ride."

"It's a long walk, mum." And it was, probably half a mile.

"I love a bracing walk," she said. But she stroked Fairweather's head and murmured to him, "What made you behave so badly, hmmm? What did I do?"

"It warn't you, mum; 'e's an ornery bugger." After many reassurances that she did indeed wish to walk back, the stable boy started off on his mount holding fast to Fairweather's reins in one hand.

With the cold settling upon her, she set off on the return walk. The sound of the horses' hooves faded, and she was left in silence. The sunny sky was giving way to grey as heavy clouds approached from the south, and she quickened her pace. But pleasure in the walk never failed to brighten her spirits as she surveyed the wide avenue with its snow-tipped firs. Dark green limbs peeked out beneath white blankets, and spotted starlings with yellow beaks flitted amongst them, landing here and there like shimmering jewels glinting in the light. It struck her as sad that so few guests came to Toadingham, or ever enjoyed the pretty sight that even the most jaded aristocrat, Margaret felt, would surely have to acknowledge as pleasant.

It was with a feeling close to amazement then, when she heard the sound of a coach behind her and realised a vehicle was approaching. Visitors? At Toadingham? No one was expected. More likely someone had made a wrong turn, or got lost from the nearest turnpike.

Just as Margaret wondered if perhaps she should abandon the road for the safety of the woods, a closed travelling carriage came rumbling past, slowed, and then came to a stop. She had been spotted. Seconds later a postilion jumped off the back, let down the steps, and a naval cocked hat, followed by the figure of a tall man, stepped out and down. Margaret watched curiously, fingering her whip in one hand.

The man surveyed her a moment and bowed. He was ruddy, not unhandsome, surely under thirty, and his blue frock coat with gold buttons, white facings, and epaulettes at the shoulder should have told her instantly who it was, but it wasn't until she got closer that she knew. He had a long lean face, dark hair, and a sea-tanned complexion. His lively eyes, regarding her with interest, held an inner glow, like two opals. She recognised those opals. It was her cousin, her intended, Captain Gabriel Rempeare.

CHAPTER THREE

Until his recent indiscretions, Captain Rempeare had been a near legend to Margaret; partly because of his heroic rescue of her in the past, and partly from his long absence. To find herself looking into his opalescent eyes, so clearly remembered, which now were attached to a quite different face—one that had matured and bore the ruddy lines and colour of sea air and sun, wave and waft of ocean—was almost a shock. She had always thought to be in raptures if he were to visit, to adore his every look and word. But such indiscretions! Jilting her when he should have called, without a word of explanation. And now to be so unfeeling as to descend upon them without warning: both, to her mind, equally fractious. Didn't he know guests must furnish notice? That arrangements must be made, servants apprised, or that young women liked to prepare themselves to be presented to their long-promised husbands?

The London rumours about the captain, his losing a fortune at cards, the long years of hardly a word from him; these, too, swirled tempestuously in Margaret's mind, so when he made a graceful bow and said, "Captain Rempeare, your servant, ma'am"—she revealed not the merest feeling.

"I surmised as much," she said, not warmly, and without offering her own name. Nor did she curtsey but gave only a curt nod. Her sense of fascination at meeting the long lost hero was swallowed up in his list of transgressions. Even his handsome uniform and the beautiful eyes fastened on her in lively curiosity, failed to rouse her better nature.

He raised a brow. "You surmised as much? You know, then, that I am a family relation."

When Margaret said nothing, he glanced at her riding dress. With the hint of a smile he asked, "Have you lost your mount?"

"No," she said, not in the least inclined to explain. Wisps of golden hair had strayed from beneath the straw bonnet during her ride, and high colour in her cheeks made him wonder, but with a glance at Toadingham, he said, "Well, as you are heading to the house, I should be honoured to have the privilege of supplying you transport." He motioned at his carriage.

For a moment Margaret was tempted, but grant him an honour? Indeed, not. She'd gladly freeze walking back, before that. Besides, she needed time to contemplate his astonishing sudden appearance. She moved past him. "Thank you, but I enjoy the walk." She quickened her pace, for she must be alone to think. *Captain Rempeare! Here at Toadingham!* Was she unwise to punish him for his past neglect? He seemed fine and polite, now. It should have pleased her to find him handsome and gentlemanlike, but somehow it added to her vexation. Nevertheless, she was behaving badly. When she reached the house she would receive him properly and give him all due respect. He was, after all, the duke's nephew and her betrothed.

"May I ask who I have the pleasure of addressing?" she heard suddenly from beside her.

Margaret gasped. She hadn't realised he'd kept pace. She turned and saw the carriage slowly following them. "You...you needn't accompany me," she said, flustered.

"If you insist upon walking, I'm afraid I must." He clasped his hands behind his back and looked at her innocently.

"And why, pray, is that?" She fell back into step.

"A gentleman feels obligated to protect a woman alone."

"I am quite safe on the duke's property."

He searched her face, and Margaret felt glad of her light lace veil. The soft clip-clop of the horses behind them was the only sound. "Can it be? Are you...my cousin, Miss Tavistock?" He said it as though it were the most unbelievable thing in the world. Margaret said nothing, while he hurriedly added, "I would not have known you!"

"Do explain your meaning, sir," she said.

"The little cousin of my memory was fetching," he said with a gentle smile, "but in a homely way." A dart hit Margaret's heart, for she had, indeed, been quite unattractive until her womanhood.

"Fetching—*and* homely?" she asked, in an icy tone. "They hardly go hand in hand."

"So homely as to be fetching," he said with a grin. With a faraway look, he added, "I dare say, there never was a creature more freckled, and with such hair—quite red!" He cleared his throat. "I shouldn't have said it, I suppose, but as you are so wonderfully changed—even through that veil I can see—surely, it cannot cause you pain now. I am quite amazed at the...er...*sea change* in your countenance."

Early ugliness had been a heavy blow to a girl with a romantic heart. Before she knew what she was doing she said, with an acid smile, "I am sorry to disappoint, sir, but I am not Miss Tavistock."

His expression dropped. "I beg your pardon. I spoke out of turn. Whom, then, do I have the honour of addressing?"

Margaret turned, frantically trying to decide how to style herself; he didn't deserve to be told the truth. Had he called to begin with when he said he would, he would have known her already. Had he not ignored her for a near decade he might have known her.

"Are you a friend of the family?" he asked.

She gave him a reproachful look, still trying to decide how to answer. But was he truly so dull? Who else could she be except his cousin?

He stroked his chin. "Are you Miss Tavistock's governess? Or companion?"

She looked crushingly at him. A governess! When she had sent away her last governess more than four years since!

He smiled. "I am quite out of conjectures. If you please, whom do I have the honour of addressing?"

Without knowing she was about to say it, the words tripped off her tongue. "Call me Lady X," she said, with her nose in the air. As soon as she'd spoken, her cheeks flushed. *What a plumper!* But surely the captain had no idea of there being such a person, certainly not one supposed to have been the duke's mistress. *The Herald* had a smaller readership than, say, *The Times*, and it must have escaped his notice.

"You?" He stopped. He looked almost injured.

Margaret shuddered inwardly. So he did know of Lady X! She'd been foolish to claim that identity. As such thoughts roiled in her brain, he asked, "Are you not—young—for the duke?"

Margaret swallowed, but pride caused her to reply only, "*He* doesn't think so." His stare of disbelief almost made her laugh and confess all, but instead she hurried forward. At the house she'd explain everything, for she had no thought of maintaining such a gammon. But the captain, with his tall stride, kept pace, and suddenly his presence was plaguing. Why hadn't he sent word of his coming? She'd have been ready to face him, then. She wouldn't have been rushed into telling a bald-faced lie.

"Young for such a profession, then?" he asked, through tight lips.

High nerves made her laugh at this. "You know nothing at all," she said. *What a lark it will be when he discovers the truth!* She had no idea of keeping up her farce, but it was rather fascinating to find that he disapproved of a mistress as much as she and Mrs. Filbert did. Later she'd confess, curtsey prettily, even forgive his past transgressions. They would laugh over this meeting, laugh at her pique and folly, and even at his earlier neglect. That was her plan. Until, with an eye that seemed suddenly grave, he said, "*You* are the reason for my call, my lady—if you are, indeed, to be styled a lady."

Indignation rose afresh in Margaret's breast. He hadn't even called to see *her*, his cousin, his long-promised bride? The girl chosen by his deceased mama? She turned her face away and hurried along. "I, the reason? When it is your cousin and uncle you *ought* to be calling upon?"

She pursed her lips. "Or is your homely cousin not worthy of your condescension?"

"That...that isn't it," he said, frowning. "There were circumstances." His look wavered. "Is she homely still?"

"She is quite the pudding face, if you must know." She felt a wild thrill of abandon, a wicked glee upon saying it. She'd never felt such before. She was misbehaving, but he was so mortifying!

He swallowed and stared towards the house. Looking back at her he said, "That is of no consequence. Be so kind as to accompany me in the coach. There are things I must say to you that should rather be said in a closed carriage than...than, outdoors, or at the house."

"What could possibly require a closed carriage?"

"Madam," he said coldly. "Yorkshire does not escape the notice of London papers. Your object is known: that you mean to bilk an old peer of his fortune."

Margaret stared at him in consternation at such a falsehood. "And you believe such a thing?"

Without answering he said, "Five minutes of your time is all I ask." Again he motioned at the coach. But the house was coming into view with its high-turreted roof and north tower. Margaret put a hand on her hip. "There is no need for your closed carriage." She was about to add, "For I am not Lady X, foolish cousin; I am, of course, Miss Tavistock." But she never got the chance.

With eyes that hardened before hers, he said, "So be it." And in the next moment the captain lifted her like a sack of flour and threw her over his shoulder. She pummelled him with her fists, calling him a scoundrel, an ungentlemanly cove, a blackguard! After opening the door of the coach, he said, "Out, Glick"—to which his valet hastily responded by jumping up and exiting the carriage, looking suspiciously like he was endeavouring not to laugh. *More humiliation!*

The captain tumbled her inside the coach unceremoniously. It was unfortunate that his action sent a blanket about her conscience, for

Margaret was in need of a conscience just then. She righted herself on the cushion and stared at him. "You are no gentleman! How dare you, sir!" she said.

"But you are no lady; how dare you, madam," he returned calmly.

"Oh!" This response was so much more infuriating that Margaret forgot this was her cousin, superior to her in both age and rank, and that she was obliged, by all sense and propriety, to be as agreeable as possible to him. At the very least, goodwill and honesty were required. But he had just nailed shut the door of goodwill, nay of good breeding, and all Margaret could think was how to make herself as odious to him as he was now to her.

He said, "Are you aware that your every hope of gain will be thwarted? My brother Earl Stafford will inherit the duke's estate, even if by some miracle you are successful in your scheme and persuade my poor uncle to marry you."

Through compressed lips, she said, "Your brother will inherit. So why does this concern you?"

He looked away and then back at her, his lips pursed. "Suffice it to say that I act on behalf of my family's ancient home and name. And I am further motivated to protect an uncle who has little capacity, or so they say, to protect himself."

"You evidently know not the duke. And I suppose you think your cousin is incapable of guarding his interests?"

"Feodora? A young sheltered woman? I fear not."

Margaret's nostrils flared prettily. "You know nothing at all!"

He eyed her with sudden doubt. But Roderick had assured him repeatedly that the duke was an empty garret; Feodora, he said, was sheltered and not wise to the ways of the world. He feared this Lady X could easily dupe the both of them. With a reproving eye he said, "My object in coming was to apprise the duke of what the papers seem to know, madam, that you are a fortune hunter. Since we have met, however, I can offer you an opportunity to drop your scheme, with a settlement, instead of going to the duke."

Margaret's lips firmed into a thin line, her anger growing yet more.

He added, "The gossip flying in Town says His Grace is too feeble to know he's being fleeced. Surely, you would not wish to prolong such speculation."

"If your uncle's reputation concerns you, why do you not put an end to such gossip? You have merely to deny it. Indeed," she said, warming to the subject, for she despised the odious rumour as much as the captain. "You should let nothing prevent you from doing so!"

He stared at her. "Your existence prevents it. You have been discovered."

She bit her lip, wondering silently how such a lie could have begun. She tried a different tack. "I think you lack the power to put an end to the speculation," she said, to goad him.

"Lack the power? No man has power over a rumour amongst the *ton*, once it's in circulation. One might as easily tame the sea."

Margaret stood to leave. "You mean to say, sir, that *you* lack the power. That you are, in a word..." She thought for the merest second. "Impotent."

A look of incredulity swept over the captain's face. He'd never imagined a woman capable of such an insult. He almost laughed but merely said, "I will overlook that ill-chosen word, knowing you meant only powerlessness regarding the rumour."

"I am sure I meant it in every way it could possibly be meant," said Margaret, whose better sense had vanished from the moment of their meeting. She was digging herself deeper and knew it, was breathless with the knowing, intoxicated with it, and could not stop herself. Her only aim in life had somehow become to vex Captain Rempeare, for he had mightily vexed and plagued her. Hadn't that term from Mr. McCluskey come in handy—except suddenly the captain had her about the waist, and he forced the riding whip from her with one hand, though she saw him wince in pain. Of course: his bad arm! But speechless with surprise and confusion, for she knew not what he was about, he turned her over upon his lap and took the whip and used it against her backside twice.

"Naughty girl!" he said. "If you were a man of my crew, you'd be flogged for that impertinence."

The indignity brought tears to her eyes, but the second his grip lightened, she sprang to her feet and grasped the whip back. She would have struck him with it except he caught her arm in the air with a lightning move. Again, his bad arm, but if it caused him pain, he did not show it. Their eyes met, inches apart. Hers, full of unspeakable wrath. His, with determination but also surprise.

"What a roller you are!" he cried, with a look in his eye not far from mirth. "A wild cat!"

"You are insupportable!" she hissed. "The duke will hear of this!"

With that, she swirled about and marched from the coach, almost falling over the steps in her haste. She rushed into the house, and panting with anger, summoned the staff.

CHAPTER FOUR

"That man," Margaret said, after hurriedly gathering the butler, two footmen, and two housemaids. She pointed towards the front of the house, "is not to see my face! Tell Captain Rempeare whatever you like—tell him I've *died*! But do not bring him near me, and be sure to say I am most decidedly indisposed!" She strode hurriedly up the stairs, still heaving great breaths. She needed Mrs. Filbert. She must see the duke—no, she must not see the duke, for she could never tell him what she had done. But Mrs. Filbert would understand. She would be a comfort.

In full riding habit, Margaret headed towards the library. Mrs. Filbert's ague had improved, but she favoured that room after breakfast for she loved to read.

Below stairs, the servants stared after Margaret, frozen with surprise. The butler recovered first and nodded at the others. "You heard what our young miss said. Inform the others." There was no question of disobeying Miss Tavistock, for like Mrs. Filbert, all the help adored her. She was kind and generous and never denied them any consideration she felt was within the bounds of her station to bestow. She was especially thoughtful on Boxing Day; they would never betray her.

At just that moment, the door knocker sounded. The butler gave a grave nod to the footmen and maids who were present, and went to open the door. Eyeing each other with suppressed grins as if it would be a lark to follow such orders, they went their way.

"Mrs. Filbert!" Margaret rushed to her companion who almost dropped her novel, *The Forest of Montalbano*, in surprise.

"My dear!" she cried, with a hand upon her heart.

Margaret threw herself into the older woman's arms and could only say, "He's horrid! Oh, he's odious! I can't tell you how monstrous he is!"

"Who, my love?" asked the companion. "Who is horrid and monstrous?"

Margaret blinked at her. "The captain! He's *here*."

"Captain Rempeare?"

An earnest nod.

"He's come to apologise, I warrant," said Mrs. Filbert, with a satisfied smile.

"No such thing!" said Margaret. "He hasn't come to see me at all! He came to see...to see Lady X."

The companion's eyes widened. "But there is no such lady," she said.

"*He* thinks there is. And I...I'm afraid I was not agreeable." Her eyes darted to her companion's face and away again. She sniffed. "I allowed him to believe that I...that *I* am...Lady X."

Mrs. Filbert's eyes popped wide, but she said nothing. She was too stunned to speak.

Margaret wrung her hands. "Oh I own I shouldn't have. But he was so *provoking!*" She turned injured eyes to her companion. "He is the last man I could ever agree to marry, Mrs. Filbert! I dare say Roderick had the right of it. I will go to London and meet many another, more suitable, prospects."

Mrs. Filbert ventured, "I dare say you did clear up the faradiddle...his misconception? Before you parted?" Margaret merely met her eyes and shook her head.

"Well, 'tis easily done," she said. "At dinner we shall disabuse him of that notion."

But Margaret shook her head. "I will not go down. I will not see his face if he stays however so long. I *refuse* to meet him."

Mrs. Filbert said, "I fear, my dear, if you do not come clean to the captain now, this will be an Icarian adventure."

"Then call me Icarus, for I will surely drown rather than enlighten such an odious being!" With amazing energy she hurried to the window but stood aside, peeking out at the front of the property. "Call me a crosspatch, or—or ill-tempered, whatever you will, I..." She could see the carriage, and then added, "Oh, there he is! Odious man!"

Mrs. Filbert hurried to her side. There were two men, but the captain was tall and handsome in a blue naval uniform with its white breeches, black shoes, and cocked hat. While issuing orders to his servant, he even had what looked like a pleasant countenance.

Margaret stared morosely out at the scene and then turned to the older lady. "I forbid you to tell him who I really am, Mrs. Filbert. I positively *forbid* it." Mrs. Filbert put her head back to study her charge. She frowned and returned to her seat and then patted the spot beside her. "Perhaps you should start from the beginning, my love."

Half an hour later, in the duke's private study, Gabriel Rempeare held a glass of sherry in one hand while sitting before his uncle, who sat behind a ponderous oaken desk. Glick, his valet since Gabriel had been made post captain, was seeing that his travelling boxes were transferred to a guest bedchamber. The duke's groom had led his horses to the stables.

After exchanging more than the usual formalities, for neither had set eyes on the other for a decade, they were relaxing, helped not a little by the sherry. Gabriel was pleased to find the duke was nothing like an "empty garret," as Roderick said. While His Grace had no pretensions of entering society, that didn't preclude his being a reasonable man. He was not cheerfully conversant, perhaps, but neither did he discourage the captain from taking up the slack.

Gabriel stayed on safest ground: the navy. He had wished to stay in service for he'd been made post only two years prior, was entitled to a larger share of prize monies, as well as having command of an excellent thirty-two-gun vessel, HMS *Navigator*. That is, until the Battle of Lissa, when the ship was pummelled mercilessly by fierce man-of-wars, the damage so extensive that the vessel was now decommissioned. It was a blow to a man who knew the direction of his ship by the feel of the waves beneath him. He'd awakened from his berth once when the course was changed by his first lieutenant. The injury to his sword arm was also a grave disappointment in wartime, as sea battles often became contests of sheer strength, such as when an enemy boarded one's ship.

He grew animated telling the duke about the battle, bringing the scene to life: the blockading ships, the mad chaos of guns pounding, smoke and debris filling the air and hitting the deck and his men, the smell of blood and sweat mingling with the acrid clouds of powder. An overheated gun, he explained, had exploded (killing one seaman), sending a hot shard of iron directly into the captain, resulting in a permanent weakness to the arm. He drew off his navy coat and rolled up the sleeve of his right arm, revealing a long nasty gash, still reddened at its edges where the burning iron had entered his flesh.

He sighed upon admitting that his shore leave might be for an indefinite period, as the navy list was overloaded with post captains awaiting vessels. The Admiralty notified him, moreover, that he'd been put at half pay.

But he moved matters to a thing most pressing upon his mind. Miss Tavistock. He had long ago stopped writing her, for she had not graced his efforts with a single reply. The duke had written only a handful of times, short letters, but with an allusion to a certain future event, when his "dear gel" as he called Feodora, must be given to the captain in holy wedlock. If not for those rare words, the captain would have thought the union was no longer desired. But was it Feodora's wish?

He had told the admiral during the last dinner in the wardroom of his ship, he "believed" he was promised in marriage to the duke's niece. The admiral, upon returning to shore, had given it out in Town that it was most decided. Gossip amongst the *ton* was wildfire; what was heard in one ear moved swiftly to another so that when he found himself ashore and shipless, he also found that his reputation of being spoken for had preceded him. It bothered him not, for he had no experience with women, no desire to court anyone. He'd barely developed land legs for one thing. Certain prize monies were hung up in the courts, and above all, until he was formally notified that the alliance with Miss Tavistock was ended, he was honour bound to it.

He began by reviewing his state of affairs. If he were to marry Miss Tavistock, it was only expected that he should have a respectable standing and income. He laid out his current holdings; he was honest about the fortune in prize monies he'd won from enemy merchantmen and not a few French man-of-wars, adding that more prizes might be forthcoming depending on the verdict of the prize office. Explained, lest the duke had forgot, that if a ship was ruled as "neutral," its prizes were null, returned to the owners and seamen; therefore, a backlog of legal challenges filled the rolls of the office, including a few for ships that Captain Rempeare had taken.

The duke said, "Sir, it is enough. My sister, Feodora's mother, had a share of monies set aside for her daughter, which she kept in the funds even when her husband took off to America with the child. I have held it in trust for her ever since."

"Surely, you drew upon it to raise her?"

"Not a whit, sir. It sits secure, earning interest, seven percent, I dare say." He paused. "Between the two of you, there should be no trouble in setting up a comfortable household." He did not state the amount of the trust, but that wasn't Captain Rempeare's concern. He shifted in his seat. "Your Grace, does Feodora look favourably upon the match?"

The duke blinked at him as if the question was not to the point. "She has always expected it, sir." He paused. "Do you wish to cry off?"

"Not at all. I am prepared to fulfill the dearest wish of my mother, and hers, I believe. I only supposed...having no word from my cousin, that is—"

"Rest easy, sir," said the duke. "She has never had any thought but to fulfill those same parental wishes, I assure you."

With this burden off his mind, there was only one further matter that the captain could not forget. Looking gravely at his uncle, he said, "Your Grace, I must tell you that I met your...er, your *lady love*, on the drive."

The duke blinked in astonishment and then became troubled. Momentarily he seemed bereft for speech. A slow flush crept up his cheeks, a red stain that prominent sideburns could not hide. Finally, he said, "I wasn't aware you knew. Are you sure?"

Rempeare wondered at his surprise, though not his embarrassment. "She told me so," he said simply.

The duke cleared his throat and rearranged himself on his chair. "That's deuced odd. How did you—"

Gabriel said, "Sir, the London papers have found it out." The duke seemed unsurprised. Captain Rempeare leaned forward and cleared his throat. "They maintain, Your Grace, that Lady X, as they call her, is a fortune hunter."

"Lady X!" he cried. "That's rich. Lying coves!" said the duke, his eyes suddenly afire. He stared at the captain in perplexity. "They have it wrong, sir. My lady is not without a fortune." He paused and added, "And you well know my estate will pass to Stafford, as I have no heir."

Rempeare looked up quickly. "Is that your purpose? No wonder... I did think her amazing young. It does give fodder to the gossips, but no doubt she will fulfill your wish with a number of strapping sons."

"Eh?" said the duke, with a puzzlement that turned to a laugh. The laugh brought on a cough, but he managed to choke out, "My lady would be much diverted at your saying so, sir. Much diverted."

Gabriel merely stared at him oddly. The woman on the drive had seemed ridiculously young to be the duke's love interest. But she positively glowed with health, high colour, and spirit. It would have been fascinating had he not been forced to censure her. But he saw now why she had been so angry. The gossips had been wrong about fortune hunting. She had independent wealth. He owed her an apology. He rubbed his chin, not quite sure how to respond. Why would she find it diverting? "Quite the lively one, too, an't she?"

The duke stared at his nephew. He rubbed *his* chin. "Where is my lady?" he said, rising from the chair. The captain came to his feet. "She entered the house ahead of me," he said.

The duke looked astonished. "By Jove!" he said. "You must excuse me, sir. We'll talk after dinner, if that suits you."

"That's fine, sir. I'm sorry to say I can only stay this night. But I look forward to meeting my cousin," he said with special emphasis.

"Haven't met her yet?" he asked. "You've got a surprise in store, sir!" He chuckled, and then before Captain Rempeare could ascertain what kind of surprise the duke alluded to, the man hastened from the room.

He can't wait to see his lady, reflected Gabriel. And no wonder, for even through the veil, he could see she had the face of an angel. He hoped the duke would not be too angry when he heard the account of his rash behaviour with the woman. But she had been unaccountably impertinent, nay, insulting. Despite the duke's assurances, he still must wonder if the mysterious Lady X was, indeed, a fortune hunter, for why else was she so quick to take offense? Or was it the title she craved? Many a young woman, he thought ruefully, might sacrifice herself to be a duchess. He must get her real name. Why hadn't he got it from the duke, so his man of business could run an inquiry. Then he'd know what was what.

Meanwhile, he must leave Toadingham on the morrow, for his brother was in London doing his brown best to burn through the last bit of the Rempeare fortune. Disgraceful, it was. Gaming and low living were his favourite pursuits. Had the earl been a seaman beneath his authority, the captain could almost see his way to having the cat on him. A few of those lashes were known to reform a man quicker than a Sunday sermon.

He'd been remiss not to visit Toadingham for so long. His shore leaves were rarely on English soil, and when they were, he'd been forced to play nursemaid to his deuced reckless brother. Even now he hadn't escaped that fate. He'd been charged by a dying father to be his brother's keeper, to ensure the earl didn't game away the ancient family estate, theirs since the days of Charles II. Stafford had come perilously close to losing it forever, just as he seemed hell-bent on drinking himself to an early grave, and it was Gabriel's charge to stem the folly by any means possible. At times he wished he could leave the earl to his fate, to his mad gaming and other vices. But he'd given his father a promise.

And if there was one thing a sea captain *meant* to do well, it was keep his word.

CHAPTER FIVE

Mrs. Filbert met the captain on the stairs and instantly stopped. She couldn't help surveying him head to toe: the man who had injured her charge. He fit her idea of a sea captain, with his swarthy complexion, muscular build, and bright eyes. Indeed, Margaret's description of those eyes as "opalescent" seemed quite right. He did not seem a good candidate to make a May game of, she thought, noting his uniform with admiration. He bowed lightly. "Captain Rempeare, ma'am."

"Mrs. Filbert," she said, curtseying. "Miss Tavistock's companion."

An unreadable expression crossed his face. "I look forward to meeting my cousin," he finally said, with another light bow. He would have passed on, but Mrs. Filbert said, "I regret to inform you, sir, that Miss Tavistock is indisposed with the headache. A severe case, I'm afraid."

He stopped, considering. "I am sorry for it. Do these afflictions last long?"

"For days, sir." Mrs. Filbert eyed him steadily, but her heart quickened. His searching look made her blush, moreover, for Mrs. Filbert was a terrible liar and feared every second that he would see through her.

He cleared his throat. "In light of the...er...arrangements for our future, I do hope Miss Tavistock will consider making a brief appearance. I think it only fitting, indeed, high time that we meet."

Mrs. Filbert smiled too sweetly. The captain had broached a subject where she felt him to be exceedingly in the wrong. "High time?" she asked, in a dry tone. "*I dare say.* But I am afraid, sir, that you must not expect it."

Gabriel caught the censure, but what could he do? He'd been tied to London since his blasted retirement on account of meetings with prize agents, solicitors, and the Admiralty, not to mention his wastrel of an elder brother. If he hadn't changed his plans to visit Toadingham on the last occasion, the Rempeare family seat, Redmonton, would have been gamed away by that worthy. He'd been in time to prevent it, been forced to offer a good portion of his own fortune: spoils of war, prize money—hard won—to replace the foolhardy wager his brother had made. He hadn't given an explanation because he loathed to reveal the extent of his brother's folly to his relations in Yorkshire. It was his unhappy burden to bear, but upon reflection he now realised he should have done more than sent off a hasty message. Too hasty—he now reflected—too late.

"Please ask her," he said, bowing. "She needn't leave her bed for more than a few minutes."

"I assure you she will not come down this night, sir." The captain stared at her strangely, feeling something wasn't quite right about such certainty. But he only asked, "Is there a portrait of Feodora I might see?" Mrs. Filbert shook her head, frowning. "Indeed, there ought to be. I hate to speak against the duke, for he is wondrously generous to Miss Tavistock, but he has never commissioned a portrait."

"A miniature, perhaps?" he asked hopefully.

She shook her head. "None."

Rempeare's brows knitted, and he nodded. "Pity," he said. "Perhaps I will send an artist myself—"

Mrs. Filbert curtseyed, signalling the end of the interview. She did not wish to inform the man that Miss Tavistock was about to embark on a London Season and would not be available for an artist's sittings. He said, "If you please, ask Miss Tavistock to make every effort to come to dinner, if only for a few minutes. I cannot stay longer than one night, I'm afraid." The look on Mrs. Filbert's face was apparently unpromising enough that the captain added, "If it would be permissible; if she is not equal to making her way to the dining room, perhaps I could pop in to her bedside—only long enough to extend a greeting?"

"Oh, sir!" exclaimed Mrs. Filbert, with real alarm. "Surely, you comprehend the sensibilities of a young lady are too delicate to allow such an interview. She is indisposed, and her complexion, her powers of conversation, are not at their best. I believe I may say it would cause our young lady a great deal of distress to—"

But the captain heard enough, and held up a hand. "So be it," he said, with patience, shaking his head. "I beg your pardon for suggesting it." He continued up the steps feeling properly chastised for the audacity of wishing to behold the woman he was bound to marry, but his curiosity to meet his mysterious cousin was so strong that he turned back and looked down at the companion, who had not gone far. "Mrs. Filbert, please convey my best wishes to Miss Tavistock for a speedy recovery, but pray, do ask her if she would condescend to make every effort to appear at table later. I am anxious to speak with her."

"Make every effort?" fumed Margaret, pacing her bedchamber. "Fire and brimstone! The way that man cuts up my peace!" She turned indignant eyes to her companion, her pretty face contorted in pain. "Did I not tell you he was provoking?" She crossed her arms and strode to the window. "I will sooner remain a prisoner in my room than make the least effort to please such a man!"

Mrs. Filbert frowned. "I must say, my dear, that he did not seem overly provoking. Indeed," she added, "he was very gentlemanlike."

But Margaret turned decidedly and said, "I charge you, Mrs. Filbert, to make our plans to leave for London with all haste! I long to see Town, and...and I long...for the first time in my life to meet other gentlemen! I am determined not to give another thought to Captain Rempeare. He is *not* gentlemanlike. He is not at all what I imagined."

"What will the duke say, my dear?" Mrs. Filbert thought it advisable to point out that Margaret's marriage arrangement with the captain was not, strictly speaking, to please herself. "He expects it. Your parents wished it. Your father returned to England on the promise of it: to see you marry into a noble family."

Margaret turned pained eyes to her. "Pray, do not speak of my father! He returned to reconcile with my mother—not on my account!" Margaret knew it was her mother's letters to America that had convinced her dear papa to return her to England. In those letters, for Margaret had them in her possession still, her mother had indeed declared that Margaret's "destiny" was in England, was to marry into the Rempeare family. But there was an equal amount of sweet entreaties to return for the sake of reconciling their differences—they'd not sought a divorce. And in gratitude for his return, her mother had met them at the wharf, waiting at a distance in a closed carriage for the ship to dock and unload.

That both parents had died in that carriage, almost the moment of their return, was still a painful point of contemplation. She did not wish their deaths to be in vain, but she could marry another nobleman, couldn't she? Her papa, at least, did not so much have his heart set on the captain as upon knowing his little girl would be securely settled. But Mrs. Filbert continued, "And the captain's mother wished it."

"I *beg* you," pleaded Margaret. "Do not remind me! These things are not to the purpose. My parents, God rest their souls, were they to know the captain, would understand. Even *his* mother, I dare say, would excuse me under the circumstances."

"And the duke?" said the companion.

Margaret was silent. In a lower tone she said, "He shall be brought round. He has ever granted my every wish," she said simply. But she looked waveringly at the older woman. "Has he not?"

The captain was off the next morning, after enquiring—to no avail—if he might have an interview with Miss Tavistock. There was no sense denying he felt positively gloomy about his future bride. The comments of all confirmed his worst suspicion: that she was not only plain, but quite ugly. Lady X—that maddening woman—had called her "a pudding face." The duke had chuckled, actually chuckled, upon saying Gabriel was in for a surprise when he met her. What could that mean except it was not a *good* surprise? And she had not a single portrait. Not even a miniature! They were all colluding, it seemed to him, to keep her hidden from his sight. He decided that he would return to Toadingham at the soonest possible time and demand an interview. He had a right to see a woman before marrying her, by Jove.

Margaret was pleased to be granted instant approval by the duke for her London scheme—until she learned it was because the captain had business in Town, and His Grace considered she could best further her acquaintance with him there. With increasing dismay she learned the use of the monies in trust to her by her mother—monies wrapped up in the funds, which she had never touched for the simple reason that the duke hadn't required it—were attached to a condition. There was only one, but it was dire—that she marry Captain Gabriel Rempeare! A release from the condition could be occasioned only if he chose to marry elsewhere. Margaret's mother was the duke's sister, and had been fast friends with her in-law sister, the countess, the captain's mother. Together, they'd hatched the scheme, adding the monetary incentive to encourage the likelihood of its fruition. Margaret hid her alarm from the duke.

"In light of my nephew's assurances," the duke had said, "his willingness to fulfill the dearest hopes of his relations in your regard, I will write my London solicitors to allow your use of the funds. Direct your invoices to them." He winked at her. "Once you marry, the fortune will belong to your husband. I dare say the captain has made his own— won it in battle—he don't need your blunt. There can be little harm in enjoying Town, being fashionable, and so forth."

So Margaret was embarking on a Season that she would pay for with money she was entitled to only if she married the captain. *How unfair!* She pushed it from her mind. She was fully deserving of one Season in Town with all the delights of the metropolis no matter whom she planned to marry.

The duke had questioned his staff closely the preceding day and felt assured that Lady Frances Hopewell, the love of his life (provokingly called "Lady X" in the papers) had not entered Toadingham Hall either before or after Captain Rempeare. If his butler insisted no one but Feodora and the captain with his servants entered the establishment, he could believe it. Lady Frances knew better.

He didn't understand how or why the captain had said he'd met her. A quick assignation with that lady had assured him that she'd been nowhere near the big house. Lady Hopewell was a long-standing neighbour of Toadingham, had been so for two-and-a-half decades, since coming to the area when she married Sir Thomas. For all that time she and the duke had seen little of each other, however, as Sir Thomas was an ogre to her, keeping her almost under lock and key. Indeed, she had scarcely any society save her three offspring, and even they were seldom home, being sent to boarding schools and then to get their certificates at Oxford.

Five months after Sir Thomas passed away, her ladyship and the duke crossed paths while riding horseback on their neighbouring lands. That first happy meeting led to many more; they were both equally astonished to discover kindred spirits in one another. Her sons, however, catching wind of the new friendship, were fiercely disapproving. They wanted a proper mourning period before their mother could further what she called "a happy acquaintance" with the duke.

Thus began the secret liaisons—innocent meetings, to be sure—but of necessity kept under wraps on account of her disapproving brood. Their dearest hope was to marry. The duke, indeed, was in raptures over it, for he'd thought himself a confirmed bachelor and had been reconciled to that fate. It was a delightful surprise to find he might enjoy conjugal bliss with a woman he adored. But since he needs must keep quiet on account of Lady Frances's children, he hadn't told Feenie about his lady love. In truth, he feared she might welcome it as little as did her ladyship's family.

The newspaper gossip was a nasty shock, for the couple was alike in despising a scandal. And neither could account for how the paper got word. The duke tried to allay her ladyship's fears, for her sons held considerable sway over her—but she bemoaned and lamented. Someone had discovered their relationship—but who? And why had they dubbed her Lady X? It was an odious mystery! And to fashion her as a fortune hunter! While Lady Frances's husband was a lout, he was a rich lout and left his widow with a comfortable jointure.

It played havoc upon an otherwise steady set of nerves. Fortunately, her ladyship was not so blue devilled as to call off their meetings. And he was utterly convinced that Feodora hadn't the least inkling of his secret goings-on. Already one person too many had somehow caught wind of it. To protect Lady Frances, he would not be party to telling another.

On a dark London street, Roderick hurriedly pocketed a guinea from a surgeon, nodded a hasty parting to his fellow resurrectionists, and found the mail coach heading toward Cambridge. An ugly business, it was, stealing corpses, but he had debts of honour to pay, and comforted himself with the thought that it was to further medical science. It was for the good of mankind.

He'd soiled his best double-breasted coat, however, when the third body they dug up turned out to lack a coffin. The poor lifeless relic was merely robed in linen caked with dirt, and he'd had to help cart it to a wagon and then lug it from the equipage into the home of the medical man who would pay for their trouble. The surgeon was afraid of being caught and hurried the business mercilessly, making it worse. Now Roderick would have to find a cleaning woman with reasonable fees. He'd tell her he was laid upon by highwaymen, and happy to come out with his life intact, if not his coat.

At school, fellow students were more worrisome. One in particular, a Mr. Jones, vowed to discover Roderick's frequent business when he left campus. If he were followed and discovered, he could face expulsion. Worse, gaol. Men sometimes spent six months in "city college," as they called Newgate, for stealing bodies of the dead. Not only that, but his brothers were likely to take fits over the business. Not that he cared what they thought. Neither the earl, who was in deep at the gaming tables, or the captain, had come through with funds for Roderick's upkeep. A man had to live, didn't he?

The upshot of it was that he simply must never be caught.

CHAPTER SIX

After the captain had safely departed, Margaret and Mrs. Filbert descended upon the breakfast room, where the former busily perused advertisements in the paper. "Mrs. Filbert!" she cried, pointing one finger delicately at a spot on the page. "To let on account of a bankrupt…an excellent dwelling house on *Tavistock Place.*" She looked up, smiling, moving aside the lace of a morning cap that was a trifle too large. "Can you conceive of it? What a lark!" she said. "But it appears a very nice establishment…six bedchambers, two drawing rooms, parlour, two kitchens, cellarage, and yard. And only twenty guineas per annum. That sounds reasonable," she ventured, glancing at her companion uncertainly.

Mrs. Filbert rested her cup on its saucer and surveyed her charge. "I regret, dearest, that Tavistock Place is not in Mayfair. You will of course wish to be in Mayfair."

"Of course," said Margaret, nodding sagely. A minute later she said, "Here's one at Turnham Green, only four miles from Hyde Park." She peeked wistfully at her companion.

"Four miles!" exclaimed Mrs. Filbert. "That's a world away from polite society, dearest."

"I see," said Margaret, who didn't see at all. Four miles didn't sound so very far.

"Shall I scan the advertisements, my love?" asked Mrs. Filbert, who had lived in London just at the outskirts of Mayfield with her husband of fifteen years until his sudden passing. It was on account of her widowhood that she had been lowered to seeking employment.

"What about this?" asked Margaret, studying the page with a look of rapt concern. She read, "Elegant town residence. No. 29 Berkeley Square. A very commodious, substantial, and elegantly fitted-up leasehold, with four spacious apartments on each floor, two staircases, two drawing rooms, breakfast room, library, housekeeper's, butler's, and footmen's rooms, servants' hall, wine cellar, and 'every other requisite accommodation for a family of the first respectability.'" But here her voice fell off. "Oh, 'tis for a family."

Mrs. Filbert smiled. "My dear, you can afford that; 'tis expected that a duke's ward should live in style."

"I shan't be known as the duke's ward on account of Captain Rempeare; I beg you remember," Margaret said, passing the paper to the lady, who reached for it, raised a lorgnette to one eye, and found the listing. Her thin brows rose. "It includes, for a small additional sum, all the elegant household furniture, French glass, a sideboard of plate, table and bed linen, china and glass, stock of very choice wines, about fifteen chaldron of coals, and numerous other articles." She lay down her lorgnette.

"I think you have found what you need," she said, to Margaret's smiling delight. "I am above astonished that it is available this far into the Season! Walking distance from Gunter's, too. Think of the tea and cake!"

Margaret stood with excitement. "I dare say we must notify my uncle's solicitors at once! That house shan't be vacant for long. We must nab it!"

"Agreed," said Mrs. Filbert. "We haven't a moment to lose if you are to find your way onto invitation lists!"

Margaret scurried off to write a letter to the solicitors. She would get the duke's signature and signet on it, and bid a messenger ride like the wind to get it on the mail coach. Nothing moved faster than the mail.

Two weeks later

A stop at the offices of the duke's solicitors was necessary before Margaret could occupy the house on Berkeley Square. Some of the staff from Toadingham had begged to accompany Margaret to London. Others, like the butler, were too loyal to the duke to desire the change. Margaret brought only her lady's maid and three footmen. For the rest, the solicitors—using "the best references"—had hired help who waited for Margaret at the house.

Mr. Primpley, the chief solicitor, a stout balding man with bushy sideburns, had stood and bowed to receive Margaret, but now sat before her behind a desk with a grave look upon his countenance. Margaret had said, "Please be advised, sir, that for all our interactions, on paper and otherwise, you must style me as Miss Margaret Chrissendon—not Miss Tavistock."

"Is not your name, legally and otherwise, Miss Feodora Tavistock?" he asked, looking down his spectacles at a paper before him.

"Sir, I desire to have my come out using my second name of Margaret, and the surname of Chrissendon; it comes from an ancestor, I assure you."

He stared at her impassively. "Everything I am authorised to supply you with is in the name of Miss Tavistock."

"And since I am Miss Tavistock, that is of no matter," she countered. "I merely beg you to understand that I do not wish to be *known* as Miss Tavistock whilst I am in London."

He cleared his throat and was about to speak, when Margaret, sensing further opposition, said, "Sir, if this is too intricate for your office to manage, there are other solicitors I could—"

"Not at all, ma'am," he said, glancing at her with a wily expression. He took a handkerchief and wiped his brow. "Am I to understand that if enquiries are made…?"

"Then you must assuredly *not* give out who I am by any name other than Miss Margaret Chrissendon. May I have your word on this, sir?"

Scanning the papers before him, he said, "There is a stipulation, ma'am, concerning your trust and a Captain Rempeare… I take it you are amicably engaged to this gentleman?"

Margaret's resolve wavered. Colouring, she said, "That gentleman, sir, is my very reason for using a different name. You must understand that I am intent upon…meeting the captain…and learning his character…quite apart from our formal understanding." She was making a mess of the explanation—or perhaps he understood too well, for the man's brows rose considerably.

Again he cleared his throat. With a pained expression he said, "I think I understand you…" He gave Mrs. Filbert a doubtful look. Is this, indeed, the wisest course, ma'am?"

"You are engaged, sir, to act for the duke on my behalf," Margaret said stiffly, though her cheeks flamed. "Please to keep your focus on that only."

"But ma'am," he said, sitting back and spreading his hands before him. "The stipulation—if the arrangement is in doubt—"

"You have the duke's assurance upon it. That must suffice you."

He took a breath, resignedly. "You do know, ma'am, that the captain is also my client."

Margaret did not know. She stared. "Does that mean you cannot be trusted to keep my confidence?"

He pursed his lips into a frown and sighed. "Your name is safe. Miss *Chrissendon*." Again he looked sourly at Mrs. Filbert, as if to imply that she ought to put an immediate end to such foolishness.

Mrs. Filbert merely smiled at him serenely. Goodness knew, she had plied Margaret during the three days of their journey with perfectly good reasons why she must not use a different name. Society would welcome a duke's ward with a dowry in her own right. As his ward, she could easily squash the rumour concerning His Grace and that supposed "Lady X." The captain would call upon her first thing if she were known to be in Town. But despite all she said, Margaret did not waver. Never had she seen the girl as adamant upon a thing as she was upon this point. Therefore since she adored her and could not dissuade her from the course, Mrs. Filbert resolved to support her in it to the full.

Mr. Primpley took pen and ink and added something on each of numerous sheets of paper before him, then pushed the papers towards Margaret while dipping the pen in the pot and handing it to her as well.

"I beg you to sign *both* names, madam," he said in a heavy tone. A few minutes later as he bowed them out of the office, he said, "Ma'am, as you are new to Town and without the benefit of your relation to the duke—which was your ticket into the most exclusive households, I must say—" He waited for an answer, but as none was forthcoming, continued, "Allow me to send a gentleman to introduce you to society. A man of the first respectability, I assure you." To her doubtful look, he added, "An introduction from the right man will greatly improve your social acceptance."

Margaret hesitated, but saw only impassive gravity on his features. A glance at Mrs. Filbert assured her that it must be a sound idea.

"Thank you, sir. I shall expect him."

"An exceedingly respectable gentleman, of course?" asked Mrs. Filbert, just to be safe.

"Of the first water," he said, bowing.

"What is the gentleman's name, if you please, sir?" asked Margaret.

He eyed her with the same impassive countenance. "I have a few prospects in mind, ma'am, as I must ascertain who will be available. I assure you, 'twill be an upstanding member of the *ton*."

The *ton*—the cream of high society. The words were enough reassurance for both ladies, and in a minute they headed to the waiting coach.

"My dear, you have crossed the Rubicon," said Mrs. Filbert. Margaret felt it a victory as well, as she entered the carriage and sat on the cushion. It had taken a surprising amount of energy to get through that interview. But she had pin money, an establishment on a respectable Mayfair street, a household and furniture, and was having her come out! No scruples over using a different name could outweigh the joyous expectation in all that.

So it was that Miss Margaret Chrissendon, not Miss Feodora Tavistock, let the house in Berkeley Square, and it was upon Miss Chrissendon that the respectable gentleman of good standing called the following day. Margaret and Mrs. Filbert sat in the best drawing room to receive their first guest, Margaret with an almost painfully erect posture. Even Mrs. Filbert could not deny a sense of anxious anticipation for how it would go off. They had discussed this gentleman at length during breakfast; both hoped for an elderly man, a wise and gentle guide with excellent connexions, who could steer Margaret towards the best company and away from the questionable.

Finally, Stevens the new butler came to announce the arrival of the man: "Captain Gabriel Rempeare, ma'am," he said in stentorian tones, ushering him into the room. Margaret was struck with such surprise that she nearly froze. Colour shot into her cheeks. Mrs. Filbert's brows rose as far as they could. She looked from the captain to Margaret with amazement.

The captain, coming into the room with a pleasant countenance, also seemed struck, stopping nearly mid bow for a second while he registered the surprise. His look changed to consternation, and he straightened quickly.

"You?" cried Margaret.

"You!" he cried, with equal surprise.

For a second, Margaret wondered if she should order him from the house or if he would simply turn and leave in disgust. But Mrs. Filbert was sending her the direst looks and motioning. Yes, she must be polite.

"Please, Captain, I beg you have a seat," Margaret said with severe politeness, extending a hand to him. He glanced at her, came and took her hand and held it before his face while making another bow. The opalescent eyes searching hers were not filled with reproof. Dropping her hand, he went to an opposite seat, so they faced each other, adjacent to the hearth.

"So I learn your name at last," he said, looking faintly amused.

For response Margaret said stiffly, "You are sent by Mr. Primpley?"

He paused. "I understood my services were needed?"

"I expected a gentleman—not a brute," she said, with a cold smile.

Mrs. Filbert looked on tensely, but when the captain merely smiled in response to this provocation, her heart warmed to him. It wasn't a malicious smile; he seemed amused.

"I dare say I must apologise for our last, er, encounter," he offered. "I'm afraid a sea captain is accustomed to a certain manner of respect…which I found you did not share." He gave a wry grin. Then, looking to Mrs. Filbert, he said, "Am I to understand, from your presence, that Miss Tavistock is with you?" Margaret blinked in alarm, but Mrs. Filbert rose to the rescue.

"Miss Tavistock, sir," she said, "was unfortunately not able to join us due to…er…the headache. She remains in Yorkshire at present, but I warrant when she is quite recovered she will make an appearance." She looked meaningfully at Margaret, whose eyes sent their thanks.

"The headache again? I am sorry for her." He paused, then added, "I believe I understand now why Primpley sent me to you, however." Stevens and a maid entered the room with a tea service. Margaret cast a look of alarm at the servant. As the butler put the tray down before her, she asked under her breath, "This is the pekoe, Stevens?" No secret it was that many forms of spurious coloured leaves were sold on the street to the unsuspecting. Some were discarded tea leaves, resold as fresh. Green tea might be coloured with poisonous Prussian blue to achieve a fresh look, so Margaret had instructed her staff to buy only the finest green Hyson, or pekoe.

"Bohea with pekoe, ma'am," he said. "From the Prince Regent's supplier. An outstanding blend."

"Very good," she said, nodding with relief. She did not want the captain to find her lacking in housekeeping. While she began to pour the brew, which she did with perfect grace—tea being a popular libation amongst the country folk surrounding Toadingham—Stevens stood aside and quizzed the maid, who was tasked with taking the filled cups and handing them to first the captain, and then Mrs. Filbert.

With that done, a tray of dainty biscuits, seed cake, and Yorkshire cakes made the rounds, after which the servants left the room. The captain took a sip of tea, surveying the appealing spread before him. "You run a tight ship," he said, in what was meant as a compliment. Looking about at the tasteful décor he added, "And a fine establishment."

Margaret had to bite her tongue not to remind him that she'd been mistress of Toadingham most all her life, dispensing with the help of a housekeeper even; only a dull-witted woman, a cork brain, would not have learned to govern the kitchen, or know the best ingredients from the vulgar. She said tightly, "Of course."

He cleared his throat. "I was told to introduce you to the best circles. But unless you keep your identity—as Lady X, that is— quite under lock and key, you will not be accepted. Were you aware of this?"

Mrs. Filbert clung to the arms of her chair. She wanted nothing more than to set the captain straight right then and there, but Margaret said sweetly, "I am sure, sir, I can rely upon your discretion as to that? As it is understood that Lady X means to wed the duke, I propose we allow that lady's name to rest whilst Miss *Chrissendon* endeavours to enjoy a Season, for I've never had one."

His face wavered, then hardened. "May I speak with you privately for a moment?" He turned and looked at Mrs. Filbert.

Margaret's curiosity was piqued, so she nodded at her companion, who rose on the instant, though with a reluctant heart. "I'll be in the corridor," she said, with a short curtsey.

"If I am to be your escort," he said gravely after watching the companion leave, "which I can countenance doing only with respect for the duke and my fiancée—for she evidently approves of you enough to lend you her companion—then I must know; are you betrothed to the duke? Will you marry him? Is it a love match?"

"So many questions," Margaret said, hedging, while she surveyed him impassively. "I think, sir, you wish to know the extent of my feelings for your uncle." She looked at him with warmth in her eyes and said, "I assure you, I love him with all my heart!"

The captain could not deny what he saw in her earnest eyes, nor what he heard in her voice—utter feeling. Miss Chrissendon might soon be his relation by marriage, then; any thoughts of not being of service to her must be discarded. Any other kinds of thoughts, for she was undoubtedly beautiful, must also be thoroughly suppressed.

"But I must ask you, Captain, to please stay silent regarding my connexion to the duke; it needn't be made plain to society, lest it bring censure upon me or His Grace. I wish to enter the polite world as any other young woman. Indeed, it is all my hope to have one short Season of carefree frivolity before taking on any other role, such as wife or mother."

He stared at her. "You mean, of course, that you wish to dance and flirt and not be encumbered with a prior connexion." He spoke in a clipped tone, with narrowed eyes.

She gave him a wide-eyed look, though a fresh blush rose in her cheeks. "Is that not what all young women wish when they have a come out?"

"Young women who are not in line for becoming duchesses, I think," he countered.

Margaret looked down. "Despite my love for your uncle," she said, studying the carpet, "His Grace has not made an offer. I have no assurance that he will."

One brow rose on the sanguine face. "So you are intent upon trying the waters…testing the wind for a new direction…ready to up-anchor and set sail, are you?"

Margaret's lips firmed into a line. With surprise, the captain realised he enjoyed it when she was angry. There was something sweetly comical about a beautiful face glowering at him.

"As I said, sir," she huffed. "I want only the diversions of a single London Season. I do not see why that should seem odious to you." Their eyes met with equal strength; neither would be stared down.

"And you have the duke's approval for this scheme?"

She nodded. "Of course."

He looked about. "I take it, then, that his purse is financing this establishment?"

She recalled that her trust monies were available only on account of an expected alliance with the captain himself, and her cheeks suddenly blazed with colour. "Not—not—no," she said, clutching her slim fingers together in agitation. "You needn't concern yourself with my finances." His gaze still brimmed with what she took as reproof, so she added, "But as I am not agreeable to you, I shall write to Mr. Primpley at once and beg another name, another gentleman—"

He came to his feet, straightening his naval blue uniform jacket. "That won't be necessary." The captain was tall and held a certain aura in his bearing that only a man of authority in uniform could give. Margaret hastily looked away.

Secretly, Gabriel was instantly determined to keep his eye upon this woman; was she running the duke a merry chase? Was she determined to find a younger man of means and abandon His Grace? On the one hand, he wished she would; if she gave him up, he wouldn't have to worry about his uncle being taken advantage of. But on the other, the duke had shown real affection for this lady. Were his hopes to be dashed? Either way, he must keep an eye on her. He would be certain to warn his uncle if it seemed necessary.

He told her to expect him the following evening, for he would see that she and Mrs. Filbert were included on the guest list of a private ball. Society loved to hear tales of sea captains and war, and sadly, tales were all he could furnish now, after being stripped of his ship, but it made him popular with society hostesses. He'd even been granted a voucher for Almack's, that sanctum of the *haute ton*.

He left with every intention of writing to both Feodora and the duke. He'd find out whether this vastly fetching woman was to be trusted. But for now, for the sake of both his relations, he would treat this lady with all due respect, though trust her not a whit.

CHAPTER SEVEN

Margaret's green eyes sparked daggers after the captain left. She turned to her companion. "How perfectly monstrous of Mr. Primpley to send me *him*, of all men!"

Mrs. Filbert said, "I dare say he thought to do you a service. You said your aim was to meet the captain and ferret out his character. Well, now you have met."

Margaret put a hand to her head wearily. "Do a service? Like the Greeks bearing gifts! I warrant Mr. Primpley must think it the veriest lark. I will have words with that man next I see him; depend upon it."

She remained unusually quiet for the next hour, even when Mrs. Filbert suggested a trip to Bond Street, which famously overflowed with highbrow shops. Margaret agreed at length, and during the carriage ride, stared dejectedly at the busy London roads until the newness of it all brought back something of her usual spirit. Now and then she exclaimed such things as, "My, but I never dreamed of so many people walking a street together!"

"The duke would have an apoplexy in this crowd."

"See there—" she said, motioning at a lady on the pavement who was looking into a shop window. "That fashionable pelisse in shot silk! I dare say we ought to get new ones. My word! Look at those *faces*, Mrs. Filbert! The poor angels!" This, about a duo of large-eyed, ragged but beautiful children holding hands and waiting to cross the busy avenue. Margaret actually turned to catch a last glimpse of the cherubs from the coach's rear window. "I suppose there must be charities aplenty hereabouts? We must find one or two to sponsor," she murmured.

"No trouble at all there," Mrs. Filbert said. "We have only to ask the nearest vicar."

Margaret sat back thoughtfully. "I suppose we'll attend St. George's Hanover Square?"

"Most definitely. We ought to see a few stars of society there on a Sunday. But only a few," she said meaningfully. "Most of the *ton,* I dare say, do not take their religion in weekly installments."

When they exited the carriage on the busy street with its shops bursting with fripperies and falderols, laces, parasols, perfumes, stockings, china, books, fabrics, furniture, and jewellery, Margaret became almost merry. She looked at Mrs. Filbert and could barely repress a grin. "How does one contain oneself? Oh, Mrs. Filbert! Market day has nothing to this! I am all aflutter."

"Recollect, dearest. You haven't the duke's endless purse to fall upon, as at home."

Margaret clutched her reticule with its pin money with real appreciation.

Nevertheless, when they returned to Berkeley Square three hours later, two footmen carried in a large assortment of parcels and band boxes, and Margaret spent the evening going over her treasures. A new silk shawl with gold thread was especially fine. She would wear it on the morrow when the captain called. But when Mrs. Filbert asked if she would consider enlightening him on her true identity, she said, "The captain? I refuse to give that man so much as a thought, I assure you." And she proceeded to refuse to give him a thought to the extent that if she closed her eyes, she saw him in the drawing room, all handsome and polite. And she imagined herself in conversation with him—almost wishing to be herself, Miss Tavistock—his promised bride. But that was out of the question—all she need do was recall that terrible scene of unspeakable manhandling in his coach, and her present course was confirmed.

That night, she continued to refuse to think of him while tossing and turning, so that she saw him only somewhat constantly in her mind's eye, his opaline eyes and sea-tanned face looking earnestly at her.

A message came the following afternoon as the ladies took tea in the library. He would call upon Margaret at eight forty-five that evening. Mrs. Filbert, unfortunately, could not be included.

"Well," said the companion, hiding her disappointment, "you must certainly take a servant as chaperon. And I shall find out whose ball this is before you put a slipper into his carriage, I warrant you."

Margaret pursed her lips. "I should never have let this happen," she said. Mrs. Filbert was delighted to think she was seeing the error of her ways, the needless difficulties associated with a subterfuge, but she added, "I have no wish to spend time with the captain. As soon as I make other acquaintances, I shall dispense with him."

"My dear, he does us a kindness in introducing you. Without your tie to the duke, you are a virtual nobody in society. And society is notoriously cold to virtual nobodies."

Mrs. Filbert put a hand to her chin. "Dearest, I must ask you to consider again the difficulty you are bound to encounter. If you are introduced as Miss Chrissendon now, how will you ever avoid scandal later when your real identity must be revealed?"

It was a question fit to make Margaret toss and turn when she tried to rest. How indeed?

She was only mildly filled with dread when the captain's coach slowed at the kerb precisely on time. She could not deny he was dashing in his naval coat, starched neckcloth, and tight breeches, his tanned face still alive with the motion of the sea, dimpled, slightly creased around the eyes, as if from studying endless horizons stretching out to the ends of the world, as, indeed, he had. Neither spoke after initial greetings, until they hit a street congested with a crush of carriages. He should inform her, he said then, what to expect at the home they were about to visit: Lord and Lady Farramore's. The company would be Whigs, so she'd best keep any Tory sympathies to herself. The duke, he understood, was a Tory.

She only nodded in reply, for Margaret herself was mostly a Whig. She and the duke seldom conversed about anything of a political nature. He added, "The navy are all Whigs, you know."

"But not Mr. Yorke," she said, referring to the First Lord of the Admiralty.

The captain blinked at her in surprise. "Do you follow naval matters?" he asked.

Margaret had forced herself to learn much of the navy in view of one day being a captain's wife, but saw her mistake and checked herself. With a wave of a hand she said, "I caught a whiff of something to that effect in the paper, I suppose."

He regarded her, noting a flush of colour infusing the soft cheeks prettily. Miss Chrissendon was absurdly appealing, a more youthful-looking face he'd have never imagined on someone known as Lady X. How could something so fresh and vibrant be entangled with his middle-aged uncle? Was it an error of judgment on her part? Did she now rue the mistake? Undoubtedly that was the reason she had come for the Season, to make it known she was available for marriage to younger blood. He cleared his throat, and she looked at him expectantly.

"I must tell you," he said. "My solicitors were reticent regarding your history, so much so that I had the presumption of looking into your background myself."

Her chin went up, though Margaret was not aware of it. Her eyes grew veiled. "Yes?"

"I can find no history of your family," he said simply. "What am I to say to enquirers? I must offer something by way of family."

Margaret inhaled, thinking. He was right, of course. No one could be welcome in society unless their background was not only known, but known to be respectable. This was precisely the problem Mrs. Filbert had intimated she would encounter.

"Happy you mention that," she said, amazed to find that a solution had just that moment occurred to her. Her face shone with the sudden inspiration. "Your cousin regrets to inform me that she continues unwell; she fears she cannot enjoy the Season in her current state and therefore wishes to cry off—in short, she has no plans to leave Yorkshire." Did he look faintly relieved? If so, that relief was followed by a crease of worry flitting across his brow, but he remained silent. She continued, "It occurs to me—in order to protect the duke, and to account for my background— can we not say that I am Miss Tavistock?" To his confounded look, she hurriedly added, "I am well acquainted with your cousin and can vouch for her complete approval of such a scheme. You may write and ask her, if you doubt me."

Margaret had left strict orders for any correspondence received at Toadingham to be immediately forwarded to her London abode, so she had no fear of such a letter going unanswered.

"That could help if I might have a reply upon the matter this minute," he said with a hint of irritation. Miss Chrissendon's pedigree must be lacking, indeed, he thought, for her to desire such subterfuge. His eyes clouded. "Her hand is promised to me; you do understand that?"

"I understand the alliance is not set in stone."

His mouth evened into a firm line. "The duke has just confirmed it. I have every expectation of being wed to Miss Tavistock, and I cannot have my future bride's name tarnished with unseemly behaviour; besides which, I should certainly look the fool whilst you dally with other men."

Margaret took a deep breath, colouring yet more. "Unseemly behaviour?" she asked, while her face transformed into that adorably angry glower. "I only mean to enjoy myself, sir, with the sights, with culture and the arts, and to broaden my acquaintance, of course!" She paused. Looking down, and with a sorrowful voice, she added, "My case has been not very different from Miss Tavistock's, you see. I long to be a part of society, even if for a short period."

Margaret felt as though she had just dug herself a grave. She did, indeed, wish to meet other gentlemen. But what chance of that, if she had an unknown background? She needed to be introduced as respectable. Her real name was not only her best guarantee of that, but how else could she continue an acquaintance in the future unless her true name was given out? Mrs. Filbert had been right about that.

Surveying her, the captain said, "It would cut the Gordian knot for you, wouldn't it? Solve your most pressing difficulty?" He stared at her, but Margaret could not bear the scrutiny and turned to survey the street, lined with the lower class curious who were out to watch their betters as they exited their coaches and entered the illustrious houses of the wealthy.

Finally, she said, "You need not own that I am your…intended. After all, you haven't seen Feodora in nigh a decade. Despite the duke's approbation, it may be that you no longer suit."

"I comprehend that," he said, wincing inwardly at what he thought was an oblique reference to his future bride's lack of good looks. "But what you are asking—you are the duke's mistress—"

"Not a mistress, sir!" The fire in her eyes surprised him. "The papers often get things wrong," she said crossly.

He put his head back to survey her. Leaning forward he said gently, "But you are Lady X."

"No one else need know that." The coach stopped moving, and the door opened. He waited for a footman to hand her down and then followed, his eyes glued with a strange light in them, upon her. Despite her protest, the duke, he recollected, had not denied that she was his "lady love." Something wasn't adding up, but he'd have to figure it out later.

She accepted his arm as they moved to the house. In her ear he said tersely, "Very well; Miss Tavistock it is, the duke's ward. If you end up his duchess, it will be your part to enlighten society upon how a niece may marry her uncle."

CHAPTER EIGHT

Despite the captain's ominous words, Margaret went on with a great sense of relief to be introduced by her real name. She met far more people than she expected to remember, received the utmost courtesies from both ladies and gentlemen, and even had a chance to address the pernicious rumour concerning her uncle when Lady Farramore approached her. Lowering her voice, her ladyship enquired, with more than a little curiosity, whether Margaret had met the mysterious Lady X.

Her question had not gone unheard despite the lower tone—or perhaps because of it—and the surrounding area fell quiet. Knowing other ears stretched to listen, Margaret said firmly, "There is no such woman, my lady. My uncle has never had a female acquaintance of that nature, you must know." She was quite happy with her reply, too, until she turned and met the eyes of the captain. There was something in them she did not relish. *Of course. He must think she was shamelessly shamming the company.* Soon, he approached with two glasses in hand and gave her one.

"Are you not doing it too brown?" he asked. "Denying that you are Lady X is one thing, but to extinguish her existence... I wonder you should go so far."

She coloured but could think of no apt response.

He said, "I must say, I begin to regret agreeing to your scheme. The longer you are known in Town, the less wise this course will appear to be. If my cousin decides to join you—"

"She will not," Margaret said hurriedly, making him turn and search her eyes for a moment.

"How is it you are that certain?"

"Recollect, I had that letter from her, sir, only this morning." But her cheeks flushed again. Why was it Margaret could not say a word that wasn't true without her colour rising?

At that moment—it was almost eleven and dancing had commenced—a gentleman approached and begged the honour of her company upon the dance floor. She gave the captain a relieved glance along with the glass and walked off, feeling his eyes upon her. The man was a plague, to be sure. How free and easy she might feel if only he wasn't there at every turn, watching her, listening to her.

The floor was elegantly chalked in a baroque design, most of which was still intact. Margaret had read of chalked floors but never seen one; she pitied the fact that each footfall of the dance obscured yet more of it. Her partner, a Mr. Crenshaw, was all courtesy in his manner and looks, following her gaze to the region of their feet with patient affability. But when he bowed and left her after the dance and she turned to accept a new dance partner, she felt a small disappointment not to see that plaguing captain looking on. After she had stood up for four dances, and he was nowhere to be seen, she took a purposeful walk about the rooms. Curiosity, she told herself, merely curiosity to know what he did, propelled her.

But a gaggle of older women in a circle motioned for Margaret. Only half of those in attendance, it seemed, were standing up for the figures. Many more were seated about the sides like these ladies. When she arrived and curtseyed, and was introduced to each by a Miss Turnbull, she found herself the object of curiosity. Was the duke as reclusive as they said? Did he never come to Parliament? Had she read in the papers about Lady X? For that question, Margaret was grateful, for it afforded her an opportunity to quash the horrid rumour a second time. Other questions followed: Did she see much of the captain since his return from sea? Did she know how much he'd won in prize money? (Asked by a younger woman with a guilty smirk, for money was considered a vulgar topic, not fit for polite conversation.)

When at last the talk moved away from Margaret and on to the shocking lack of corsetry in the younger generation, she listened politely, but Miss Turnbull approached and asked for the honour of taking a turn about the room with her.

Miss Turnbull was tall and slim and wore a trailing gown with a low décolletage that emphasised an ample bust. Her high-feathered turban was intertwined with a strand of pearls and quite pretty, Margaret thought. She was pleased by the invitation to promenade, taking it as an offer of friendship.

"So, Miss Tavistock, the reclusive duke's ward, you must know we are all quite ablaze with envy of you."

"Of me?" Margaret turned large eyes to her.

She smiled, nodding. "'Tis quite the catch you have in the captain." Margaret wanted to protest, to say, "There is no certainty to the match," but the captain's words, *I have every expectation of being wed to Miss Tavistock*, haunted her ears and prevented her.

Miss Turnbull looked about to be certain they were alone. Then, covering her mouth with one hand as if imparting a great secret, she added, "His prize monies, of course, are far and wide spoken of." As Margaret thought how to reply, the young woman continued, "But 'tis his constancy we envy. He is almost disagreeable in it; he has not an ounce of the flirt in him. The admiral assures us 'tis because of his long-standing alliance with you."

Margaret nodded, as though she'd known for an age that the captain had not an ounce of the flirt in him. And that was all she could do for response, for she had nothing to say to it. This assessment of the captain was, in fact, startling. Why, if she didn't know better, if she hadn't experienced brutality at his hands, she might even be forced to consider that perhaps the captain was a good catch. Heaven forbid.

But then she remembered what the papers had intimated, and what Roderick had reminded her. "I understand the captain quite enjoys women," she said, blushing.

Miss Turnbull blinked at her. "Oh, you have read the papers!" She waved a hand in the air. "The papers often get things wrong, you must know."

Margaret's face flushed, for she had said those very words to the captain. *The papers often get things wrong.*

Miss Turnbull continued, "Now, his brother the earl has mistresses enough, but the captain is that category of naval officer who stays wide of women, and particularly those of disrepute; I recollect he says they weaken a man." She looked benignly at Margaret and continued, "Such a credit to our naval force, he was: that victory at Lissa. A shame about his arm, though; he is quite out of spirits, almost in the doldrums."

"I nearly forget he is injured," Margaret replied honestly. "He says nothing of it."

"Just like him, that," she said. "For he wouldn't, would he?"

When they had circled the room and the young woman went her way, Margaret was left with thoughts roiling in her head. Was the captain, indeed, in the doldrums? What had Mrs. Filbert said? The sea got into a man's blood? She wondered if Captain Rempeare was unhappy. He'd been put on extended shore leave on account of his injury, forced out of service. She'd been so occupied with herself, her pique and pride that she'd not taken time to notice whether he was unhappy or not. The thought of him being dispirited was strangely unsettling. And was it true, that he stayed wide of women? Earlier, Miss Turnbull said he was almost disagreeable in that he refused to flirt. This was not the ogre she had painted in her mind.

She took nourishment in the supper room, welcomed by the Dowager Countess Reardon and her son's wife, the new countess. The young woman, a plump and pleasantly countenanced girl, said not a word, but the dowager spoke in spades, wanting to know all about the duke and the estate and whether His Grace regretted having no heir of his own, particularly as Stafford, as she called the earl, was an utter wastrel.

Before Margaret could form a reply, she waved a hand at her. "Oh, I dare say you care not; you have the captain and his hundred thousand to console you—such prizes he won!"

Margaret's eyes widened. Surely if the captain had won such a fantastic sum, the duke would have mentioned it. "Ma'am, you must allow that prizes are divided amongst all the officers of a ship, as well as the admiral; the captain may well have taken that amount, but he would not have been entitled to keep it."

The lady touched Margaret's arm with her fan. "You have the right of it, of course," she said, turning to nod at the countess, who nodded in reply. "But I warrant he took a great deal; indeed, as post captain, I am sure only the admiral had more; they say he is swimming in prizes. And how he cares for his brother!"

Margaret nodded blithely, continuing to listen politely, though she was surprised at what she heard, especially "how he cares for his brother." Was it Roderick she referred to? Roddy had always intimated that he didn't get on with his brother. The lady leaned in confidentially. "That is, if the cards don't put him to ducks and drakes, like they did the earl."

Margaret smiled weakly. Her head was aswim with all the gossip, and she did not wish to care whether the cards put the captain to ducks and drakes. If he gamed away his fortune, it would serve him for being foolish enough to risk it. But suddenly the ball felt wearisome. The excitement of her first social outing had somehow devolved into an unknown discomfort of heart. Indeed, when Lady Farramore approached to introduce a gentleman wishing to stand up with her, Margaret thanked him prettily but cried off, claiming the headache.

Hoping to leave, she returned to her search—no sense denying it. She was searching for Captain Rempeare and circled the room, but to no avail. Lady Farramore found her. "Do you look for the captain, Miss Tavistock?"

"I haven't seen him for this age," Margaret murmured, blushing faintly.

Her ladyship smiled and touched Margaret's arm with the tip of her fan. "Surely, you know where to find him, poor man?" She took Margaret's arm and led her to a corridor off the main rooms. Margaret realised her ladyship must have drunk a great deal of negus, for she hung rather too much on her arm for support. She hoped she would explain why the captain was a "poor man," but all she said, clinging to her arm and frowning was, "He has too strong a sense of duty, your captain." She forced them to a stop in the corridor. Whispering in Margaret's ear, she said, "Perhaps, when you wed him, you can prevail upon him to cease being his brother's keeper? Hmm? Surely, he must see the merit in conserving his fortune for his own family." This last was said emphatically, as though none could disagree.

"Yes, surely," Margaret said, but she was all at sea. She knew the captain engaged in gaming, but what that had to do with "too strong a sense of duty," she hadn't an idea. And now that she thought upon it, why hadn't her uncle cautioned her against the man, instead of encouraging her to see him in London? Surely, he didn't want her to marry a gamester and a wastrel. He'd banned the earl for such reasons, hadn't he? The earl, it was true, was a renowned rake, and the captain, she knew now, was not. But didn't an addiction to gaming warrant concern enough?

It was with a head full of such questions, led by Lady Farramore, that she turned into a card room with four tables spread about. The captain sat at one, his face creased in concentration. To Margaret's mortification, Lady Farramore announced loudly, "Here is your lady love, Captain! The poor creature was searching for you." Margaret's features froze, but her cheeks coloured rosily. Captain Rempeare raised his head of dark locks, and met her eyes. Lady Farramore mercilessly dragged her forward; she was soon deposited at the captain's side, and a man even vacated a chair for her use, though she did not sit.

Any thoughts of regret on the captain's part for being relegated to land fled her mind as one thought alone took its place—that he was, indeed, a gamester. He hadn't even asked her to stand up with him before hastening to this room, where men pitted fortunes against luck.

A man and a woman, as well as four onlookers surrounding the table, surveyed her with curiosity while Lady Farramore drifted away.

"Who's the tart?" asked the man sitting across from the captain. Margaret was astonished that anyone in good company would refer to her in such a manner. The man was elegantly dressed and looked somehow familiar, but had a sallow complexion and shadowed watery eyes; furthermore, he was in need of a shave. Overall, there was an unwholesomeness about him, though a pair of faintly iridescent eyes studied her with a mocking look.

Ignoring him, the captain turned to Margaret. "I beg your pardon for my absence." Before she could answer, the man asked again, in a louder voice, "Who's the tart, Gabriel? I ask you." His words were slurred.

Captain Rempeare turned to him and answered in a clipped tone. "Hold your tongue, my lord. You forget your manners. All in good time."

He turned back to Margaret who instantly said, "I am sorry to disturb you. I only wondered, Lady Farramore…"

"I understand," he said. "Forgive me; I'll have to play out the rubber."

Margaret gave him a dubious look, raising her chin. "Of course." She turned to go but the elegant, faintly sinister-looking man said quickly, "Introduce her to me, sea rat." He came to his feet and stood, swaying.

"You'll have to excuse my brother, Miss Tavistock," said the captain. "The earl is in his altitudes, I'm afraid, and forgets himself." He looked severely at the man. Margaret's eyes widened. *His brother! Earl Stafford.*

"Miss Tavistock?" spouted the earl. "Miss *Tavistock!* How delightful," he said darkly. "Why, my girl"—he rose with effort and stumbled around the table towards her—"how I have long wished to meet you, coz!" He came around to where Margaret stood, and taking her hand, made a fine deep bow. It would have been fine, that is, except the weight of his torso almost sent him crashing against her, but for the hasty intervention of the captain, with help from another man who was observing the game. Together they managed to lift him by the arms and drag him back to his seat.

"He's too hocused to hold his cards," said the captain.

"He'll kill himself, yet," said the other man, surveying the earl sadly. The earl's head hung down. He raised it enough to survey his brother, looking as if he wanted to argue, but in a moment his head swayed heavily and then fell again, confirming that he was all done in.

"Has a physician seen him?" asked the captain.

"I was with him only yesterday when the surgeon came by. Says he mustn't touch a drop." He looked at the earl and sighed. "Your brother, sir, is not one to take doctor's orders."

"We'll stop here," said Captain Rempeare. He took out a roll of bank notes and counted out a handful then put them carefully in front of the lady card player. "That covers it," he said.

The woman nodded and collected the notes, smiling. "Thank you, indeed, Captain. Always a pleasure to have you join our game."

Margaret stared at the bank notes. If she married the captain, her own trust money would fall into his hands. No doubt it would end up being spent, bill by bill, game by game, and disappear just as this handful of notes had done.

She was now grateful beyond words for the duke banishing the earl from Toadingham. Such an unpleasant man! And stone drunk. She would be certain to stay wide of Earl Stafford; she hadn't come to Town to meet the likes of him. His brother was more troublesome a matter. She had to think of a way to dispense with him, too. She could not reconcile why he was considered a great catch if he was addicted to much gaming...but perhaps standards in London were not the same as in provincial Yorkshire.

Before leaving, Margaret was assured of numerous invitations to follow, though she felt dazed at the thought of sitting through more interrogations. Society, it seemed, was merely an excuse for gossip. She could only hope that curiosity about her, the duke, and the captain, would now subside. And if nothing else, she had the supreme satisfaction of knowing that Lady X had been put decidedly in the grave.

The following day, Captain Rempeare went unaccustomedly to Grosvenor Street to the earl's townhome. His lordship's friends had seen him home and to bed the previous evening, but Gabriel had burning words he wished to rid himself of: words he had rehearsed during the night, which were meant for his brother's ears. He would have his say.

The earl was still abed but awake by the time Gabriel got past his servants and up to his bedchamber. After expressing his surprise to see his "affectionate brother"—spoken with his usual surliness—so early in the day, and asking to what he owed the honour, Gabriel said, "I've come to make something clear to you."

"Tsk, tsk," the earl said, eyeing him coldly. "Did I misspeak myself to our cousin?" Without giving him time to answer, he continued, "A delightful sight, that. A prime article."

"Collect, she isn't a doxie, Stafford."

"I had no thought of forgetting it. But I dare say I shall call upon her, and do my cousinly duty."

"Which is precisely why I've come," said Gabriel. "Do not think of calling upon her. The duke, you remember, forbids you her company. "

"This isn't Yorkshire where my eccentric uncle must be obeyed," he said, disdainfully.

The captain flushed. "*She* will obey him here as well as there." He paused and levelled a severe gaze upon the earl. "Keep your distance."

The earl feigned offense, putting a hand to his heart. "You wound me, dear brother. My intentions are only honourable. Indeed, high time I did something honourable, wouldn't you say?"

"Be as honourable as you like. With anyone else. Recall, if you would, that Miss Tavistock is my intended."

"Intended," repeated the earl. "Funny thing about intentions," he said, with a wicked gleam of amusement. "They seldom come to pass."

CHAPTER NINE

"So now you are Miss Tavistock again?" asked Mrs. Filbert, with a hand upon her heart.

"To society, yes. I'm afraid I'm still Miss Chrissendon to the solicitors and to the captain, though he introduces me as Miss Tavistock."

"So he has it all topsy-turvy," Mrs. Filbert said, nodding with a small frown and taking a sip of tea. They were seated in the morning room.

Margaret frowned into her cup. "I dare say."

Mrs. Filbert eyed her with affection. "My dear," she began, "why do we not both sit with the captain, and explain it from the beginning? Surely, he has a right to know—"

"Out of the question," she cried. "I have not decided upon my next course yet. I have not decided whether I even like the captain, much less wish to marry him. He must not know I am Feodora."

With a shake of her head, she turned to the morning paper and read silently for a minute. "Those horrid resurrectionists are at it again," she said presently.

Mrs. Filbert grimaced. "One can hardly bury a body these days and expect to find it safely in the ground the next. But I dare say 'tis our surgeons who encourage such grave robbery by paying good money for the corpses."

Margaret said, "It says here the practice in London grows quickly; 'tis almost as widespread as in Edinburgh." With dread in her heart, she turned to the society pages. Morbid curiosity made her scan it impatiently until she gave a gasp and set down her cup of chocolate so hurriedly it splashed. While a footman shot from his place near the door to wipe the spill, she said to Mrs. Filbert, "Good heavens! More of Lady

X! I spent the greater part of last night killing her off, I assure you. But someone is determined to darken my uncle's name in a dubious affair with that lady." She slid the paper to her companion.

Mrs. Filbert read the column and said, "Perhaps if we speak to the newspaper directly. I dare say their London office must be accessible."

Margaret said, "Will they listen to us?"

"They'll listen to *you*," she said.

Margaret came to her feet. "Let us go directly! That soirée this afternoon will have the captain here by three o'clock."

By the time Stevens located a coachman, it was going on noon. When Margaret instructed the man to take them to the office of the *Herald*, he said, scratching his head, "The office of the *Herald*? Cain't say as I know where t'find it, mum." A short jaunt through Town, during which Margaret stopped and enquired of different well-dressed individuals, led to the information finally, that the offices were in Middlesex.

"We cannot go today, then," said Mrs. Filbert, "or we'll miss the captain."

Margaret's little planned speech, during which she meant to level a severe combing upon those responsible for printing such Canterbury tales of a Lady X and her uncle, would have to wait.

Later that day when the captain called in a freshly starched naval jacket and neckcloth, worn above tight buff-coloured pantaloons and Hessian boots, Margaret greeted him cordially but with every intention of notifying him, before the day was over, that his services were no longer needed. She had been introduced already to a large number of upper-class families; and today's soiree promised to add to that number of London acquaintances. She was sure she would feel only relief at his absence, for he alone regarded her as a deceptive young woman with dubious aims.

Mrs. Filbert was allowed to join the party and sat beside her charge in the carriage.

Presently the captain turned to Margaret. "Mrs. Filbert is aware that you are going by Miss Tavistock's name?" he asked, casting a curious eye on the older woman.

"Why, of course," said Margaret. Mrs. Filbert nodded, though she could not keep a small frown from appearing. She wished that Margaret's identity was as open and clear to the captain as the midday sun.

"I am sorry to say—and I think, Mrs. Filbert, you will have the same mind on this matter—'tis a great mistake for you to meet new acquaintance under a false name. I wonder that I agreed to it; 'twas ill-considered."

"What is your fear, sir?" Margaret asked, not to be polite, but because she really wanted to know. Using her own name, she was sure, could only be a good thing. But since he did not know it was her real name, she could understand his hesitation—perhaps. He must enlighten her.

"If, in the end, you marry the duke, it would be unremarkable if you are anyone but Miss Tavistock. But to be Miss Tavistock and marry him—the whole thing is impossible. And even if you do not become his duchess—at what point do we give out that you are not, in fact, Miss Tavistock? A scandal will follow, I assure you."

Margaret listened with a slight puckering of her lips. As if he found her reaction lacking, he added, "Your scheme is fatally flawed, Miss Chrissendon."

"Miss Tavistock, if you please, sir," she said quickly, making him frown. Margaret was having trouble taking his concerns to heart. They would have been breathtakingly accurate if in fact she was not really Miss Tavistock, but she was—none of his dire predictions would ever come true. Only she too wondered, now that he had made plain the implications of using a false name, how it was that he had agreed to her scheme.

"I would leave for Yorkshire to see my cousin on the morrow if there weren't pressing matters keeping me in town," he said.

"I understand you have always had pressing matters keeping you from Toadingham," she retorted, with a cold smile. "It seems your future bride isn't worth the effort of a visit. I wonder not that she prefers Yorkshire to Town."

He looked searchingly at her. "I have rarely touched upon English soil this decade," he said. "And when here, my elder brother and the Admiralty both required my attention. Between the two, I dared not leave London." After a pause, and perhaps because Margaret's face hadn't softened, he added, "I hoped my letters would intercede for me—"

"You refer to your annual letter, I suppose?" she asked, with disdain.

He looked at her with surprise. "You are evidently not as informed of my business as you suppose. I wrote far more than once per year, though mail from sea ships is often delayed by months at a time. Surely, you...that is...she, knew that."

"You did not write to *her.*"

He stared at her. "For the last five years, no. I took her lack of a reply to mean she had no wish to hear from me."

Margaret looked faintly astounded. "Her lack of a reply? Reply to what, sir? I understand that Miss Tavistock has never had a letter direct from your hand addressed to her."

Captain Rempeare frowned. "That is incorrect. Ask Miss Tavistock when next you see her."

Margaret's lips firmed into a line, but the captain continued, "Granted, I wrote little my first year on the waves; a midshipman is hardly given leisure, and I was a mere youth. But I was in mind of my parents' wishes regarding the alliance, and after my father the earl's death, I began to think more seriously about things of that nature. I wrote to Toadingham numerous times per year, and to Miss Tavistock particularly."

Margaret frowned. Either the captain was lying, or he had written letters which she'd not received nor set eyes upon.

The carriage stopped in the street in a long line of equipages. The captain, looking out at the crush said, "Excuse me." He opened the door to peer out to survey their situation. Had he waited, he might have noticed the look of stark doubt that had crept upon the faces of both Margaret and Mrs. Filbert. The companion looked at her charge. Whispering forcefully, she cried, "Upon my word! He is most emphatic."

Margaret frowned and whispered back with equal fervor. "How could it be so? Why, if we received any letter from him, would we not have received all?"

In a moment, the captain jumped from the open door and then turned and put the steps down. He held out a gloved hand to Margaret, who came forth with scarcely concealed puzzlement and allowed him to hand her down, followed by Mrs. Filbert. "We'll get there faster on foot," he said.

"Sir," Margaret said, as he led her carefully through a throng, "I maintain that Miss Tavistock never received a letter from your hand; how do you account for that?"

He looked at her in consternation. "I enclosed my letters in packets to Redmonton. I dare say Roderick, or any one of the staff, should have had them sent on by mail coach." With a much-raised brow, he asked, "Do you mean to say"—and his look moved to Mrs. Filbert—"that she never had a letter from me? Not a one?"

Both ladies shook their heads. The captain looked ahead and whistled to himself. "I wonder she is still amenable to the marriage."

Margaret exchanged a look of surprise with her companion. As soon as she had the chance of speaking privately and not being overheard, she said, "I do not regret the mix-up, if indeed, he wrote me, for then my heart might have been subject to deeper injury, whereas now I am able to let him go, freely and with a clear head."

"But must you let him go?" asked Mrs. Filbert, with real regret. She had seen nothing in Captain Rempeare but good humour and gentlemanlike behaviour.

"He is addicted to much gaming," Margaret said. And then she fell silent, for she realised that her other complaints against the captain were fast falling to the wayside. He had been nothing but gentlemanly in London, was now known not to be a womaniser, and if he were to be credited, had even written her numerous letters, which had somehow got lost. The day they met, he had been provoking, to be sure, but had not she also been provoking?

Soon, they were mixing in a very crowded townhome, and Margaret found it reassuring to have the captain's arm to lean upon amid the crush. He was courteous, quick to introduce her (and this, she knew, despite his remorse at her using what he thought was a false name), and he was equally thoughtful to supply her with a welcome cold drink, stopping the occasional footman with a tray to present her and Mrs. Filbert with refreshments.

Miss Turnbull appeared and dropped a curtsey. "Miss Tavistock, my brother begs an acquaintance with you. May I present Mr. Joshua Turnbull?" she asked, turning to a light-haired gentleman of a neat and pleasing appearance. Smiling in a friendly manner, he bowed politely. He and the captain exchanged a nod of greeting.

In minutes, Margaret learned that Mr. Turnbull was all amiability, as he spoke admiringly of the North Country. Miss Turnbull chatted with Captain Rempeare while Margaret warmed to the subject of Mr. Turnbull's conversation, for she loved the hills and dales of Yorkshire.

"Most people find the country harsh and the winds too fierce to take pleasure in," she said, smiling. She was so caught up in their conversation, telling eagerly of adventures on horseback, that she failed to notice the captain had fallen silent and was listening.

Mrs. Filbert touched her arm as a warning, but Margaret missed it. She said, "Mrs. Filbert does not approve of my riding; I dare say she thinks I am like to break my neck, but my uncle enjoys a good gallop with me. 'Tis one of the few things we do in common, I dare say."

Mr. Turnbull said, "Whenever I am next in that country, I must join you in one of those gallops, if you will allow it."

"I should be delighted," said Margaret sincerely. "The duke has a respectable stable, though nothing like—" She stopped suddenly, for the captain was staring at her with a look on his face that she hadn't ever seen before. Colour infused her cheeks. She had completely forgot to speak as though she wasn't really the duke's ward. Something in her manner had alerted him; she was sure of it. But he leaned in and said, for her ears only, "You play your part well." And then, resuming his full height, his face cleared, and with a small wave of his hand, just like a ship's captain would say to his crew, he said, "Carry on." He turned aside to give his attention elsewhere, but despite Mr. Turnbull's continued amiability, Margaret had lost her appetite for speaking about Toadingham.

She was issued an invitation to the Turnbull's drawing room the following day. Upon reflection afterwards, she felt Mr. Joshua Turnbull was a delightful acquaintance.

The captain was stiffly polite when escorting the ladies home. Margaret had thought better of relieving him of the duty of introducing her further to society, for certain guests and their talk of an upcoming fête at Carlton House put her in mind that she very much wished to attend. And the captain, she reckoned, was her sole means of being invited.

Before leaving the carriage, Margaret thanked him prettily for his escort, and then, saying she wished to speak with him on a matter, invited him in. The captain hesitated, but then said, "If it pleases you."

They sat in the best parlour. Mrs. Filbert had disappeared for a few minutes, but now entered and took a seat upon a wing chair facing the hearth, as if to give them privacy, limited though it was. The captain looked expectantly at Margaret. "Are you invited to the Carlton House fête?" she asked. "I am all agog at the regent holding the largest celebration dinner in history the very year I am in London and may have a chance at attending it! A banquet for well-nigh two thousand to sit at table!"

"Four hundred at the main table," he said. "The other sixteen hundred will be disbursed beneath tents on the grounds." This didn't dampen Margaret's enthusiasm, for her face lit with excitement as she cried, "The royal family, Queen Charlotte, the French royal family all shall be there, but invitations are for gentry as well as nobility. I wondered if you—"

The captain said regretfully, "I'm sorry to disappoint. I'm afraid I gave away my invitation." In point of fact, he had given it in lieu of a thousand pounds his brother had lost at cards. The winner, a man not of the nobility, eagerly accepted it in place of the blunt.

"I dare say you could apply to Lady Hertford for another; you have too many friends to be excluded."

He gave her a quizzical look. "If I had the least ambition to attend, I might, indeed, speak to her ladyship. But I have no aspirations to be dazzled by the pomp, or should I say the pompous?"

Margaret's jaw might have dropped. Captain Rempeare was clearly not impressed by mere finery. And was he poking fun at the rich upper classes, most of whom were chomping at the bit to attend?

"They say His Royal Highness has commissioned every artist and craftsman in England for the event; Rundell's accepts no orders for silver or gilt, until all the pieces commissioned by the prince are finished. There will be wonders to behold, I am certain." Margaret's eyes shone at the thought of them.

"There will also be a crush. Every man and woman, regardless of rank, hearkens for an invitation."

Their eyes met. "Truly, you have no curiosity to attend?"

"None whatsoever."

Margaret's eyes clouded. "But—Carlton House—on such an occasion! After such preparations! Under normal circumstances 'tis considered lavish. They call it Byzantine luxury," she said. "The richest rooms in the world, to rival any royal court in Europe, even Bonaparte's!"

He nodded. "They also call it an experiment. To entertain so many at once, the prince is determined to stand out amongst the courts of Europe but thinks little of the inconvenience and cost to his country."

"Mrs. Filbert says"—and here she nodded towards the older woman—"he gives much work and income to manufactory. He asks his guests to wear apparel that must come only from British tradesmen, so that every weaver, tailor, mantua maker and milliner is engaged. And the porcelain, glass, and silver, and gilt-work—'tis all done in England. Cooks and confectioners, architects, painters, why most every trade is put to work."

"And all well and good, except the cost is still carried by the treasury, which is to say, the people."

Margaret realised his point, and her face lost some of its glow. His countenance softened. "I'll make enquiries for your sake. But with the guest list already bloated, I suggest you do not pin your hopes on going." He cleared his throat. "You might find a peer who will be happy to have you upon his arm." His eyes suddenly held a look of something—a wavering look directed at her that spoke of some inner longing, a regret, something wistful and heartfelt. But it vanished in a moment, and he was once again an impassive presence. Perhaps she had imagined it.

Studying him, she had a thought. "Is the earl to attend?"

The captain stared at her. "You would not wish to accompany him. I couldn't advise it in good conscience." Softly, he added, "Nay, I could not allow it."

Margaret smiled. "I thank you for your concern," she said sincerely, "but I should be safe enough at a public fête."

"In the earl's hands you would be anything but safe."

"He is my cousin! Surely—" She stopped, aware that she had slipped. The captain's eyes narrowed, so she hurriedly added, "That is, he will think we are cousins. Surely, that must constrain any improper notions."

The captain's face became granite. "On the contrary, Miss Tavistock is the duke's ward, and he is to inherit all else that His Grace owns. If I know my brother, he would jump at the chance to add her to his acquisitions." He paused, studying her face. "And if he finds out you are not his cousin, you still risk everything a woman can risk. He has no scruples and no fear of law, for his title inoculates him against it."

"Is he, indeed, so much a blackguard?"

"I am told."

Before he left, he asked for a copy of the *Times*. Paging through it, he assured Margaret there were numerous other London attractions which he would be more than honoured to escort her to. There was the British Gallery on Pall Mall open to the public, where she might purchase new paintings by renowned artists. There was the European Museum, brimming with historical art and artifacts, including figures by Vandyke and artists such as Corregio. There was "Kendrick's Collection of Rare and Foreign Beasts and Birds." Bonaparte's black tiger, "the only one seen alive," was on view. He added though, that "Kendrick's Menagerie" opposite St. James's Church on Piccadilly was possibly superior for it had the only large crocodile in England, and the "only mountain lion in Europe," amongst other exotic species.

"Du Bourg's Exhibition of Cork Models" of antiquities could be seen on Lower Grosvenor Street. And on New Bond Street, there was an exhibition of Velvet Paintings, under the "benign patronage of Her Royal Highness the Princess of Wales."

Margaret had read these listings but hadn't dreamed of discommoding the captain with requests to see them. Her head swam with delight at knowing he was willing to take her to such things. Indeed, the mere thought of seeing them sent a pretty sparkle of colour into her eyes and cheeks. With an appreciative glance at her interest, he went on to cite

"Barker's Panorama" on the Strand, currently showing numerous Italian scenes and quaint villages in art.

"There isn't a diversion you've mentioned that I should *not* like to see," she conceded, for it all sounded vastly exciting. He peered at her over the edge of the paper.

"I am happy to hear it. You'll never miss Carlton House with so much to amuse and interest you."

"Oh, but I must see Carlton House, too!" she returned instantly. "I only mean I'd like to see all of it. Everything there is to see!" She smiled at him so brightly that Captain Rempeare could not find it within himself to demur. He rested the paper upon his lap and glanced at Mrs. Filbert. The companion had lips pursed in amusement.

The call upon the Turnbulls the following day in their fashionable upper rooms on Hanover Street was a happy and comfortable outing. With Mrs. Filbert accompanying them, they walked to Gunter's and had tea and cake. Afterwards, they went on to Berkeley Square so Margaret could show off her fine establishment. She was particularly happy with the French-style drawing room with its Oriental carpet, and the corridors, lined with wainscoting, as was the library and second drawing room. The Turnbulls were properly impressed, and Mr. Turnbull was even so kind as to remark upon her good taste in books, at which point Margaret had to allow that the room came furnished.

They agreed to stay for dinner, during which the banquet at Carlton House occupied much of the conversation. The Turnbulls, alas, had only two invitations. But Mr.Turnbull gallantly offered to take Margaret to see the place the following day. According to the papers, it would be open to the public for guided tours through the public rooms and part of the grounds. Any royal subject who could squeeze his or her way into line and pay the guinea to get in might get a glimpse of the splendid luxury of their exalted regent.

Margaret retired that night happy with the thought of that coming day. She was happy, too, in that she had found a way to see the palace quite apart from Captain Rempeare. To her knowledge, he hadn't called at Berkeley Square that day. To her chagrin, once she thought of it, she tossed and turned, wondering why.

CHAPTER TEN

Margaret and Mrs. Filbert left the house the following morning to find the *London Herald's* office. Margaret was still exceedingly eager, for the duke's sake, to quash the rumour of a mysterious Lady X. As they entered the carriage, another equipage rolled up behind them. Mrs. Filbert said, "I think we have a caller."

Margaret turned to peer out the back window and gasped as she saw the tall, aristocratic figure of Earl Stafford emerge from a coach.

"The earl!" she said.

Mrs. Filbert said, "Let us off! We needn't entertain him." But in another second the earl was at the door of the vehicle and knocked, then opened it without preamble. He was elegantly dressed and had a strange similarity of appearance to Captain Rempeare, except where the captain's face was sea tanned and healthy, this face was sallow, the eyes more sagacious, almost unnerving. A smile curved the man's lips, though it did not reach his eyes. And he seemed to hold to the door almost as if for support.

"Miss Tavistock," he said, "you will pardon my intrusion, I trust, for I could wait no longer to meet my delectable cousin."

Margaret swallowed. "You have caught me on my way out, my lord."

"A morning call?" He glanced at Mrs. Filbert and looked her over with a bored air.

Margaret hesitated. "What else, sir?"

"Ah! But she doesn't tell us who she calls upon. My cousin is all mysterious," he said, as if speaking to a third party.

"Can I help you, my lord?" Margaret asked, with growing impatience.

"You can, indeed," he said, with a humorless grin. "I am come to offer my escort to Lord Malcolm's dinner tonight. The princess is to make an appearance. I thought it would please you to meet her." Margaret met Mrs. Filbert's eyes with a look of amazement. Princess Charlotte! At a Town dinner! Mrs. Filbert, pressed against the wall opposite Margaret, shook her head with a look of high alarm.

"I almost sent a note but came in person, dear coz," he continued, "to impress upon you the honour of this opportunity. Her Royal Highness is seldom in attendance; you don't wish to miss her." He stopped and had to cough here, a deep hacking sound that made Margaret's toes curl. She suddenly realised her cousin was ill looking not only on account of living a low life, but because he was, in fact, physically ailing.

Margaret bowed her head towards the earl. "I am obliged," she said. "Unfortunately, my lord, I expect the captain to call this evening."

"The captain cannot bend Ulysses' bow, my child. He isn't on Malcolm's guest list."

Margaret's heart beat quicker, but she hid her alarm. "Nevertheless, we have a previous engagement," she explained.

"Break it," he said, levelling a hard stare upon her. "When one is to see the princess, no one wonders at a broken engagement. Her company is prized."

Margaret glanced at Mrs. Filbert and then answered, "My lord, the duke would never allow it. I am afraid, sir, he has forbidden me to keep company with you."

The earl, holding a handkerchief over his mouth to cover another cough, nevertheless exerted himself to enter the carriage and sat beside Margaret. Mrs. Filbert's eyes bulged. He looked at the companion. "I wish to speak to my cousin."

Margaret said swiftly, "Mrs. Filbert may hear anything you might say to me, I assure you." The earl grimaced, but turned and took Margaret's hand. "Your uncle has been severe upon me," he said. "But he is in Yorkshire. And surely he would be loath to let you miss the opportunity of meeting our princess." He raised her hand and lay a lingering kiss upon it.

Margaret swallowed. "I am obliged," she said. "But I never break an engagement." The earl met her eyes. She saw gleams of steel in his.

"As your cousin, your elder, your superior, and your uncle's heir, I insist you make an exception."

Margaret pulled her hand free, trying to decide how to answer. She didn't wish to make an enemy of the earl. She wondered if he were really as untrustworthy as the captain had intimated.

"I will speak to the captain" she began to say.

"Do not trouble yourself. I will take care of him, I will arrange everything, I assure you." He made to leave but turned back to say, "Be ready at half past eight."

Margaret leaned forward in consternation. "My lord—"

But he was gone. She blinked at Mrs. Filbert, who cried, "You will not leave the house alone with that man. I am your chaperon. The earl will not win the day."

That afforded some comfort to Margaret but there was another worry on her mind. What was the earl going to tell the captain? Would he think she had cried off? She was surprised to find that she did not wish to displease him. She decided she would write him a note as soon as they returned from their morning mission.

The venture to *The Herald's* offices turned out to be a great failure, since the newspapermen were supremely unimpressed at Margaret's insistence that the duke was not engaged in a secret affair with a mysterious Lady X. They pointed out that since the affair was "secret," it wouldn't be known by her, now would it? Her ignorance of it only proved their allegation.

"But you profess to know of it," she cried, stamping her foot in exasperation.

"On account of an informant," he said.

"And who is your informant?" she asked indignantly. They refused to tell. No amount of protests would convince them to abandon the story, so she left with Mrs. Filbert in a lowering mood. As soon as they were home she put her mind to writing the captain. She ordered a cup of pekoe and sat at her escritoire. She wrote,

Dear Captain Rempeare,

Your brother the earl is quite insisting upon my company this evening to Lord Malcolm's house, where he says I may meet Her Royal Highness, Princess Charlotte."

She paused here and frowned. She would really like to meet the princess. Should she tell him that? No, best not. She wrote,

"Please advise. My uncle has forbidden— "

—she scratched that out, crumpled the paper, and fetched a clean sheet. She amended it thus:

Miss Tavistock's uncle has forbidden her to know the earl. And I remember your own ardent warning, sir. What would you have me do?

I am,

Yours most sincerely,

Margaret Chrissendon.

She sent the note off with a footman and waited. But while she and Mrs. Filbert leafed through catalogues from furniture merchants and then went over the month's fashion magazines, Margaret worried. Slowly she came to terms with her feelings and concluded two things. One, she did not wish to accompany the earl that evening. No longing to meet the princess could overrule the aversion to Earl Stafford in her heart. She tried to reason it away, to trust that a member of the nobility could not be bent on a dastardly course, but still her misgivings did not cease, and especially as the day wore on and she did not hear from the captain. The second realisation was that she quite looked forward to seeing Captain Rempeare!

The realisation was startling. She had said she wished to be rid of him, to "dispense" with him as soon as she met other gentlemen. But she enjoyed his company. The captain had an air of elegance and quiet dignity, whether from the uniform or his very proper manners, she did not know, but he garnered respect wherever he went. There was nothing of the coarse seaman in him, such as one might find in a common sailor. He was evidently well bred, and his manner towards her had softened a great deal since their first encounter, and even since their meeting in London, so that he seemed as fine an escort as she could desire.

Except he might behave more warmly towards her, but Margaret supposed his reserve was on account of her being Lady X. The very idea that she had claimed that identity suddenly filled her with remorse. And had she not only that morning, emphatically insisted to the *London Herald* there was no such lady? She had not managed to make them agree to print a retraction under her authority as the duke's niece, but perhaps it was just as well, since the captain would certainly have found it hard to comprehend her doing so.

When Mrs. Filbert entered her chamber, she said, "Mrs. Filbert, I think you had the right of it. I must tell the captain my true identity. I only need the right moment."

Mrs. Filbert nodded. "You will be much relieved when you do so!"

"I dare say," Margaret murmured. She turned a page of the catalogue but hardly saw the illustration of a diaphanous gown described by the editors as "evening dress." In her mind, instead, was the captain. His dark locks, curly on top, with his serious eyes and trim sideburns; his blue uniform—he was a captain of the blue—ornamented with its gold epaulettes and high collar edged in gold trim. At times, she could almost wish to run her hand along the length of gold buttons that ornamented his coat in two elegant lines. When he was amused, he smiled gently; there was no loudness or unseemly behaviour on his part. Contrasting him with the earl, his only failing seemed to be his addiction to gaming. Other than that, she saw a truly good man—a man worthy of respect. A man she had lied to in the most horrifying manner, it now seemed. A sigh escaped her.

"My dear," Mrs. Filbert said. "The captain hasn't answered your note. Soon it will be time to dress. What do you propose to do?"

Margaret stared at her, still frowning. "I will dress for the evening," she said. "And hope the captain calls upon me as planned."

"Perhaps that is his plan," said Mrs. Filbert. "To precede the earl and whisk you away before he arrives." She tried to sound confident, but wondered if the captain, indeed, had a plan, or had he bowed to the wishes of the earl? Surely, his lordship had contacted his brother. Had Captain Rempeare given up Margaret so easily, then? Now it was Mrs. Filbert who sighed.

She and Margaret were both in full evening dress, sitting stiffly in the parlour at half past eight when sounds below signalled the earl's arrival. Margaret cleared her throat nervously. "I suppose I cannot blame Captain Rempeare for not coming. He may not have seen my note," she said.

"Mayhap the earl browbeat him with rank," said Mrs. Filbert.

Margaret looked exquisitely feminine in white, sprigged jaconet muslin, bolstered at the bust with short stays. She had insisted upon keeping her décolletage modest, but the revealing fashion of evening wear could not disguise the sweetly rounded tops peeking above the bustline. To offset the low square neck, she added a lacy tippet about her shoulders. Her lady's maid, Clarice, had risen to new heights with hair fashions this night, taking special pains with Margaret's shining locks on account of her possibly meeting Her Royal Highness. A fillet of twisted satin and pearls circled twice around her head, ending with a hanging tassel at one side.

The butler scratched at the door, and it opened to reveal, not the earl, but Captain Rempeare. "Captain!" exclaimed Margaret with a sincere smile that lit her features.

"Your servant, ma'am," he said, eyeing her with surprise as he took a deep startled bow. His eyes swept over her and he swallowed.

"My dear sir," said Mrs. Filbert. "How relieved we are to see you this evening."

The captain stared at her a moment. "The earl barked at you, did he?"

Margaret stood, motioning to her companion to do the same. "He did, indeed. I sent you a note—"

"Which I received," he said, opening the door for them. "I found my brother and took care of the matter." He hesitated while surveying her. "I wasn't quite certain what your wishes were, or how you wanted me to proceed. I feared you might be disappointed at my arriving rather than him."

"Disappointed?" Margaret asked. "Not to meet Her Royal Highness, you mean?"

He nodded. "That's it."

"I would be gratified to meet her, I confess. My maid took extra trouble with my hair on her account," she added, smiling. "But I have enough aversion to the earl that I can pass this opportunity without regret."

"Your hair is lovely," he said, with mild eyes.

She looked curiously at him. "Thank you."

When the butler produced a hooded cape for Margaret, the captain took and helped her into it, studying her face the while. He waited as the servant helped Mrs. Filbert into a pelisse and then led both ladies to his waiting carriage. As they walked, she said, "Surely, with your connexions, there may be another opportunity of meeting the princess?"

He took a breath. "That's possible."

When they were seated with the captain across from them, Margaret looked at him quizzically. "How did you put off the earl? He seemed most decided about my accompanying him."

Captain Rempeare studied her, thoughts whirling behind his eyes. "My brother seems beyond redemption, but he's not so removed from sense that he doesn't understand what's in his best interest."

Margaret blinked. "I do not understand you, sir. How is that to the point?"

He explained. "He is in my debt; I had merely to remind him." He did not mention to her the two hours it had taken to locate his brother at a shadowy game hell in a low district of the city or the fifteen minutes of heated discussion between him and the earl, during which he'd threatened to never come again to his rescue at cards. His brother had cursed him for a useless sea rat and threatened to have his half pay stopped: a threat the captain utterly ignored as empty, for the earl had no standing at the Admiralty. He told him in no uncertain terms that he was not to approach Miss Tavistock on this occasion or toy with her on any, and he'd left while his lordship flung oaths at his back.

Without knowing any of those details, Margaret was still impressed. Any younger brother would normally have a hard time putting off an elder one, and especially a titled elder one. She eyed him gratefully.

The ball that evening was filled with glittering, bejewelled, and boisterous people. To her pleasure, the captain asked Margaret to stand up with him. She enjoyed the cool eyes upon her, the quiet presence of him, and appreciated the grace of his movements during the figures. Afterwards, she enjoyed the quick manners that made him introduce everyone who came their way, or on occasion, introduce her to those of rank.

To her surprise, he remained in attendance all night, though there was a card room. She caught more than one glimpse of people in it, intent on their game, and looked curiously at the captain to see if he felt the draw of the room, but he seemed utterly oblivious to it. She was relieved to know Earl Stafford wouldn't be there; he was at Lord Malcolm's. The Turnbulls were nowhere to be seen, unfortunately, but Margaret spoke with many another young woman or older dame, and Mrs. Filbert sat contentedly against a far wall, looking on and nodding, and engaging in conversation with dowagers and other older women.

The captain asked her to dance a second time towards the end of the night. Margaret blushed when she caught Mrs. Filbert smiling at her idiotically. She had read that being asked to dance a second time by the same gentleman signified special interest on his part. But of course, the captain was only expected to dance with her twice. She was thought to be his intended. Margaret found her heart beating faster during this dance; she could barely meet the captain's eyes for fear he would somehow know it.

They promenaded the room afterwards. Upon passing the doorway open to the card room, Margaret said, "You do not play this evening, Captain."

He glanced into the room. "Thank God, no!" Margaret eyed him curiously. He was aware, she thought, of how unhappy a pastime it was, gaming. She wanted to ask why he engaged in it at all, but found she lacked the courage.

Just before they left, Earl Stafford arrived, along with an entourage of loud, bedecked men and women. Margaret heard his cutting voice. She had been engaged in conversation with a Miss Allen, but hurriedly excused herself to find Captain Rempeare. She saw him standing and speaking with another gentleman, but she could not contain her anxiety over the earl and floated to his side. "Excuse me, sir," she said. Hardly knowing what she did, but with much relief to have found him, she entwined her arm within his, and felt instantly safer. He looked at her in surprise.

"The earl has arrived," she said in explanation, not trying to hide her alarm. Her cheeks had filled with colour, and she swallowed nervously. There was no denying she had somehow developed a strong fear of his lordship.

The captain's eyes were soft as he put his other hand protectively upon hers. "Have no fear of Stafford," he said. "I can manage him, I assure you."

"Thank you, sir," she said, and her eyes shone with real gratitude. He met her gaze searchingly for a moment before turning to the gentleman.

"My lord, have you met Miss Tavistock?"

The grey-haired man, with a kind and easy face, said, "I have not had that pleasure, sir. Pray do me the honour of an introduction." He twinkled a smile at her, and Margaret returned it. If only her cousin Stafford was a kindly old peer like this man instead of a frightful roué. She learned he was Lord Agerwood. He said, "So you are the fortunate lady promised to our captain here, eh?"

Blushing, Margaret nodded; what else could she do? His lordship turned to the captain. "I dare say, sir, there is fortune on both sides. If she comes equipt, sir, you are doubly blessed!"

To Margaret's look of horror, for "coming equipt" wasn't a familiar phrase, and lent itself to several blushworthy meanings, the captain hastily said, looking at Margaret, "She does, indeed, sir, but *dowry or no*, any man who weds Miss Tavistock must be blessed."

Margaret smiled regally as though she were perfectly at ease, but was inwardly filled with surprise. Did the captain really think any man who wed her must be blessed? Had he changed his opinion of Lady X? Or, more likely, he referred to the *real* Miss Tavistock, not knowing it was she. She could only murmur, "You are too kind, sir."

"Kind? Nothing of the sort," said Lord Agerwood jovially. "He's a man in love, I warrant!" The captain looked away. Margaret looked down uneasily.

Afterwards, they found Mrs. Filbert. The room was beginning to thin as the evening had worn on into the early hours of the morning. Captain Rempeare enquired if they were longing for their homes and firesides yet. Margaret looked up to find Earl Stafford looking sourly in her direction. When she met his eyes, he bowed his head in greeting, but even that gesture seemed coloured with surliness.

During the ride home, Mrs. Filbert appeared to be brimming with news, but constrained by the captain's presence, had to keep it to herself. She kept eyeing Margaret and looking to the captain in the most curious way. By the time they were back at Berkeley Square, Margaret could see the older lady was ready to burst. With the captain safely gone, and even before the butler had helped them from their coats, Mrs. Filbert cried, "My dear! The captain nearly came to fisticuffs with the earl today!"

Margaret's eyes widened. "What on earth for?"

"To prevent his lordship from calling for *you!*"

"How do you know this?" asked Margaret.

"A man who was there; he spread the word to his wife, who spread it to her acquaintance, who spread it to—"

"I see," Margaret said, moving slowly to the stairs.

Mrs. Filbert climbed the steps beside her. "He championed your cause," she said, pressing her point, "even though he thinks you are— you know—Lady X."

"He protects me for the duke's sake," Margaret said. "'Tis only that."

Mrs. Filbert fell silent, for perhaps that was true. But then she said, "He stood up with you twice. There was no call for that."

"Society thinks we are betrothed to be married. There would be much surprise if he did not stand up with me."

Mrs. Filbert fell silent again, though secretly she was sure there was something to it. She had been watching the captain this evening. He kept an eye upon Margaret even when she was speaking to other people. There was something in his look that made Mrs. Filbert sure it was more than duty at work. Somehow Margaret must be made sure of it.

CHAPTER ELEVEN

Before sleep came, Margaret found herself replaying the evening in her mind. Most especially the look on the captain's face as they danced...or when she took his arm...or when he said any man who married her must be blessed! The severe countenance of the disapproving captain seemed a thing of the past. It pained her heart that she wasn't being honest with him. Captain Rempeare was not a man to trifle with.

She now saw that he might, indeed, be dispirited about losing his sea command. When a naval officer by name of Lieutenant Northcote spoke with him, she could hardly help but notice how his face lit with animation. She'd gone to dance with a gentleman and returned to find them still deep in conversation and the captain alive with feeling. Yet not once had he complained about having lost his command in her hearing. And she had forgotten to ask about it. But she felt she was learning to know him. And there was nothing she'd learned that she disliked—saving his addiction to gaming.

It was indisputable, for she had discerned a pattern in his behaviour. Despite the captain's fine manners and attentiveness, he often disappeared after an hour or two to the card room. Stafford was always there. What had Roderick called them? *Wastrels.* Just the other day she had read a moraliser who said, "Gambling is one of the strongest passions in the human breast," and that "no warning, no exhibition of fatal examples" would ever stop the indulgence. But what right did she have to judge the captain? When she herself had him hoodwinked about her identity due to a falsehood!

She was drawn from her thoughts when Lieutenant Northcote enquired where she was from, to which the captain replied, "She hails from Yorkshire."

"A smuggler's paradise," he said, glancing at Margaret with a reproving eye as if she herself were guilty of importing goods by night in secret coves along the wild shoreline.

"I suppose it is," Margaret said. "But you can hardly expect the populace to complain; we have all the tea and sugar we need in that region."

"The problem, ma'am," he said, "is it keeps the enemy in the blunt. We're trying to bankrupt them, don't you know, which means it isn't in the national interest to allow it."

"But it hurts our own nation and economy when we forbid it," she said. "I can understand not exporting items, but to stop imports—"

"From enemies, ma'am, only from enemies," said Lieutenant Northcote. "Though I should say," he added, with a smile to Gabriel, "that if all our populace were as lovely as you, Miss Tavistock, I shouldn't want to deny them anything."

Captain Rempeare said, "The duke, I am sure, would never allow his land to be used by smugglers."

"I am sure," agreed Margaret, though she had often wondered at how well supplied they were with black-market items. But the lieutenant suddenly asked her to dance—if Captain Rempeare would allow it— putting an end to further thought of smugglers, tea, and sugar. As they moved to the floor, Margaret said, "I notice how well the captain enjoys another seaman."

"Oh, aye," said the lieutenant. "No one understands a tar like a fellow one. Poor devil," he added, looking at the captain. "Injured in a skirmish that ought to have made him a hero, and the Admiralty sets him ashore, decommissions his ship, his command. No wonder he seems out of sorts."

"But he is considered a hero," said Margaret.

"Small comfort, that," he said. "It won't feed a man. He has his prizes, of course, but will he take a merchant ship, you think?"

The idea had never occurred to Margaret, that Captain Rempeare might miss the sea so much that he would captain a commercial vessel since he couldn't get a naval one. Or that he might need the income to such an extent that he would. "I—I don't know," she said. And during the remainder of the dance, she wondered.

Afterwards, she went to check on Mrs. Filbert to see if the dear lady might be bored. She found, on the contrary, that she was happily engaged in conversation with other chaperons, and having, in fact, a merry time. But Captain Rempeare was once again speaking to his friend Northcote, and the depth of feeling in their speech, evident even at this distance, made her linger in order to give them time. Let the captain enjoy his seagoing friend, she thought.

Lieutenant Northcote checked to be certain Margaret wasn't in earshot and said, "Well, sir, if I may say, your intended bride is a Juno! Another prize to add to your conquests."

The captain's eyes strayed to where Margaret sat with her companion. His expression grew serious. "A Juno? Nay, a Helen of Troy. A beauty to start a war if ever there was one. She starts a war within me."

Lieutenant Northcote almost gasped. "Indeed, sir?"

Rempeare continued in a tone tinged with remorse. "She is the siren I never met at sea. Her presence mocks me."

"Why, sir!" Lieutenant Northcote showed real surprise. "Why do you say so? When you are betrothed?"

"Our arrangement is…less certain than it might appear."

Lieutenant Northcote rocked on his heels and nodded understandingly.

"You must strengthen it, then," he said quietly. "You're the kind of man can do it, sir. A good, dependable husband you'll make." He nodded again towards Margaret. "Don't want to lose a good thing, eh?"

The captain merely looked back at Margaret with a serious expression.

The next morning, to Margaret's delight, invitations came trickling in to Berkeley Square, filling the little, gilded, hallway card tray. Whenever the white-gloved butler, Stevens, delivered a new one into Margaret's hand, she practically held her breath to see what fine establishment now begged the honour of her presence. To her dismay, she saw that wherever she was invited, the captain was too. Society hostesses, it seemed, were going out of their way to invite the pair as a couple. Margaret and Captain Rempeare were a known commodity.

"This accounts for why the gentlemen are admiring and polite," Margaret said, "but treat me as though I'm spoken for." In an injured tone, she continued, "If the captain is in the room, they hardly talk to me in deference to him. I dare say I am as constrained by it." Mrs. Filbert did not think it was that bad, but as she formulated an answer that would serve, Margaret added, "It's as though I'm betrothed to be married!"

"But, my dear," said the companion, not hiding her surprise. "you *are* betrothed—you and the captain."

"I begin to wish we were," she said, blinking. "He is not—not at all the ogre I thought him at first. But he thinks of me as the dubious Lady X. I am neither here nor there, Mrs. Filbert. I am not the duke's lady, and I am not really the captain's lady, for he thinks I belong to his uncle! The rest of society thinks I belong to the captain." She turned large sad eyes to her companion. "All my swans are geese, ma'am."

Mrs. Filbert made a tut-tut sound. "But you *are* the captain's lady. All you need do is let him know it."

"He has said not a word in all this time about me—about Feodora, that is—his actual betrothed, who is supposedly in Yorkshire. He neglects me most horridly."

"Neglects you?" asked Mrs. Filbert. "He calls upon you almost daily and shows you the utmost respect."

"But he does it only to keep an eye upon me, I am sure of it. He does it only for respect of the duke."

Mrs. Filbert was at a loss for words. "Did you not say it was time to let him know?"

But Margaret was in the throes of indignation. "And why does he not enquire after his sweet, homely cousin in Yorkshire? It is past time for *that*, I dare say!"

Captain Rempeare showed up that afternoon with the express purpose of taking Margaret to Hyde Park at the popular hour. She felt a surprising flutter in her stomach at his arrival. Seeing his tall good looks, the dignified uniform, and knowing his mild nature, she felt suddenly grateful for him and his agreeableness in helping her. He had such goodwill and loyalty, when he might have despised her for being Lady X.

He helped her atop the board, feeling he lifted a mere cloud of soft muslin in a spencer, before going around and climbing up to drive.

Seated together in the small gig, for the first time it seemed to her that his demeanour was, indeed, dispirited. He was polite as always, but on their way to the park she studied the quiet profile of his face and thought it troubled.

"Captain," she said, as they rounded the corner onto Park Place, "tell me, are you quite dispirited to have lost your command, your ship?"

He glanced at her in surprise. "I beg your pardon," he said. "Have I been preoccupied? Forgive me."

"You are perfectly polite, sir," she said. "But it occurs to me that it was perhaps not what you would have wished, to be plunged into shore leave?"

He kept his eyes on the street as he handled the horses, a team of matched greys, and thought for a moment before replying. "It is kind of you to enquire," he said. "I will confess that no sea captain takes it easily—losing his ship—no willing seaman, for that matter. A sailor learns to love the sea. She is a wild mistress, but predicting her turns and tides is a vastly stimulating endeavour. I've not yet found anything equal ashore." He turned suddenly as if remembering whom he spoke to; he cleared his throat and bade her look at the park, as they swept through the great Cumberland Gate into its busiest thoroughfare.

Already Margaret saw familiar faces and was inordinately pleased to be waved at and called to, and to wave and call in turn. Clusters of people in gaily coloured clothing went by in open carriages, barouches, gigs, and curricles, all dressed in high style. As they clip-clopped past, Margaret cried, "'Tis like a veritable fashion magazine!"

"'Tis exactly that," the captain said, with a wry grin. "The upper class comes here to see and be seen."

She glanced at him and again thought she discerned low spirits. "It must be very hard for you then," she said. "Losing your commission?"

He stared for a moment, as if gathering his thoughts. Then, looking afar off, he said, "To a sea captain, the ship is his domain, his realm. He is king." He paused. "Ashore, he is given respect, to be sure, but there is no honour to be gained, no chance of routing the Corsican's ships, no battles to be won, or prizes to secure." He met her eyes. "No crew to manage or win the heart of, to encourage when necessary, and control at all times. Sea life is regular, ordered by discipline, and protocols, and requirements that can be met and done with." He met her gaze. "Life ashore lacks every bit of it. The regularity, the discipline—the honour."

Margaret saw a shadow in the depth of his eyes that seemed vast, indeed, like the ocean he so missed. It cut to her heart.

He said, "There are days I awake and expect to feel the roll of the sea beneath my feet, but am met with hard earth. At night I see the heights of the rigging with the sun behind the sails, or the horizon in a blaze of light as it sets in a wide sky in a glory of colours. I do wonder if life on land shall ever compare or can afford the smallest sense of the freedom and beauty oceans alone possess." He looked at her and added, "Forgive me; I ramble on."

"Not at all, Captain," she said quickly. She added, "I own I have never thought much about what it must be like, life aboard a ship."

"Shall I tell you a story from my days at sea?" he asked.

"Please," she said, with a little smile. It rather fascinated her to discover that she wished very much to hear such a thing. "A story of one of your skirmishes, if you please."

He hesitated. "You'll think me a shameful boaster, if I do."

"No, I assure you," she said, with a small laugh. Their eyes met, and she enjoyed the mirth she saw in his gaze.

Considering what tale to relate, his look became distant then he said, "Very well." And he began a tale of an expeditionary landing upon an unknown island in the West Indies. He and his crew saw evidence of past human occupation but nothing that looked recent. Nevertheless, they drew swords, a few readied pistols—a necessary action, it turned out— for no sooner had they stepped inside the lush growth of a tropical stand of trees, than they were set upon by a band of pirates and bounty hunters!

Their attackers were armed with cutlasses, clubs, and pistols, and a nasty skirmish ensued. The captain lost two men in the event and gained a permanent scar, and a thing unknown to Margaret—a gash beneath his right ribs. It happened that the rogues had been about to bury a stash of treasure they'd just stolen off a French frigate. After winning the fight, they discovered from a prisoner that the French ship was becalmed on the other side of the island. The captain and his men recovered the prizes, took five prisoners, and in the end, engaged the French vessel in battle, winning a ship for Britain and many French prisoners. It was quite the feather in the captain's hat.

What a thrilling tale!" cried Margaret. "Like something from the pages of a novel!"

"I assure you, such things—or worse—happen regularly in the navy," he said.

"And your arm," she said gently, as they turned onto a quiet lane, empty but themselves. "I should like to hear of that battle."

His expression seemed troubled for a moment, but he said, "Would you?" At her assurance, he relived the battle as he had done for the duke and countless drawing rooms. He hurried past the moments of his injury, not lingering on the pain he must have felt, or even the subsequent afflictions suffered on account of that battle, losing his ship and his command.

But Margaret remembered how, in his carriage, on that fateful day of their meeting, he'd winced when using that arm to restrain her. She glanced at him, and with a pounding heart, asked shyly, "May I see the scar, if you please?"

The captain looked at her searchingly; Margaret felt surely she had made too bold a request. But in a moment he undid his jacket. They were still quite alone on the path, though the sound of voices and equipages could be heard in the distance. He shrugged off only one side of the jacket and then undid the button at the wrist of the white shirt sleeve covering the injured arm. As he rolled up the linen, she saw the scar: a wide ugly gash on the inside of his arm with its permanently reddened edges. It was long, running from his upper arm to well beneath the elbow.

She was drawn to touch it. She reached out a hand, stopped to remove her glove and then gently touched the scar, letting the tips of her fingers feel the depth of how it had ploughed up muscle and skin on an otherwise strong arm. Suddenly the horror of warfare became real to her.

"How you must have suffered!" she exclaimed softly.

"This wound is nothing next to what others endured," he replied. But it was wound enough for Margaret. She took a shaky breath. Her eyes filled with sorrow and met the captain's eyes. They beheld each other for a moment as if they were just any man and woman, not a captain betrothed to another lady, and not a woman romantically connected with his uncle. The meeting of their eyes seemed like a meeting of minds, of hearts. But suddenly both seemed to recollect themselves, looking away. He hurriedly drew down the sleeve and closed the button. She helped him back into his coat and put her glove back on. A minute passed in silence. .

Margaret was lost in dismal contemplation, feeling painfully drawn to the Captain. She turned to him. "Captain," she said. "The day I met you at Toadingham—you do recall?"

He glanced her way with a veiled expression. "Of course."

"I am flummoxed, sir. I am all at sea." Here she blushed, for the pun was not intended. "I beg your pardon; I am at odds to comprehend a change in you. What seemed like ease, like good spirits that day, has been lost in you."

He looked at her thoughtfully but said nothing, so she hurried on. "I mean to say that I am sure I am still a plague to you." She swallowed, staring hard at the scene ahead. "I wish to let you know that I have no further need of your escort. I am greatly obliged, but you are free to cease calling upon me." She turned serious eyes to him. "You are free to return to your better nature, sir."

He reined in the horses to pull up alongside the road and then made them stop. Turning to Margaret, he said, "Am I to understand that I have displeased you?"

"No, sir; that is not my meaning." She bit her lip and again stared hard at the road ahead.

"Am I to understand that my presence is tiresome? For I can assure you I find no punishment in accompanying you about Town."

Margaret frowned. "No, sir, not that."

"Pray, be plain with me, then."

Margaret swallowed. "You are too polite to say it. But I remember how free and easy you were that day on the drive—before our disagreement. And yet in my company, you are reserved and—and unhappy. I know I am the cause of it." She shook her head and looked away. To Margaret's shock, she was blinking back tears. "I dare say you wish you were in Yorkshire and could see your—your intended, rather than being chained to Town in order to introduce a plaguing woman."

She dared to glance at him and found him looking at her with a troubled expression. He said, "I am subdued on account of losing my ship; the sea was my life. It is practically all I know. I must say, however, Miss Chrissendon"—his voice grew soft—"that what began as a duty, that is, introducing you to society, I now undertake willingly. I dare say it must cause *you* grief to be known as my intended, for it prevents other offers coming your way—"

"No, sir, I assure you!" she cried, with perhaps more feeling than he expected, and definitely more than Margaret herself had been aware of. She blushed lightly; he fell silent, regarding her with unreadable eyes.

They rode in silence then, heading back to Berkeley Square. At length Margaret asked, "Should you like to dine with us this evening?" She'd never invited him to dinner. She hoped he would accept. She would ask him more about his life at sea, about his exploits and conquests; how little she'd troubled herself to consider such things in the past. How little she'd known or understood Captain Rempeare!

He seemed surprised at the invitation and almost at a loss for words, keeping her waiting for long seconds. Finally, he said, "I thank you, no. In fact, I should tell you I am off for Yorkshire in the morning. I have just recollected; I failed to see my cousin at my last call. I am determined to meet her; and suddenly I feel it cannot be too soon."

CHAPTER TWELVE

Margaret's heart dropped. He was determined to meet Miss Tavistock in Yorkshire? She wouldn't be there, and he'd find out everything. Her mind raced for a solution. She must not let him go! But how to keep him from it? She had no claim upon him as Lady X. The captain slapped the reins to reach a smarter pace, and her mind sped to think of what to do. As they manoeuvred through traffic, and then stopped to let a rushing line of carriages hurry past, she wracked her brain for a solution.

The right thing to do, of course, would be to tell him at once that *she* was Miss Tavistock, that there was no need, no need at all for him to travel to Yorkshire. She'd been increasingly sorry for having misled him. But how to say it? The words would not come.

He turned to her. "I must ask you to stay wide of the earl, Miss Chrissendon," he said. "Particularly while I am away." He was busy with traffic or might have seen her stricken face, for she was still in agonies of indecision. It was no more a matter of wishing to keep him in the dark, but how to tell him? How to confess that she'd been deceiving him all this time? In truth, she saw now that she was a stubborn, quick-tempered minx of a woman!

A carriage flew towards them suddenly, and only the captain's quick handling of the team prevented a head-on collision. As it sailed past, for it hadn't bothered to so much as slow, a woman waved gaily from inside the equipage. Margaret didn't recognise her, but the captain said, "That is Lady Hempley. Sir John, her husband, was quite deceived in her, poor man."

"Deceived?" asked Margaret, wide eyed. "How so?" Her fingers gripped her reticule.

"She claimed to have ten thousand pounds in the funds. He married her for them. She had less than five hundred."

Margaret swallowed. "Did it not serve him for marrying her only for her dowry?"

"Oh, he loved her," the captain said, casting a knowing look at her. "Says he would have married her anyway, but he still laments the loss." He shook his head. "I think 'tis the knowledge that she fed him a Canterbury tale that really galls him."

Margaret said not another word; she was too, too lost in gloomy thoughts to speak. As they pulled up to number 29 Berkeley Square, she felt herself a condemned criminal. It was only a matter of time. The captain would know that he too had been lied to. And would it not gall him, as it had done Sir John? What would be her sentence? Besides calling off the nuptials, would he let it out in Town that she was a deceiving shrew? Would the whole world know, as it knew about Lady Hempley, that she was so wicked?

Her face must have betrayed such tumultuous thoughts, for he said suddenly, "My dear Miss Chrissendon, are you unwell?"

She looked at him like one coming out of a dream. "Oh! I beg your pardon. I am only just thinking...your leaving tomorrow...'tis very sudden." She tried to control the doldrums from showing on her face.

He gave her a searching look. "Perhaps I may return with Miss Tavistock, if she is well. Is that what troubles you? Because you have used her name?"

She was so confused how to answer, that she merely stared at him. Finally, she said, "Must you go tomorrow? Can it not wait a few days more?"

He looked surprised then stared out ahead of them. "You wish me to put off my trip so your subterfuge will not be discovered?"

"I do!" she said, very earnestly. "I realise there is no merit in my plan. Nothing in it for you to like. But the Season is almost at an end, and there is the Carlton House fête, which Mr. Turnbull has graciously offered to accompany me to see on the public day. I am sure Feodora would not deny me the opportunity."

"Turnbull?" he said, a little sharply.

"*He* has no fear of the crush," she said, almost reproachfully.

"He has no sense of it, then. You must know every cit in Town longs to be there, which means every cove, scoundrel, ruffian, and whipjack will be on hand as well, hoping to relieve you and everyone else of the contents of your pockets or purses."

"But Carlton House, sir, will surely have foot soldiers on hand, if not the prince's guard—"

He said, "The fête is in ten days, after which all the best families will leave London for their country estates. As I have written to Miss Tavistock, I will hold off my return to Yorkshire, unless she bids me come. Is that agreeable to you?"

Margaret's eyes shone with relief. "Quite agreeable! You are very kind, Captain." She glowed inside with the thought that a letter from his hand was en route to her, even if it would have to reach Yorkshire first and then be redirected to Berkeley Square. A letter, from his hand!

He said, "May I ask? After the Season ends, do you plan to return to Yorkshire?"

"I have no other plan," she said quietly.

"And to the duke," he said, with strangely veiled eyes.

An awkward silence fell, until Margaret said, "Are you quite determined that you cannot join us for dinner? I would be very pleased if you did."

His mouth hardened. "I'm afraid I have business to attend to, but I thank you. Princess Esterhazy promised me you'd get a voucher for Almack's."

Margaret nodded eagerly. "Yes, it came! Thank you for arranging it."

"I'll call for you tomorrow evening, then."

Margaret's groom had arrived and held the reins while the captain helped her down and gave her his arm. Before they'd reached the door, however, a street urchin raced towards them, followed by a merchant calling for his capture. The man was red faced and huffing; the captain instantly caught the boy and stood holding him. The sooty child, stuffing bites of apple into his mouth as fast as possible, kicked and fought against the captain's hold. Even an injured arm did not prevent him from holding the boy securely, but with a kind of evil genius, the urchin spit out a bite of apple and went instead for the captain's arm with his teeth. In a stifled exclamation, he had to let go of the boy, but Margaret had come close to inspect the child, and she instantly took hold of him.

He continued to fight and kick, but she held him fast. Why, it was no different than grasping one of the duke's great hounds. Two footmen rushed from the house, and the child was apprehended. Margaret brushed off her gown, quite unperturbed. The captain stared at her with a look of near amazement, but it was an admiring look, amused, even: a look she caught glancing up at him at the last second before the merchant arrived, panting and sweating. He wiped his face with a handkerchief and nodded at the captain. "I am obliged, Admiral," he said, guessing at the epaulettes on the captain's uniform. "For catching this thief. I'll 'ave his 'ide for this!"

"Captain will do," said Gabriel.

"What did he take, sir?" Margaret asked.

"Why, he's eaten the evidence," the man said. "But he's done it afore—taken my apples, 'e 'as."

Margaret reached into her reticule and took out a guinea. "Here," she said, handing it to him. "Let the child go." She eyed the boy, who had suddenly ceased fighting, and stood, staring at Margaret in astonishment. "Hunger drives him to thievery, cannot you see it?"

"Aye, mum," said the man, who now took off his hat in deference and held it against his chest. "But it cain't be 'elped; I cain't give away my living, now, can I, or I'd be no better off than he'n."

She took out another guinea. "Allow this child two apples a day. And then apply to me when the money runs out. I am Miss Tavistock, and here is where I live," she said. The man took the second coin meekly, bowed low and said, "As you wish, mum." The captain released the boy, who, after taking a last, wondrous look at Margaret, darted off for freedom.

When both had gone, the captain said, "The boy is better off, I suppose, but all the guineas in the kingdom will never rid us of the poor."

She nodded. "The poor you shall have always with you," she quoted. "But it doesn't follow that we shouldn't do our best by them."

"No, indeed," he said.

"If he musters the courage to come, I'll have cook feed him proper meals," she said, looking in the direction the child had run.

"What you have done already was prettily done." His look of approval sent Margaret into the house with a happy glow. She'd come near disaster that day, for if he'd gone to Yorkshire, her game was up. But somehow it was avoided, for the time being, and her small act of kindness seemed to please him.

Seated in the solicitor's offices on Conduit Street, Roderick Rempeare scratched his chin and levelled a puzzled stare upon Mr. Primpley, his family's man of business.

Mr. Primpley had to repeat himself to Roderick and was fast growing annoyed at the whole business. "I repeat, sir, you must call upon Miss *Chrissendon* in Berkeley Square. She will direct you to Miss Tavistock."

"I never heard of a Miss Chrissendon," Roderick insisted. "'Tis Miss Tavistock I wish to see, my cousin, sir, and I cannot understand," he added through gritted teeth, "why you should direct me to this Miss Chrissendon instead."

Mr. Primpley came to his feet, signifying that the interview was at an end. "Call upon Miss Chrissendon," he said, with a most determined and indecipherable look, "and all will be made plain, sir. Miss Margaret

Chrissendon, of Berkeley Square." Suddenly Roderick's face cleared. His eyes widened.

"Miss *Margaret* Chrissendon, did you say?"

"Miss Margaret Chrissendon."

When Roderick left the solicitor's offices, he did so with a strange puzzlement. Miss Chrissendon must be his cousin! She had always implored him to call her Margaret. Why on earth she was choosing to use a name other than her own perfectly respectable one, he did not know. But no matter. So long as he could find her, he was sure she'd lend him the blunt he needed to pay off a debt of honour. Blast it, why had he sat down in that gaming hell? He'd enjoyed it, of course, but he didn't have the means to keep up. Nevertheless, he was in London and meant to make the most of it. Sadly, he'd been expelled from Cambridge, knew it was bound to happen, but he'd hoped to have more years of eternal scholarship before facing life as an independent gentleman. Being an earl's son didn't translate into having an income, not in his case. But now independence was upon him. He almost wished he'd heeded the captain's advice and accepted an army commission when he'd had the chance.

Adding to his present discomfort was the fact that the night business was falling off. Two resurrectionists had recently landed in gaol, and the rest were on tenterhooks. The fear of the law would soon wear off, and they'd be back in operation. Why, merely getting a good set of teeth from a body could earn him thirty pounds! But in the meantime, Roderick was in the basket, dry in the pocket. It would take three days to reach the duke and lodge a plea; besides which, he'd drunk from that well not long ago. He had to find Feodora; she was always flush in the pocket. He didn't mind hanging on a woman's sleeve if it kept him from being all done up and dished. A petticoat pensioner, they'd call him, but what cared he? His brothers were not to be considered as sources for help. Stafford was in dun territory himself and hadn't a feather to fly with. And the captain was a last resort, being too high in the instep for Roderick's liking.

Feodora, however, was just the thing. He could manage her, he was sure.

Margaret and Mrs. Filbert were reading in the library on facing sofas when Stevens came in to announce that a Mr. Roderick Rempeare awaited Margaret's pleasure in the parlour. She looked at Mrs. Filbert in alarm. "Roddy!" she cried. "Here in Town? I am undone!" He knew her to be Miss Tavistock—that meant the captain would soon know it, too.

Mrs. Filbert came to her feet with a look of regret. "'Tis for the best, my love. He had to know sooner or later."

Still, Margaret dreaded the revealing. What would such an upright man as Captain Rempeare make of her prolonged deception? Would he not feel like Sir John, "sadly deceived?"

Roderick stood when they entered. "I knew 'twas you!" he said triumphantly. "So now I must call you Miss Chrissendon?" he asked doubtfully, as he made a bow.

Margaret hesitated, and a taper lit in her mind. "Of course not," she said. "You must call me by my proper name, Miss Tavistock." She gave Miss Filbert a meaningful look, for a wild hope had filled her breast. Since she was already known as Miss Tavistock, there should be no harm in Roderick calling her thus. The captain would think he was merely keeping to the rules of the game.

Roderick's eyes narrowed. "Why'd Primpley call you Miss Chrissendon?"

Margaret waved her hand. "A misunderstanding, I assure you. Do not give it a thought," she said dismissively.

"I must say, Feodora, you're not in your looks."

Margaret had had spent a sleepless night trying to formulate the proper way to end the charade and confess all to the captain. Light shadows about her eyes attested to little sleep, and then she'd grown pale upon hearing of Roderick's arrival. She cleared her throat and said nervously, "Nonsense. I have a strong constitution." She gave him a severe look. "But you must call me Margaret! It cannot be too difficult for you, Roddy!"

He held up his hands. "Don't raise a breeze about it! Margaret it is, coz." He would happily call her Margaret—he'd call her Queen Charlotte if she chose—so long as she took kindly to him.

She rubbed her hands together as she took a seat across from him. "Now, what brings you to Town and away from your books?"

Roderick, it turned out, desired to stay for a sennight. Margaret almost insisted he stay with one of his brothers—they were both in Town—but she was alarmed at the thought of his leaking the truth somehow if he saw either of them at length. She wondered why it was not his thought to stay with a sibling, but she said nothing on it and merely assured him he was welcome.

At the first moment possible, though it meant missing Almack's, she wrote a hasty note to the captain, explaining she was indisposed for the evening, and he must not think of coming for her. She apologised prettily, claiming the toothache. She knew it was only prolonging the inevitable—Roderick's meeting the captain—but even one day's respite gave her relief.

Roderick soon revealed that he was short in the pocket. He thought it wise not to mention his student days had ended in sad disgrace or that Mr. Primpley had reminded him, maddeningly, that the monies for Roderick's upkeep were conditional upon his being a student in good standing or attaining his certificate of degree. He only grumbled something to the effect that Primpley was being tight-fisted with funds, not granting Roderick so much as a farthing. Word of his expulsion had somehow preceded him to London, but Margaret didn't know.

She assured him of a sum to meet his pressing needs. When she learned he had a debt of honour, however, she frowned. "You will get no further help from me for such debts," she said. "I'm afraid this odious habit of gaming plagues your family, but you must rise above it, sir." She looked at him seriously. "Surely, your superior learning must inform you of the sheer folly in it."

"Indeed, cousin, indeed," he said, nodding contritely. He went on to bemoan the earl's poor example, and how even the captain was prone to sad bouts of extreme gaming with disastrous results.

"Disastrous?" asked Margaret wistfully.

"I should say so," Roderick said, as if he knew every last detail of the captain's financial affairs. He gave her a curious look. "Still planning on getting leg-shackled with him?"

Margaret frowned. "You lapse into vulgar language, Roddy; do not say they are now encouraging it at Cambridge."

"Speaking of the captain," he said, examining his fingernails as if they held acute interest, "I suppose he'll be by presently?" He looked up with a bored air.

"I...er...not tonight," Margaret said. But she suddenly remembered something. "Why did you tell me he was in the petticoat line? I have learned quite the opposite of him."

Roderick shrugged. "Saw it in the papers, I suppose."

"The papers often get things wrong!" Margaret cried, realizing she'd said that before. How true it was!

Before going down for dinner, the captain's letter arrived, addressed to Miss Tavistock at Toadingham Hall. It had been forwarded from Yorkshire after arriving there from London. Margaret opened it with fumbling fingers. It was the first letter from his hand written expressly for her that she'd ever received. In a gently scrawling hand, he wrote:

My dear Miss Tavistock—Cousin,

I hardly know where to begin, having just learned that my past letters to you (and I assure you there were dozens) have never reached your hand or eyes; nor therefore, your heart. I know not what happened to prevent their reaching you, and can only express my regret for what must have seemed a monstrous neglect.

But more to the point, I am, as you know, recently come ashore and hoping, therefore, to begin a life on land. This life must include a family. As you are aware of the long-standing hope, the dearest wish of both our parents, I will only say that I am, for my part, ready to fulfill it. I apologise for the pressing matters that have kept me in Town since coming ashore. And allow me to express my sincere hope that you are much recovered from the ailment that prevented our meeting when last I came to Toadingham.

I urge you to instruct me. I am your servant, ma'am, and will obey your word. Shall I come to Yorkshire for our long awaited reunion? Do you prefer to join us in London (The "us" I speak of being your acquaintance, Miss Chrissendon, and your servant, Mrs. Filbert).

I must inform you that Miss Chrissendon is using your name. I can hardly express how aghast I am that I lent her scheme my approval, for I'm sure it is a disservice to you. She assured me of your complete approval of it, but why should it be so? There are more things I wish to discuss with you concerning this lady, not the least of which is our uncle. And 'tis on her account, I confess, that a new sense of urgency propels me to my duty concerning you.

I ask for your soonest response. Instruct me as to whether I should come to you, and pray give the duke my best compliments.

Your most humble servant,

G. Rempeare

Margaret was all awhirl. One thing in particular stood out from his letter: *'a new sense of urgency'* and *'on Miss Chrissendon's account'* propelled him to his duty concerning Miss Tavistock. A new sense of urgency: what could it mean?

While she paced and considered how to answer—there was no question of bidding him go to Toadingham, of course—another messenger arrived with a note. This, too, was from the captain!

"I am told," it said, "that my brother Roderick is in Town. Please send word if he contacts you."

Fire and brimstone! What made him write that? Why should he think it likely that Roderick would contact Lady X? But then she realised since she was known as Miss Tavistock, it would be reasonable for Roderick to seek her out. With a sinking heart, she mulled over his letter and thought how best to answer.

Finally, she replied as Miss Tavistock from Yorkshire, imploring him to feel perfectly comfortable staying in Town until the Season ended. She said she thought it a great lark that Miss Chrissendon was using her name, and it should not cause him the least uneasiness. She declared that if he arrived in Yorkshire by late June, it would be most propitious. And impulsively, she added a line to the effect that she was cognisant of the honour of being his future wife, and that nothing would please her more than to fulfill the dearest wishes of both their parents.

The ink flowed easily enough as she wrote, but Margaret had to wipe away tears. Marrying the captain had somehow become the true wish of her heart! Yet marrying him would likely be the last thing possible once he knew of her deception. He was too, too good a man to ever accept such a dishonour.

She decided to say nothing at present of Roderick. Though he asked her to, how could she hasten the discovery of her lie? If Roderick and the captain spent time together, surely Roderick would say something of Margaret from the past and then it would all be out.

She enclosed the letter inside another to Toadingham, where the butler was to redirect the one to the captain back to London. Such a circumbendibus route; how complicated everything had become! And as she dressed for dinner, Margaret realised her efforts to avoid the inevitable were in vain. If not from Roderick, it must come out some other way. Captain Rempeare was determined to meet his future bride, and then he would know all.

He would despise her forever.

CHAPTER THIRTEEN

The following morning, while her maid helped Margaret into a morning gown of white muslin with ruffled lace, and a matching robe with wide lace ruffles running its length, Margaret had a sudden flash of insight. She'd been thinking how to keep the captain and Roderick apart for another day, when it hit her. As soon as she'd tied the ribbons of her robe and adjusted her morning cap, she hurried from her chamber and down the corridor like a summer cloud blown by a wind—a cloud that found Mrs. Filbert still abed.

"Mrs. Filbert! I have hit upon it! The solution to my dilemma."

Mrs. Filbert blinked sleepily at the cloud. "Which dilemma is that, dearest?"

"The captain! He will loathe me if he discovers who I am. So I have determined to break off the betrothal, letting him go—free and clear! He shan't have to meet me at all in Yorkshire, and I will not have to own up to my horrid mistake."

Mrs. Filbert sat up. She swung her legs out from the blankets and said, "Let us discuss this, my love. He is your cousin; you are bound to meet at some time or other. A funeral, a wedding, a reunion…this won't answer."

"I am quite determined upon it," Margaret said, but then she frowned. "If only I hadn't sent that letter yesterday." To Mrs. Filbert's questioning look, she explained, "I wrote telling him I was honoured to be his future bride and happy to expect our coming nuptials. I told him to come to Yorkshire at the end of the month, after the Season is over, and that I thought it the veriest lark to let Miss Chrissendon use my name." She sighed. "Only now I see I must tell him quite the opposite. That my heart has become engaged elsewhere, or some such thing. And that he is free as a bird, free to choose any other wife he might."

Mrs. Filbert said, "But that ends it. Better you should risk his anger than lose him altogether, dearest."

"Oh, he is lost to me already, Mrs. Filbert, utterly lost. If you only knew his goodness," she said, her face creased in worries. "If you knew his estimation of honour...and I have none! None that he could admire, for when he learns of my deceit. Oh, I can hardly stand to think on it."

Mrs. Filbert said, "I have studied Captain Rempeare, and I find him a most reasonable man. I am sure he will only be relieved to know that you are no pudding face." She smiled. "And, as you will show all proper remorse, he will be only too happy to find the woman he loves is the woman he must marry."

Margaret turned astonished eyes to her companion. "The woman he loves? Why, whatever can you mean?"

Mrs. Filbert smiled. "The way *he looks at you*! And who can blame him, dear man? He might have ceased accompanying you about Town weeks ago, but he comes for you still, almost daily."

"Society thinks we are betrothed."

Mrs. Filbert said, "Fiddle! Why, the couples who are engaged are the ones least seen together. Once an arrangement is made, that is all that matters. He could easily have abandoned us. He comes because he cannot help but to come. He comes because he must see your face."

Margaret blushed but said, "I maintain you are mistaken." She shook her head. "He is all businesslike and practical with me, I assure you."

"Of course; he thinks he must be. He thinks you are involved with his uncle. He thinks he is betrothed to a different girl. He is honourable."

"Indeed!" she moaned. "Far too honourable!" She stared out disconsolately at nothing. "To think, that high morals in a man is my undoing!" She turned an agonised face to her companion. "The letter I sent won't arrive for a week or more, I warrant. I will present him with a different letter this very day from Miss Tavistock's hand, which I will say I received along with another for me."

Mrs. Filbert frowned. "My dear, you only add more lies to the other."

"I am settling the matter, don't you see?" she said, stopping to face the lady. "I could not bear it for him to find out now!" She blinked hard to fight tears. "I simply couldn't bear it!"

Roderick preceded the ladies to the breakfast parlour and was polishing off a large plate of bacon, turbot, egg pie, and guinea fowl from the sideboard, when they entered. His chewing slowed considerably as he took in the sight of Margaret, her face fresh with signs of crying.

"I say, coz," he said, "you are most decidedly not in your looks. Is there aught I can do?"

She sat across from him and looked at him gravely. "There is, indeed." Her pretty features puckered into a frown. "I require your word upon a matter."

"Anything at all," he said, relieved that only his word would be required. He put a forkful of bacon in his mouth while saying again, "Anything at all."

Margaret levelled a hard stare upon him and said in a hurried long breath, "You must never let the captain know that I am really your cousin Miss Tavistock, though you must always call me Miss Tavistock."

Roderick froze. Frowning, he said, "Say again?"

Margaret sniffed. "'Tis simple, really. You are to call me Miss Tavistock, but I am really Miss Chrissendon. I am not Miss Tavistock; I am only using her name."

He stared at her. "But you are Miss Tavistock."

"But the captain doesn't know that. And he must not ever know it." She stopped suddenly and put a hand to her head. "Oh, dear. It is no good! How am I to explain your staying here if I am not truly your cousin?" She gave him an agonised look. "Why did you have to come to Town just now? Oh, I'm sorry, Roddy, but you have no conception of the trouble I'm in!"

Roderick had slowly resumed his meal. He'd stolen a few glances at Mrs. Filbert as if to ascertain how she felt about this calling someone by one name, when they really were that person, only to be told that they were not to be called that person and must be called another. It was most befuddling.

"Lud! What a bumble-broth," said Roderick. "How'd ye get in such a hobble?" To her pained look, he said, "Here, go through it again. I don't mind keeping the wool over Gabriel's eyes."

Margaret gave him another agonised look. "Must you say it so plain?" she cried, closing her eyes in horror.

Mrs. Filbert said, "Sir, let me explain…"

About six minutes later, Roderick's laughter echoed through the room. "You are in a proper tangle!" he cried. "But I've no reason to upset the cart. I'll stay out of sight when my brother calls, and I'll avoid him in Town. We've no great love between us, you know."

Margaret did know, though the captain had never said a harsh word about his younger brother.

"But see here, coz," he said suddenly. "I might find it easier to stay low if I had some blunt to spare." He looked at her hopefully.

"Humph!" said Mrs. Filbert.

But Margaret pounced on his hint. "Roddy, you may be assured of a constant income so long as you stay wide of Gabriel...er...the captain."

Roderick smiled. "Your servant, ma'am."

Margaret took a breath of relief. Feeling the first sense of peace she'd had for countless hours, she suddenly had an appetite and went for the sideboard. Sitting down with a cup of coffee and the morning paper, she turned with a lighter heart than she deserved, she was sure, to the society columns.

After reading for a moment, she gasped. Shutting the paper, she put her head in her hands.

Mrs. Filbert said, "My dear! What now?"

"'Tis Lady X," moaned Margaret, from behind her hands. "She is back. Only now it is much worse."

"Why, my love?" said the lady, while simultaneously reaching for the paper.

Margaret looked up, her face distraught. "Because now I am a widow!"

Roderick looked at her in consternation. "What d'ye mean, you're a widow?"

"The paper says it's been discovered that the duke's mysterious Lady X is a widow! With children!"

He blinked at her. "But you're not Lady X."

"The captain thinks I am."

Roderick slammed a hand upon the table and glared at her. "You said the captain thought you were Miss Chrissendon!"

"He does! He thinks I'm Miss Chrissendon, and that Miss Chrissendon is Lady X."

Roderick thought about it for a moment, shaking his head as if it all were bothersome in the extreme. "Well, this is a deep kettle you're in," he said. But he gave her a dubious look. "A widow with children, eh? You don't look the part."

Margaret cried, "I have it! I'll tell him the papers got it wrong."

Mrs. Filbert said gently, "You could tell him the truth, dearest."

Margaret stared at her companion. Usually Mrs. Filbert gave excellent advice. But not now, not on this occasion. "That," she said, taking in a great, shuddering breath, "is the one thing I simply cannot countenance doing!" Her eyes strayed to Roderick. "Don't look at me so! Your income depends upon your not looking at me so!"

He turned away immediately and resumed eating. But in a moment his head popped up. "What about Stafford? Is the earl all at crosshairs like Gabriel? Must I watch what I call you in his presence?"

Margaret grimaced. "Oh, he thinks I am his cousin, Miss Tavistock, and 'tis fine for *him* to think so."

Roderick frowned. "If he can think you're his cousin, why should not I go on just as if you was—since you are?"

"Roddy, please!" she cried, extending a slim hand towards him. "For all the reasons Mrs. Filbert explained! The captain knows who the earl thinks I am, because we're going about as though I *am* who I am, but *he* doesn't really believe it, because he thinks I'm Lady X, who is Miss Chrissendon! Don't you see?" she asked, as if it were the simplest thing in the world.

Roderick hurriedly swallowed the last bite of guinea fowl on his plate and came to his feet. "No," he said, but he held up a hand to prevent the torrent about to escape his cousin and said, "But fear not; *I* needn't understand. Female mysteries are nothing new, I dare say, and I can keep your secret—I think. You are Miss Tavistock, although you are not Miss Tavistock, and you are Miss Chrissendon and Lady X although you aren't neither of them, either. Is that it?"

Margaret smiled beatifically. "That's it!" She held out a hand to him. "Much obliged, Roddy!" He bowed to leave but stopped and levelled a stare at his cousin. "You do know the game is blocked at both ends. He'll find out sooner or later."

Margaret's smile vanished. "I know. But I'd rather it was later, thank you."

The ladies changed into afternoon dress and were preparing to give a morning call when the butler sent a footman to Margaret with a note from Captain Rempeare.

She tore into it. He asked her to pray excuse him for that day, for he had matters to attend to concerning the earl. *They are gaming,* she thought ruefully. *And he wishes me not to know.* He added, however, that a report of an alarming nature had reached him, which he wished to discuss with her at the soonest convenience. *That horrid newspaper account, no doubt.*

She'd been in the midst of the maid putting finishing touches to her hair when it arrived, getting the curls to hang just so on either side of her forehead as was the fashion. Frowning into the mirror, Margaret told the footman, "Thank you. Pray send Mrs. Filbert to me."

In a minute the companion appeared, dressed in grey figured silk.

"Mrs. Filbert! The captain shan't call today."

She handed her the note. Mrs. Filbert read it swiftly and said, "I do wonder if his lordship's condition is worsening."

Margaret eyed her dubiously. She thanked her maid and then turned on her seat to survey the older lady. "I dare say they are bent on gaming. 'Tis the captain's only fault, but a grave one."

Mrs. Filbert considered it. "I cannot think so. I'm sure I forgot to mention this, which is most flummoxing, for it will relieve your mind, but did you know that Captain Rempeare is not a gamester—"

"But he is!" Margaret cried, her eyes filled with conviction. "He retires to the card room on almost every occasion, and I've seen him at the table, vastly intent on the game." She paused, raising her nose in the air punctiliously. "He never looks happy, and I don't know why he plays, but he does, and I've even seen him paying up."

Mrs. Filbert said, "My dear, you must know—I only wish I'd told you as soon as I learned it—the captain only plays when his brother does. And he pays up, to be sure. He covers his brother's losses, for the earl has long since gone through his own fortune. The captain bailed him out these many times or the Rempeare estate would have been lost! 'Tis an ancient family seat and would be an irreplaceable loss. The captain is a paragon of virtue to save it."

Margaret stared. "But the estate belongs to the earl, not the captain. Why should he protect it?"

"His father gave him an injunction on his death bed. I had it all direct from the Dowager Countess Besserman who knows the whole story, for her husband was a great friend of the fifth earl, God rest his soul. He charged the captain before he died that he must be his brother's keeper. Stafford was already a determined rake and gamester, and even though the captain protested that he could hardly keep him in check while a thousand miles away at sea, his father insisted that whenever possible, it was his duty to watch his brother's—and the family's—interests."

Sitting there looking at Mrs. Filbert, Margaret's countenance dropped further. The companion said, "But this is good news, is it not? He is not a wastrel!"

"He is *too* good, if you must know," she said. "This only confirms my path. I must break off the betrothal with him as Miss Tavistock." She stood up and said mournfully, "He needs a saint for a wife! I am most assuredly not of that shade."

As Mrs. Filbert followed her charge, still bearing a woebegone look, she said, "You might say, 'tis not goodness that makes him cover the earl's losses."

"How so?" asked Margaret with a sigh. She ordered the carriage as soon as they saw Stevens, also asking him if Roderick was about.

"Mr. Rempeare left the house an hour ago, ma'am."

Margaret nodded, hoping she didn't have to worry about Roderick's doings. He'd promised to stay clear of the captain and he'd better, but Mrs. Filbert was still talking. She said, "One might consider it a great fault that he spends his fortune for the estate when he has his own future to consider. Without a commission, how is he to recover the losses? He can take no more prizes, as you know."

Suddenly things she had heard weeks ago came back to Margaret and now made sense. Lady Farramore had said, "He has too great a sense of duty, your captain. When you wed him, you might encourage him to save his fortune for his own family, eh?" At the time, she could not make heads or tails of such sentiments. But now she understood. And more than once she'd seen the captain as he sat at cards; always his face bore the look of boredom combined with concern. He certainly did not play for amusement. He seemed more wretched at cards, in fact, than at any other time. Little wonder, if he spent his fortune at it for the sake of the family estate.

"I am sure he expects a new commission; this war goes on abominably!" But her face puckered in thought. "Or perhaps he depends upon my trust money to support us if we wed." But she shook her head. "Poor man. For I am about to cry off. 'Tis no good—he is far too much the paragon for me. He is soon to despise me, for it must come out, who I am."

"Then let it come out. Take your chances with that, for I maintain he will not despise you." She settled a soulful look at the girl. "Don't cry off, my dear. You will only injure him further if you do."

Injure him further? That thought hadn't occurred to her. So Margaret did not write a letter to release him from his promise. But she had to think of some way to soften the coming blow to his pride; for would it not injure a man's pride to learn he'd been bamboozled?

CHAPTER FOURTEEN

The following morning another note came from the captain, this one by special messenger. "I am sorry to inform, the earl's condition is deteriorating rapidly. I fear his days are numbered. He begs your attendance—wishes to make amends, I suppose." Margaret gasped. Mrs. Filbert was right, indeed, about the earl's health declining.

At breakfast she shared the news and said, "I believe I must pay a call to his lordship. He is apparently nearing his end, poor man... There are passages in the prayer book to read such a one."

"Miss Tavistock certainly should pay her respects," agreed Mrs. Filbert. "But when the captain thinks you are not she? You may not be admitted."

"But 'tis the captain who says he begs my attendance. And the earl knows me as myself."

"Hmmm," said the companion. "Let us try. We'll need our parasols," she added, "for the sky is grey and lowering." They turned their attention to Roderick who, all this time, had said nothing.

"I suppose I'll have to go," he said glumly. But then his face lit and he looked up. "Hey! Not if you keep my whereabouts to yourself! Neither of my brothers know I'm here. No reason for them to suppose I've had word of the earl's decline."

Margaret said with a gaze of great consternation, "Roddy, why aren't you on good terms with your brothers? Don't you even care if the earl...if he..."

Roderick shrugged. "The earl's a crusty fellow; I've no use for 'im. And the captain has no use for me. Neither of 'em ever had, I assure you."

Margaret played with her spoon but said carefully, "The duke said you didn't care for the navy."

Roderick coloured. "Well, and so I didn't! Not all bloods do, you know!" He would not, under any circumstances, tell the truth of the extent of his abhorrence of the ocean. Gabriel had enrolled him as a youth as part of his crew. But Roderick became severely seasick. He felt sicker, indeed, than an apoplectic, sure he would die before reaching land again. The captain said seasickness wasn't unusual; it would pass if he kept at it, but Roderick wanted nothing to do with ships again. Somehow he'd got the idea that his brother took him for a coward, and it was this which had started a deep, simmering resentment. Every conquest, every promotion of his brother's only served to sear into his brain that he was, in comparison to Gabriel, a yellow-bellied cove. It wasn't to be borne.

The truth was, it was Roderick who had disposed of every letter the captain had enclosed for Margaret when his mail packets arrived at Redmonton. He'd put them in a safe place, a secret hiding spot in their ancient home. He hadn't done it with thought of injuring Feodora— Margaret—that is. He'd been aware of only one desire—to thwart Gabriel's hopes. He'd sent on only the occasional letter to the duke to avoid suspicion. If the duke didn't hear from Gabriel, he'd enquire of the Admiralty; Roderick hadn't wanted that. Heavens, he hadn't thought of those letters in years…and suddenly he was hit with a sense of guilt. Feodora—Margaret—hadn't deserved to be cut out like that.

"Roddy, you should accompany me," said Margaret in that same gentle tone. "If the captain is there, we can simply say we met on the way in."

Roderick grimaced and surveyed her, unmoved. "You must do the pretties for us both, love. When you tell me he's ready to kick, then I'll come along."

"Must you be so vulgar!" Margaret cried. But Roderick was being far more vulgar than she imagined, for his mind was spinning with plans. He'd alert certain friends of the coming demise of his relation, and they'd be ready the day the coffin was closed. They'd get a pretty penny for those remains; surgeons loved dissecting a body with a known cause of death, and it was no secret that Stafford was hastening the calling of the grave by habitual drunkenness. Yes, a pretty penny, indeed. It was about time he got something from his elder brother.

When Margaret and Mrs. Filbert arrived at the town residence of Earl Stafford, a three-storey house of Portland brick on Grosvenor Street, they were informed by a haughty butler that "relations only" could be admitted to the earl's apartment.

The ladies eyed each other dubiously. "How does his lordship?" asked Margaret.

The butler returned a blank gaze. "As to be expected, ma'am."

"Are other relatives here today?" asked Mrs. Filbert, uneasy about allowing Margaret to disappear alone into the recesses of the house of a known scoundrel.

"Not at present."

Margaret said, "I'll only stay a few minutes, then." She turned to the butler. "Please show my companion to the parlour where she may wait for me."

But Mrs. Filbert cleared her throat. A sixth sense or some other harbinger spoke heavily to her mind that Margaret was not to be trusted to the earl, whether he lay dying or not; she had, in fact, no proof that he was indisposed other than the note. "My dear, I cannot allow you to go off alone to see the earl. The duke would consider me quite unfeeling to my duty. He did banish this man from your presence, recollect."

The butler cleared his throat. "The earl's express command, ma'am, was for him to see Miss Tavistock only. Pray be cognisant of his condition," he added sourly.

Margaret said to the older lady, "I cannot think there is any harm in it." But Mrs. Filbert was adamant. "Call me Ruth," she said, smiling coldly at the butler. "Where Miss Tavistock goes, I go. I dare say 'tis improper for his lordship to expect the case to be otherwise."

"Under the circumstances," said the butler tightly, "it should be understood that exceptions can be made."

"Not this one," returned Mrs. Filbert instantly. "And not with this young woman!" She raised her head and levelled a withering glance at the man from beneath her bonnet. "Either I accompany Miss Tavistock, or her visit must wait."

The man motioned them into a side parlour, saying, "Pray, have a seat if you would, while I inform his lordship." When he'd gone, Margaret met Mrs. Filbert's eyes and smiled wanly. "You are a comfort to me, Mrs. Filbert!"

"I ought to be," she said, straightening out an imaginary wrinkle in her gown. "'Tis my duty."

Margaret smiled again but said nothing. She knew it wasn't mere duty that made the older woman watch her like a mother bear. The butler arrived again within minutes.

"This way, if you please," he said starchly, motioning them towards the staircase with a tightly controlled countenance.

Captain Rempeare arrived at Berkeley Square determined to discover if Miss Chrissendon was, indeed, a widow with children, as the papers now asserted of Lady X. For some reason, it chafed at him like Paul's thorn to think it. It seemed impossible—it must be impossible. She was not above twenty, he was sure, and to have mothered offspring, nay, more than one—the paper said "children"—seemed outrageous not least because she behaved as though utterly ignorant of their existence. Could a mother be so unfeeling? But what discomfited him even more was to think that so young a beauty as Miss Chrissendon, who seemed somehow innocent despite her connexion to the duke, could have belonged to a man and had his children.

He would wholly dismiss the charge outright, except a nagging concern made him wish to hear that it was all a fribble from her own mouth. And if she could not deny it? Then it was a deuced weakness and folly in him which made him know, even now, that it would change nothing. He would still hold her in reluctant admiration. He was helpless to it. Her every movement was feminine beauty, but every word that of a firebrand's. Such spirit he'd not met with elsewhere in all womanhood!

It was with shock, therefore, that he was informed by Stevens upon his arrival at Berkeley Square that Miss Tavistock had gone to pay her respects to the earl. His lordship, said the butler with a properly sorrowful countenance, was in a sad state of decay. The captain's brows narrowed. It felt too smoky by half. "You received word of that?" he asked in surprise, for he himself had been given no such information. "From whom?"

"Why, 'twas my understanding," said the butler in surprise, "it came from *you*, sir!"

"Indeed!" he said, as his whole aspect became formidable. "How long ago did she leave?"

"A quarter of an hour, sir," he was told.

He hurried to his carriage, shouting to the coachman, "Grosvenor Street, on the double!"

Margaret and Mrs. Filbert were ushered into the earl's ponderous chamber, where the invalid lay covered in blankets upon a massive four-poster with the curtains wide, looking sadly indisposed. The butler stopped Mrs. Filbert inside the door, enjoining her to wait there.

Mrs. Filbert looked about with pursed lips, but nodded that she'd stay behind; her aim was to be at the ready if help were needed, and since she could see into the room, though the window curtains were drawn, making it darkish, she stayed at the narrow corridor at its opening.

As Margaret drew nearer the sickbed, she saw that the earl, if he were, indeed, stricken with illness, hadn't changed with regard to his eyes. They held their customary steely glint as he said, "Good of you to come." He ignored Mrs. Filbert at the door.

"We are relations," Margaret returned simply. "How are you, my lord?"

"I will not keep you in suspense," he said. "I hoped your kindness would prevail to make you come, for I've an offer to make you." His eyes watched her closely.

An alarm went off in Margaret's head. "An offer?" she asked sharply. A man suddenly appeared from a dark recess of the room, a clergyman, by the looks of him. He came and stood beside her. Margaret greeted him with a nod, feeling vastly reassured that a man of the cloth was on hand. Surely, his mission was similar to hers: to comfort the invalid before the end.

"This man is Mr. Dickson. He is a clergyman of the church and here to marry us," the earl said.

Margaret blinked at him. "Marry?" she asked, in a high tone of incredulity.

Behind her, Mrs. Filbert made a move to rush to Margaret's side but was stopped swiftly by two pairs of strong hands, one of which stifled her mouth so she could make no sound, and the other which forced her from the room. Margaret, turning to share a look of indignation with her companion, saw the last of her gown as she was forced from the room, and gasped.

"How dare you, sir!" she cried.

"You will be Countess Stafford as of today, and I can assure you." He added calmly, in a low serious tone, "Your prospects with my brother the captain are nothing next to mine."

"You, my lord, are a scoundrel!" she cried. "Have you not the least notion or principle of honour?"

Without a pause he continued, "Your future hopes with him are only to have a husband who is an idle seaman with no employment, no clear course, no income, and no fortune—"

Margaret cried, "No fortune? Is that not on your account? For you have managed to squander both his and yours!"

He smiled maddeningly. "That is of no consequence, for I have an income; my estate brings in quite more than enough to keep you in style, and—"

"Your estate? Redmonton would also be lost if not for the captain. And you will no doubt lose it eventually, if God gives you breath. That is no security, my lord."

His mouth hardened. "Nevertheless, you will be a countess with me."

"I thank you, no!" she cried. She turned on her heel, only to find that two burly footmen blocked her way. Margaret stared about her, suddenly short of breath, feeling her peril. Her pulse flitted rapidly; she hardly knew what to make of such an astonishing predicament.

Captain Rempeare banged the wall of his carriage and gave the driver new orders to stop at his townhome on South Audley Street before proceeding to the earl's. He ran into the house, hollered for Glick, grabbed his sword and holster, and ran with the valet in haste back to the equipage, shouting, "Grosvenor Street, handsomely now!" Muttering beneath his breath at what a scurrilous dog his brother was, he dug beneath the seat for the hidden box which held a pistol and four bullets, and pocketed them inside his coat.

Margaret swallowed and turned back to the earl with a grave expression. "You are too hasty, sir. Have you considered? The duke will surely disown you—"

"He has no power to do so," he said, with a little smile. "Primogeniture's a close-fisted law."

Margaret gave an involuntary gasp and turned to Mr.

Dickson. "You, sir, are a servant of God. Surely, there is no sum great enough to induce *you* to evil!"

The man frowned but looked away. Turning back, he said, "Ma'am, I consider it no evil to elevate a young woman to the nobility."

She would have replied with a sharp insistence that it was evil if the young woman despised the thought of it, but the earl chose that moment to swing himself out from beneath the bedcovers, revealing that he was fully dressed. Margaret saw his stockinged calf and breeches and said, "Was it all a ruse, then? Are you not at death's door?"

Stafford smiled. "I hate to disappoint, but I have not yet reached that shore." He turned a mean eye to Mr. Dickson as he came to his feet. "Marry us!" he cried.

Margaret saw her whole life crumbling before her. How foolish for her to rush to see the earl! Why had she not, at the very least, enquired of the captain if it were wise to do so? But the note had come from him, or so they'd been told. To think, it was all a hoax!

To her relief, sounds of disturbance reached her ears, coming from the corridor. And then—was it? Yes! The captain's voice, demanding and sharp. "I know not what sum he offers you, but is it worth your life, sir?"

In a second more, the door swung open. The two footmen turned and now prepared themselves to stop this intrusion, but the captain cried, "Whatever your wages from him—are they worth your lives?" He aimed his pistol at the region of the heart of one man. The footmen looked at each other and then stood aside.

"You hen-hearted worthless cowards!" yelled the earl. "He won't shoot you!"

"I assure you, I will," replied the captain in a cool tone.

The earl took Margaret about the waist and barked at the clergyman, "Ignore him! Marry us, I tell you!"

"You'll do no such thing," said Captain Rempeare, though he had stopped to motion both footmen to leave the room, waving his pistol to direct them. He locked the door behind them and then turned and approached Margaret and the men.

"Little brother," spat the earl, "I demand you stay out of this business!" The captain merely came forward another few feet so that he was eye to eye with the earl. Margaret could hardly contain the relief she felt, had felt from the moment she heard his voice, her heart thumping with joy. Even now, she wanted nothing more than to run into his arms.

"Let her go," he said, with quiet authority.

"I have a special licence and mean to use it," the earl replied, grinding out the words in a mean, low voice.

"May I see it?" asked Captain Rempeare. Margaret gasped; was he going to give her up so easily if it was in order? He scanned the paper when it was hastily produced by the clergyman. He turned with quiet triumph and said, "'Tis just as I expected. This licence is useless."

"It is perfectly legal!" spat the earl, plucking it from the minister's hand. "It comes direct from the archbishop!"

"If you had Miss Tavistock in your mawlish paws, I might agree with you."

"What?" he asked, startled, looking down at Margaret. He let go of her and stared. "You are my cousin, of course." But it was a question, not a statement. Margaret scooted to the captain's side where she pressed herself against him. He put an arm about her protectively as she clung to him.

"You ought to thank me," he said to the earl, in that same quiet tone, "for saving you from a doomed campaign. What you took for a well-dressed frigate lacks the prize. For this lady is not your cousin, my lord."

"That's a coker!" he cried. "Of course she is!"

"But she isn't," he said. He paused and looked from Margaret back to his brother. "She is Lady X, sir, Miss Chrissendon by name."

"What, a demirep?" The earl's face contorted and he cast stony eyes onto Margaret. "*She*—Lady X? It's a whisker! I warrant she's fresh from the schoolroom. You think me a pigeon that you can fob off so easily?" But there was dawning doubt in his eyes.

"You may enquire of the duke's solicitors on Conduit Street. Ask him the name of the lady residing at 29 Berkeley Square. We can wait here while you send a man." The captain took Margaret's arm and led them both to a set of chairs off to one side of the room. The clergyman seemed at a loss as what to do and began to sputter, "If my services aren't needed, my lord—"

The earl cried, "Quiet! I *will* send a man, by Jove! I don't believe this sea rat for a moment! He'd say anything to keep her fortune for himself."

Margaret heard those words with an inner sinking of heart. But Captain Rempeare cried, "As if that were my aim!" With a breaking of understanding upon his features, he cried, "But it was yours, no doubt! Great Joseph, that's what this is about! A grabble for that trust money!" He glared at the earl, who said nothing. In that one silent moment Margaret saw that the captain was, indeed, right. Stafford had been ready to force her into marriage for the sake of gaining her fortune! Apparently he did not know it was tied to her marrying his brother.

"I'm done with you for this," Captain Rempeare said to him. "You've always been too ripe and ready by half for trouble; I'll not save your hide again, no, not if it means the loss of Redmonton! I'm done, I tell you!" He stood up and gave his hand to Margaret, who came to her feet and took it. He grasped it tightly and began leading them from the room.

"You'll wait until I send a man to Conduit Street," yelled the earl.

"Go ahead and send him," said Captain Rempeare in a voice of dead gravity. "But we will not wait." He turned and looked back at his brother, red with rage. "She wouldn't have married you anyway, you know. Even if she were Miss Tavistock."

"If she *is* Lady X, as you say," the earl said bitterly, "why do you protect her?"

The captain hesitated. Margaret held her breath. Looking down at her, he said quietly, "Because I must."

The earl turned to Margaret with a raised brow. "I could always offer you *carte blanche*," he said, with an evil grin. "Why stay hidden in Yorkshire when London could be your home?"

Margaret did not understand his meaning until the captain said, "She's no Cyprian, my lord!" Understanding dawned upon her features in a cloud of fury. *He'd offered to keep her: the living arrangement of a...a common lady bird!*

The earl made a move as if to stop them, but Captain Rempeare drew his sword. "I won't put a bullet in you, Stafford, but I will use this if I must."

The earl's eyes suddenly lit with a thought, and he moved a step closer. "You can't fight!" he cried. "Your arm! It's weaker than a dormouse!"

The captain glared at him. "Not so weak as all that," he said in a sinister tone and from between dark eyes. "Try me."

CHAPTER FIFTEEN

The earl thought better of putting the captain's sword arm to the test, but as Margaret and his brother backed out of the room, he let out a string of colourful epithets. Margaret was a deuced bleached mort, a jade, a vixen, and a whore, the daughter of a whore, and the captain was the devil's own fool, a cursed sea rat. Keeping his sword at the ready, Captain Rempeare called back, "Behave you, sir! She's not one of your doxies."

"No, she's the duke's doxie!" he shouted, angrier than ever.

When Margaret and the captain reached the corridor, no footman stood ready to challenge their escape, and she could have thrown herself into his arms in relief—except for Mrs. Filbert, who was missing!

It took little persuasion, once they found a servant, to reveal where the older lady was, seated stiffly in a back parlour with a footman standing guard. When she saw the captain and Margaret, she exclaimed, "Thank heavens!" With tearful eyes, she hurried forward. She hesitated as she passed the footman, however. Drawing up her parasol like a baton, she rapped him soundly on the head and arms again and again. He was easily twice the size of the comfortably plump companion, but he tried to shield himself with his arms and then, yelping objections, turned and ran off.

Margaret and the captain's eyes met, both twinkling in amusement.

Glick had the captain's carriage at the kerb, the horses stamping their feet impatiently. Fifteen minutes later, after manoeuvring through a crush of traffic, they reached Berkeley Square. Throughout the drive, both ladies thanked the captain again and again, Margaret saying she hardly had words to express how *very* grateful she was, and she didn't know what she would have done had he not come, for she was almost ready to go into a faint. She hadn't actually ever swooned in her life, and added that she may not have been *really* at the point of doing so, but her horror at the prospect of marrying the earl might certainly have brought her to it. The captain smiled gently at this, however, saying, "No such thing. You managed bravely." His approving words, coupled with a warm gaze, made her eyes sparkle with pleasure.

"I never thought it would be propitious, your not being Miss Tavistock," he said mildly, "but things may have got more havey-cavey had the earl not had the wind snatched from his sails with that revelation."

Margaret knew she'd had a narrow escape and had to agree, but not without remorse, for despite his kind words, his saying she was no Cyprian, nor a doxie, he must have still thought of her as something of a wanton—for she was still Lady X to him.

He eyed her a moment and then said with a start, "Good heavens, Miss Chrissendon! Had you wanted to be a countess? Was I interfering..."

But her eyes widened in horror. "Oh, Captain, I assure you! There is nothing that could induce me to be the Countess Stafford!"

"I beg your pardon," he said. "But I recollect your saying the duke may not offer for you, and...and..." his eyes suddenly grew harder. "As you are a widow—"

"I am not, sir!"

"Not a widow with children?" he asked, searching her face.

Mrs. Filbert here made an involuntary clucking sound, for she disapproved of anything that reminded her that the captain believed Margaret was Lady X. Margaret glanced at her in alarm, but the companion shook her head and looked out the window. Margaret swallowed but said, "I am but nineteen, sir; I assure you I have neither been married nor borne children."

Relief flooded through him. He said, with a little smile, "I could hardly fathom that you had. Do you know why *The Herald* should say so?"

Her eyes blazed. "That horrid rag lives upon lies! I mean to write the duke and bid him seek damages!" They arrived at the house, and in a minute Captain Rempeare had each lady upon an arm and walked them to the door, where Stevens instantly opened it.

"I am greatly obliged to you," Margaret said for the hundredth time as they entered. She gave up a parasol, a light cloak, gloves, and bonnet to the butler.

"Perhaps I should thank *you*," he said.

She looked up in surprise. "Thank me?"

"I had a devilish time of it, trying to decide whether to cut off support for Stafford's debts, but now 'tis done, I find, at heart, that I am vastly relieved."

She looked wistfully into his face. "I am pleased, truly, if I've done you a service." Her earnest, pretty eyes met his, equally full and sincere. He regarded her a moment.

"I dare say you have," he said softly.

A look of gratification and then longing swept across her face. How she wished she had the courage to tell him, but no, it was utterly impossible. Her face grew troubled. "I think, Captain, I will remain at home the rest of the day and tomorrow. The earl quite...quite astonished me."

"I understand," he said.

"The fête at Carlton House is in two days, and then Mr. Turnbull will take me to see the palace on the next."

He frowned. "Is there no way I may yet dissuade you from that? Now it is so close, there is every expectation of a riotous crush."

She said, "Thank you, but I believe I am equal to it. I shan't bring a purse, and nothing upon me to be napped except a handkerchief."

"And it likely will be," he said, though with a kind look. "In a crush, you could lose your bonnet to sharps if you're not careful. Ladies have had them snatched right off their heads as they walk in Town."

She smiled. "I am warned. I thank you again." But her face suddenly lost its glow, and she said, "Captain!" The rest came out in a hurried spurt. "The earl will spread it abroad, do you not think so? That I am not Miss Tavistock!"

"And we will call it sour grapes, for you refused his hand," he said instantly. He regarded her a moment. "Now you mention it, the last thing you should do is hide at home. You must be seen in society, no different than before. No one will take his word, an old spent roué, over mine and yours, though he is an earl." He covered her hands with his. "Do not let it plague you. Nothing will change; you'll see."

That touch, his hand over hers, without gloves, combined with a look of earnestness, sent Margaret nearly into tears. Her regard for him had grown each time she saw him, but now, after his rescuing her, it had changed. She no longer merely admired or esteemed him; she loved Gabriel Rempeare! Yet it was a sad hopeless love, due to her own wicked lies. And he, too, it seemed to her, had a look of sadness about him, though she knew not its cause.

She drew her hand away and curtseyed. "You once said there was no opportunity for gaining honour apart from the navy, but you made a brave rescue, sir. I call that honourable, indeed."

The captain, amused, was ready to reply that taking her from a nobleman's townhome in Mayfair—a nobleman who was his brother, no less—was hardly on a keel with a naval action involving man-of-wars, guns, and powder, but she was blinking back tears. This silenced his objections, and then before he could reply in any manner, she cried, "Good day!" She hurried off towards the stairs.

As she climbed up, a pretty cloud of muslin and lace ascending, the captain motioned to Mrs. Filbert. "She's had a shock, I'm afraid. Blast Stafford! Perhaps you should summon a medical man; I don't doubt a mild restorative should help. Keep an eye on her, if you will."

"'Tis what I do, sir!" said Mrs. Filbert.

He looked piercingly at her. "What of you, Mrs. Filbert? I dare say this was an ordeal for you as well. Shall I send a surgeon? My excellent ship's doctor happens to be ashore—"

"I thank you, Captain," said Mrs. Filbert, "but Miss Tavistock loathes doctors. She and I shall manage. We always have, you know."

"You've known her long, then?"

"Two years, now, sir, since I answered her advertisement for a com—" But the word died on her tongue, and she stopped suddenly, blinking in alarm. At first the captain inclined his head as if to hear how she would finish, but her guilty countenance, combined with what she did next, made him pause. She bobbed a curtsey and said, "Good day, Captain! Much obliged to you!"

She turned and hurried towards the stairs with a hand upon her heart. Captain Rempeare was left staring after her with a very strange look on his face. Stevens, who had heard all, cleared his throat and opened the door for the man. "Good day, sir," he intoned, as a strong hint that the captain should take himself off. But Captain Rempeare said, "Stevens, how long have you known Miss Chrissendon?"

"Why, only these five weeks, Captain, sir, since Mr. Primpley directed me here to serve as butler."

The captain seemed disappointed. "Hmm, well, good day to you." But he kept sending little furtive glances towards the stairs as if he wished for the lady in question to appear once again. When he was gone, Mrs. Filbert rushed back down the steps and questioned Stevens. When he relayed the captain's sole question—how long had he known Miss Chrissendon—the lady shook her head and clucked her tongue and headed back towards the stairs, murmuring, "Oh dear, oh dear, oh dear."

Roderick was in good spirits. Thanks to Feodora, Margaret, that was—dash it, why couldn't he remember to call her that? He had no need to join the resurrectionist men, perhaps not ever again. It was a deuced nacky business, grave robbing. Margaret, fortunately, was first rate, bang up, unlike that old tabby, Mrs. Filbert. Why, if all it took was to ask, he might get by just fine as the poor relation in the Rempeare family. But before getting comfortable in that cloak, he'd ply the earl to force the solicitors to open the purse strings of his trust. He'd tried for a certificate—given it his best. He deserved the funds.

But for now, he'd paid off his two most pressing debts. As he was celebrating his newfound freedom, strutting towards St. James's Street like he was all the go, he saw some fashionable bloods he knew.

"Rempeare!" they called. "Come, you son of an earl. Join us." In minutes he'd been assured of a night's pleasure far from any establishment either of his brothers were likely to frequent, making it instantly appealing. He jumped into someone's coach and soon alighted at a neat little coaching inn called The Blue Boar, on the outskirts of Town.

Captain Rempeare reached his rooms on South Audley Street and did an astonishing thing.

He scribbled off messages to two seamen he knew to be ashore, men who were not *tonnish* or invited to the fête. He charged them in no uncertain terms, knowing they would respect their former sea captain as if they were still beneath his command, to keep the earl occupied before and after the grand event. All they need do was engage him at cards day and night until Captain Rempeare could get to Toadingham and back, for he must call upon his cousin. But the earl must be kept busy and given no occasion to smear Miss Chrissendon's name during his absence.

The captain estimated that he'd be gone at least four days, more if the duke kept him in Yorkshire. But go he must. If he did not lay his eyes upon the real Miss Tavistock of Toadingham Hall before the week was out, he'd go *mad*. There was no question of withdrawing from the betrothal. He was honour bound. But only an immediate visit to

Yorkshire would settle his mind, and nothing on earth could stop him from settling it, for Mrs. Filbert had put a glorious, terrible, wonderful, appalling, idea in his head, and he had to know the truth. She'd said, or had nearly said, that she'd answered Miss Chrissendon's advertisement for a companion; which, if that were the case, Miss Chrissendon must be Miss Tavistock.

It made perfect sense. Yet it was unthinkable. For what kind of mad folly would cause her to maintain such a fetch? Was she not in favour of the nuptial agreement? The duke had given him every indication that she was. But why else did Mrs. Filbert bite her tongue and take off as if she'd been stung by a serpent, except that she was hiding this truth?

His heart was rolling like the quarterdeck in a tempest. He couldn't keep it steady; conflicting thoughts drove it first one way then another. If she'd been bamboozling him, there'd be the devil to pay! No man should be subject to such dissimulation. But, if Miss Chrissendon was, indeed, Miss Tavistock! A wild thrill overtook him at the thought of that lovely, maddening girl being his bride! Immediately, a storm of clashing feelings returned in waves: first hurt, dismay, anger, but then joy, light, and relief! Every hour in her presence had become a battle for him; the fight was to deny feelings that he must not have for the wrong woman. All the more reason, then, to go, go while he still had it in his power to resist the charmer on Berkeley Square and honour his betrothal if it turned out his suspicion was wrong.

Quickly, he took up pen and ink again, writing to Lady Carson and Mrs. Humphries, society hostesses who were particularly infatuated with his hero status. He begged them to be so kind as to keep Margaret in company for the next few days. These ladies had loudly decried their lack of invitations to the fête, saying it was astonishing, badly done, an oversight on the prince's part, of course, but they were not granted tickets, so were available. He gave it out that he'd been called away on pressing business and wished to know that she would be entertained.

Could they send an immediate reply, if it wasn't too provoking of him to ask? They did. Margaret's social life was settled.

He wrote one last note to Miss Chrissendon. He'd been remiss not to visit Yorkshire since the Season had begun, he said, and begged leave to tell her he was en route there at last. He apologised for the change of plan, and promised to return at the soonest possible time. He expected she would have seen Carlton House before his return, recollected her to take precautions, and assured her of the attendance of Lady Carson and Mrs. Humphries during his absence.

Afterwards, while nagging Glick to hurry the packing of his trunk, he asked, "What think you, Glick, the coach with four?"

"The gig with two's bound to be faster, sir."

"Two horses faster than four?" he asked, revealing his poor experience with land travel. Now, if he could sail to Yorkshire….

"We'd have to hire two for the coach, sir, and it bein' more ponderous, will run slower, and needin' to refresh four horses at each stop'll take more time than two; you see, sir? The gig is what you want for speed, sir."

Gabriel stashed his pistol, sword, and extra money into the equipage, and they took a hasty leave of London. No sooner had they hit the road than doubts assailed him. Perhaps he was jumping ship; it must be a reckless hope, too good a thought, that the beautiful woman he'd been struggling to keep at bay was the selfsame creature he was betrothed to. Surely, if it were so, she would have come clean, confessed all before now. The not knowing lay heavily upon him.

With such disquieting thoughts filling his mind and heart, the curricle passed through the outer road from London onto a turnpike. Then endeavouring to give space to an oncoming equipage, he drove far to the side of the road, hit a small boulder, and was nearly thrown when a wooden wheel cracked and split. The horses kept on, dragging the equipage, lolling dangerously to one side, but Gabriel managed to halt the team. What a bacon brain he was! Capsized before leaving the outskirts of the metropolis.

Glick said, almost in his ear, for he'd hung on grimly as well, "There's an inn, sir, we passed, not a half mile back: The Blue Boar. We can take the horses there, sir, and send back for the curricle. I dare say an ostler, or postilion, or stable boy will know how to find a replacement wheel, sir, and we'll be on our way."

"Very good, Glick," he said. "Let's hope they're natty with wheels. It's all we can do."

Ten minutes later, the men dismounted at the inn. Two postilions came running out and received the captain's instructions about the curricle.

"Well, I've mucked up my chance at a speedy journey. We'll never make it there and back as fast as I'd hoped," said the captain glumly.

"Come, sir," said Glick, frowning. "No fault of your'n; the toll keeper ain't cleaned up his road. You've time for a pint, sir." He nodded towards the inn.

Gabriel, with Glick standing dutifully behind his chair, had hardly tasted his drink when a most surprising sight made him freeze, holding the pint in mid-air as he got a better look. By Jupiter, it was Roderick, the scapegrace! "Glick," he said. The man instantly lowered his head to his master's.

"Sir?"

"There is my brother, Roderick Rempeare; we have a resemblance. Can you make him out?"

Glick's head bobbed back and forth, up and down, as he strove to get a good view of the loud men sitting on the opposite side of the crowded inn, trying to pick out a man who might be the master's brother. Finally, seeing Roderick's dark curls and aquiline nose—not quite as distinguished as the captain's by half—he nodded and said, "I think I can, sir. Is he wearing spectacles, sir?"

The captain nodded. "For effect, most like, but that's him." Roderick was standing on the bench, holding a pint in one hand and posing like an orator, regaling his fellows with a speech.

"He looks a trifle *disguised*, sir," Glick said, "if I make no mistake."

The captain sipped his pint, surveying his brother. "A trifle? Dipping rather deep, I think, if not ape drunk." They watched while Roderick tried to climb onto the table and nearly fell backwards, but was helped by a chorus of hands that prevented an immediate catastrophe. He stood swaying on the wooden surface, spouting what was probably nonsense into the air like a statesman. The landlord arrived. Even from their distance, the captain could make out his objections, that his establishment was above the crack, not at all the place for coves and culls.

"Look here," called one of the gents, pointing at Roderick. "This here's a Cambridge man, sir, a fellow commoner, they call him there."

"A fellow commoner?" asked the landlord, with a gleam in his narrowed eyes, inclining his head as if to hear correctly.

Roderick tried to shush his friend with a finger to his lips, but as he leaned in towards the man, he nearly fell over and had to be propped up by others. "That's right, sir," the man continued, nonplussed. "Heard it with me own ears. That's what they call the Cambridge men, sir!"

The innkeeper said, "My son's a Cambridge man, sirs"—he pointed at Roderick—"an' if they call this cove a fellow commoner, 'tis on account of 'is 'aving an empty garret! Aye, an empty bottle, sirs!" he added, pointing at his head. "My son's a right gentleman, but as fer yer fellow commoner here—" He shook a cloth at him. "Get 'im off the table, lads."

"Hire a private room from the landlord," the captain said to Glick. Then bring my brother to me. Smartly now, but watch; Mr. Rempeare is in his cups. Don't let him raise a dust."

In less than ten minutes, Gabriel was in a comfortable private room replete with a table and chairs, wing chairs, another side table, and a cheerfully burning hearth. Glick came dragging in an unwilling Roderick, who was as much supported as forced along and deposited on a cushioned chair across from the captain.

The landlord himself brought in a flagon of wine, cast a dubious look at Roderick, but then enjoined the "fine officer" to partake of an excellent supper, which he assured Gabriel was this evening of the first consideration: braised quail, a haunch of venison, boiled ham, asparagus, a leg of lamb, herbed gravy, and cauliflower cream. Jellies and tarts on the side, of course.

"Not a snivelling spread, sir," confided Glick in his ear, "nor a Lenten feast, if I may say so. I've seen far meaner dinners at inns such as this, and no saying how long ye'll have to wait 'afore the wheel's replaced; may as well eat your fill now, sir, and let it take ye all the way to Yorkshire if need be."

One of the pleasures on land was the greater variety of food available. The captain had eaten a lifetime's worth of Cheshire cheese and pork pie, dried beef and biscuits with walnut catchup, and "smash," which was leg of mutton and turnips. All of it, cured hams and salted fish especially, were tiresome. He ordered enough for himself, his brother, and Glick, and assured Roderick his indignation at being torn from a night of frivolity with his friends would be redressed by an excellent meal and wine.

Managing to wobble even while seated, Roderick stared unsteadily at his sibling. "I say, Gabriel," he said, eyeing the numerous covers after they'd been brought in by two serving girls, the landlord looking on, "not shoddy by half, sir."

"Help yourself," said the captain. But Roderick could hardly lift the first cover before dropping it again. Glick, who dismissed the serving wenches with a scornful air, hurried to make himself useful and prevent further damage. While he filled the gentlemen's plates, the captain asked his brother, "What brings you to Town?"

Roderick looked faintly green as he focused double vision on his brother. *Deuced if it didn't happen whenever he drank a few too many. Which brother should he answer?* As he tried to work it out, whether it was the captain on the right he must reply to, or the captain on the left, suddenly there was one in the middle. "Are you between terms?" it asked him.

"Quit," he said simply. He looked daringly at all three Captain Rempeares. "Done with studies, you know."

The captains frowned. "Without a certificate of degree?" they demanded. "What went wrong?"

"Now see here, Gabriel!" spouted Roderick, pounding his fist, and looking angrily at first one Captain Rempeare and then the others. He'd meant to hit the table but managed to land his hand only in a mound of lamb and gravy, which Glick hurried to lift and wipe clean with a serving cloth. Roderick hardly noticed, continuing a mostly incoherent tale of how standing for exams was a deuced hobnobbery business, and studying quite beyond his powers at present, being too deep in dun territory to apply himself to anything but that which could fill a pocket with the ready.

The captain listened with a growing frown. Directing a glance at Glick, he said, "Fetch him coffee." Roderick, meanwhile, having got off to an emotional start at recounting his woes to his brother, continued in a lachrymose fashion, bemoaning the seasickness that had caused the captain to make him out a coward to begin with.

Gabriel would have objected to this, for though he thought his brother a scatterbrain and dandy prat, he'd never labelled him a coward. But Roderick was bent on finishing his monologue and went on to bitterly denounce Gabriel for counting him a lily-liver; why, if the captain only knew what he did of a night to make up for the disgraceful stipend a Cambridge man could not possibly exist upon. This evoked a raised brow from Captain Rempeare, who did, indeed, wonder what Roderick did— but the younger man hadn't finished. He divulged that he would have never pilfered those letters Gabriel had written while at sea, if he'd only given him a fair shake.

"What's that?" Captain Rempeare came sharply to attention. He could hardly credit his ears. His brother had been the cause of his letters not reaching Miss Tavistock?

"You ought to have bought me a *commishion,*" Roderick was saying, as if he hadn't just revealed that he was a traitor and thief. "I shoulda been an army captain. Lord knows," he continued. He was a *prisoner* at school, having no other situation or recourse open to him. "You," he said, pointing an unsteady finger at Gabriel. "You kept me down!" He closed his eyes and said, "Little wonder a scholar's forced to dig up the stiffs; every man's gotta line his pockets."

Gabriel leaned forward. "Can I credit my ears? Are you saying you're a resurrectionist? Great Joseph! A Rempeare involved in that. God help me, Roddy. If I hear of you involved in that business again, I'll have you hauled to Newgate myself."

Roderick opened one heavy eye to peer at his brother. "A man's gotta live," he mumbled. This was followed by some incorrigible talk of "helping medical science" and "furthering the knowledge of mankind."

But the captain said, "Depend upon it; if you're caught in that business you'll not get a farthing from me for the rest of your days."

Roderick yawned. "Won't get caught."

"That wasn't my meaning," Gabriel said. "Don't even think about taking part in it again. If you don't stay clear of it, you'll have only your stipend and not another halfpenny."

Roderick didn't deem it wise, even in his inebriated state, to enlighten his brother to the fact that his stipend no longer existed since he'd been expelled. The captain shook his head. "To think if you'd been caught heretofore! I'm not a gudgeon about reputations and keeping to points, but that business is beyond the pale for gentlemen. Nothing to plume yourself on. Leave it to coves and culls and their like."

"It's genelmen surgeons who buy the bodies," Roderick objected, deeply indignant that his brother was raising a humdudgery over it.

"It's a deuced unholy business, and I won't have you in it." When Roderick said nothing, the captain pressed him. "Do I have your word on it, Roddy?"

He nodded, opening the slits of his eyes. "My word. Fine!"

Gabriel knew he could hardly trust the word of a man in his cups, but he felt honour bound to procure it. He hadn't realised how desperate his brother must be to rely upon such an income.

When Glick finally returned with the coffee, he said, looking at Roderick stretched out with his mouth hanging open, "I think he's beyond coffee, sir."

"He's in the land of Nod. Wake him."

Glick did so, vigorously shaking Roderick's shoulder and exhorting him, saying, "Come, come, Mr. Rempeare, sir!" When the wayward scholar stirred, Glick removed the food from before him, for Roderick, despite his best intentions, had not managed to get a bite to his mouth. Glick put the steaming dark liquid in its place, but as the young man showed no inclination to avail himself of it, the valet proceeded to spoon it into his mouth. At first he had to hold it open, one teaspoon at a time. Roderick swallowed, staring out ahead of him as if in a trance. As the captain ate his dinner, finally with some peace, Glick patiently plied the failed scholar with coffee.

Minutes passed as the captain stared into the fire, thinking. Eventually, after he'd ordered port, and was served nuts, fruit, and tarts, Roderick blinked as if coming awake. He sat up straighter and hardly swayed. "I say, Gabriel!" he said. "What brings you to Town?" He was relieved that the three captains had congealed into only two.

"That was my question for you, Roddy," they returned quietly.

Roderick shrugged. "Game's up at Cambridge; time to start anew!"

"Where are you stopping?" the captains asked.

Roderick suddenly could not collect whether he was supposed to allow that he was staying with Feodora and was he supposed to call her Miss Tavistock, or Miss Chriss—Chriss something?" He hit upon a solution. Smiling, he said, "You'll never guess. With Lady X!"

As soon as he spoke, Roderick had an uneasy feeling in his breast; something at the edge of his brain wasn't quite happy with that response, but he couldn't for the life of him supply a reason either in favour of, or against having made it. The whole business was a bothersome hubble-bubble. Glick forced another spoonful down his throat, but suddenly the two Captain Rempeares congealed into one: a very glowering captain.

"Lady X? Do you mean to say you're stopping with Miss Chrissendon? How do you know her?"

Roderick hesitated. He'd got it wrong; he was certain. Why else would the captain have a thunderous look upon his face? And why couldn't he collect what it was his cousin had said to call her? "She ain't Miss Chrissendon, she's Miss Tavistock! Wait, no, no," he said, frowning. "She is Miss Chrissendon, dash it. Lady X!" But his look wavered, and he muttered, "Or is she Miss Tavistock? Pluck a feather, I don't care what she's called! But she gave me a room, and that's the lay of the land."

Again, the captain's hopes rose and fell. Roddy's reply wasn't wholly reassuring either way, and he was losing patience. It was of paramount importance he knew of a certainty.

Roderick was feeling much improved suddenly, and he eyed the covers with an appetite. He prided himself on an iron stomach; he looked up at Glick, who stood behind his master's chair, and motioned at the spread. "Would you mind, er—?"

"Glick, sir," said Glick, who got instantly to work. Roderick sat back to allow the short tidy man to fill his plate. Then taking a hefty bite of venison, he said to the captain, "'Tis all a muddle to me, all quite flummoxing." He pointed at his head. "It's all up here in the knowledge box somewhere, if I can only get it straight." He took a bite and chewing, said, "One day she's one person, and the next day, another!"

He motioned to the flagon of wine, but Captain Rempeare said quickly, "Nothing but the weakest doctor for him."

"Doctor only?" objected Roderick. "I'm not one of your crew." But he fell quiet as Glick hurried off to fetch the drink, for he supposed that milk and water with a little rum and nutmeg was superior to no spirits at all.

"Miss Chrissendon said nothing to me of your arrival. Do you know her from Toadingham?"

With sudden insight, Roderick realised his brother's interest in Feodora...er, Margaret, was so strong that he wasn't in hot water even for having failed at Cambridge, and he had a suspicion he'd gabbed something of taking his brother's letters. He'd best milk the thread. He chewed, considering. "I suppose I do."

"You suppose?"

Roderick nodded hastily. "O'course, where else?"

The captain leaned in. With a deadly serious gaze, he ordered, "Tell me all you know of her."

CHAPTER SIXTEEN

Roderick stared glumly at his brother. Why couldn't he collect what it was his cousin had said to call her? He glared at Gabriel. "Look here, whoever it is you think she is, she is. It's all my eye, all the same to me."

"Is she my cousin?" Captain Rempeare asked with dead seriousness. He was thoroughly incensed with his muddle-brained brother, for the thought that this dandy prat was lodging with Miss Chrissendon seemed insupportable.

Roderick shrugged. "All I need do is call her Miss Tavistock."

The captain leaned back, his spirits dashed. So he'd been wrong. She really was Lady X. But why hadn't she mentioned seeing Roderick, much less that she was playing hostess for him?

"You've seen the real Miss Tavistock," he said quietly, as though quite, quite resigned. "Describe her to me."

Roderick eyed him for a moment. Lud, this was an opportunity to do a little recruiting! "Look here, I'm out at the heels," he said.

The captain almost rolled his eyes. "I'll equal your stipend. Now, let's have it."

Roderick stifled his glee at such an easy triumph. Matching his stipend—why, the captain wasn't so bad by halves! "She's a fashion plate, all the go, modish to a tee. Not a missish, retiring chit, either; spirited, she is."

"Yes, yes, but what does she look like?" he asked.

Roderick cried, "'Tis as I said! She's all the crack! A prime article."

The captain blinked at his brother with cautious hope. "All the crack, you say? Not a pudding face?" he added, worriedly.

Roderick sputtered a laugh. "A pudding face? Feodora? Nothing of the sort!" He eyed his brother pityingly. "And you think *I'm* addlebrained! You are more at sixes and sevens, sir, than I." He fell into helpless laughter.

Captain Rempeare stared at his brother. He rose suddenly and went around the table to Roderick, who eyed him with defiance, though a flicker of fear swept through his gaze. "See here, Gabriel," he began, but the captain, pulling Roderick's chair out, took him by the lapels of his coat and levelled a hard stare at him.

"Tell me everything you know of Miss Chrissendon," he said through gritted teeth.

Roderick glanced at the captain's hands holding him roughly by his coat, and then stared into his hardened features. "I'll tell you what I know," he said slowly and with rare sagacity. "You *love* her! That's what I know. You're in love with—Lady X!"

The anger in the captain's face drained. He released Roderick and went around to his seat with slumped shoulders. "I am betrothed to my cousin," he said, with a deep sigh. "I'm en route to Yorkshire this very night to see her and hasten the event."

Roderick's look now became cautious. "En route to Toadingham?" As his mind grew sober, it all became clear to him, what awaited the captain in Yorkshire. He'd learn the truth about his future bride. And then he'd remember that he, Roderick, had not dealt plainly with him. Thinking of Feodora, that muddle-headed chit, and knowing now that his brother had fallen in love with her, he suddenly saw his future, and it boded disaster. The captain might be shocked at his bride's deception, but he'd forgive her. One look at that face of sweet innocence, and he'd forgive her, by Jove, and marry her, and they'd live happily ever after. But Roderick? No, his flams would not be forgiven. Indeed, with his luck, the whole muddle would somehow be laid at his door. The captain would spurn him, and then Feodora would spurn him, and the earl had already spurned him, and Roderick would have nothing. Nothing except his grisly night work to live on.

While the captain sipped port looking utterly miserable, as though the weight of the world was on his shoulders, Roderick came to a decision. Feodora wouldn't like it; she'd ring a peal at him, but he was forced to be a marplot.

"Gabriel," he said, frowning. "Don't be hulver-headed. Don't go to Yorkshire." Captain Rempeare's eyes were fastened on him, questioning. "Miss Chrissendon ain't Lady X, says there is no such lady. It's all a hum! A jig!"

The captain's eyes narrowed.

"She is, indeed, Miss Tavistock, sir: my cousin Feenie—*your bride*."

The captain had instructed that his note to Miss Tavistock on Berkeley Square should be delivered the next morning. So Margaret was only pulling on her stockings the following day when the butler delivered it to her maid at the door of the bedchamber. Upon reading his words, Margaret turned pale. She hurried into a clean chemise and then bade the servant fetch Mrs. Filbert. Shakily, she sat upon her bed and waited for the older lady, who had been reading the morning's collect (for Mrs. Filbert was a great reader of the prayer book) to come to her.

"What is it, dearest?" the lady asked a minute later, coming into the room with alarm on her features. Mrs. Filbert wore a sleeping gown of frilly white with a matching mob cap, not too unlike Miss Tavistock's nighttime apparel.

"Mrs. Filbert!" Margaret said tragically, letting the note dangle languorously from one hand while she lay back, reduced to a prone position. "I am undone at last! He will soon know it's all a fudge!" She lay a slim arm across her head and eyes. "How shall I ever face him? It is too provoking and mortifying!"

Mrs. Filbert knew she had made a slip of the tongue which had no doubt preceded this blow. She was at fault in the matter, there was no denying it. Nevertheless, she could not help but feel some relief at the thought that if the captain knew the truth, all must come to rights. "What does he say, my love?" was all she said.

Margaret held out the note. "He is en route to Yorkshire this very moment! He will see the duke. He will find Miss Tavistock missing, only to be told she is in London on Berkeley Square!" She sighed deeply. "He'll know I've been shamming it. Even the duke will be shocked at my deception, I dare say! He'll ring a fine peal over me, as will the captain." A tear rolled down her cheek.

Mrs. Filbert sat beside her on the bed, read the note, and patted Margaret's hand. Margaret removed her arm from her eyes and cried, "What possessed him to be off so suddenly? When the Season is nearly over, and he might have waited! I wrote him as Miss Tavistock from Yorkshire instructing he should wait!"

Mrs. Filbert clucked her tongue. "I warrant he has not received that missive yet."

"He gave me his *word* he wouldn't call at Toadingham until the Season ended, unless Miss Tavistock herself bade him come!"

"Perhaps the duke required him to call?"

At this, Margaret lifted the note and scanned it. "He says nothing of that. If it were the duke asking it of him, surely he'd have mentioned it." She fell back against the couch. "Ma'am," she said, "Pray send word to Mr. Wilson, the dancing master, that I am indisposed today. And send to Lady Carson and Mrs. Humphries. I am too indisposed to be taken from home. I dare say I shall be laid up the rest of my days. I will live in the 'Slough of Despond' forever!" she added tragically.

Mrs. Filbert's lips were pursed while she considered the difficulty. "My dear," she said, "why do *we* not leave at once for Yorkshire? We can meet the captain there, and have it all out far from prying eyes and Town gossip. I warrant you, he will be of a mind to accept you wholeheartedly when he learns he will be fortunate enough to call *you* his bride!"

Margaret gave her a tragical look. "I *would* leave, but I do not think you have the right of it. Captain Rempeare is a man of high principles! He will despise me when he learns the truth." Her face took on a look of tragic resolve. "In future, I won't even have the trust monies. I'll be a relic! A *toad-eater*! The unmarried, poor female relation!"

Mrs. Filbert's mighty frown was lost upon Margaret, who went on with martyr-like stoicism, "No. I must remain here and wait for the worst. In the meantime, Mr. Turnbull will escort me to Carlton House. It shall be my last delight before I am constrained to finish my days in Yorkshire not very different from how I began them. In isolation. Only now, disgrace will be added to my lot."

Mrs. Filbert fretted and cajoled, pleaded and reasoned, but Margaret was adamant. She would remain in London, let the cards fall where they would. But no word was sent to either of the ladies charged with entertaining Margaret for the days of the captain's absence, so Lady Carson's carriage arrived that afternoon, and Margaret went, pale faced and with circles beginning to darken her eyes, to an afternoon music party at her ladyship's house.

Margaret's blue-devilled appearance, it was whispered, was on account of the captain's absence. This made the women take her yet more into their hearts, and she was treated with the utmost delicacy and attention. The kindness of her friends vexed Margaret, for she knew how very different their attitudes and estimation would be when Captain Rempeare was returned, and they would learn all.

Her sorrows seemed magnified as she listened with rapt attention to the opera singer who regaled them with arias to break a heart—every melancholy note held until it swelled and broke in a wave of sorrow on her head—echoing the sad state of her despondent heart. It was all she could do not to sigh aloud. The opera singer was followed by a troupe of dancers who did a short ballet. Even this dance, augmented by a pianoforte, seemed laden with grief. The aching beauty of their movements only plucked at the guilty strings of her heart, and the dancers' sorrows, expressed in heart-rending expressions, made her blink back tears. Nothing could make her forget her troubles, though Lady Carson evidently spared no expense for her entertainments.

Afterwards, Margaret was introduced to more lords and ladies than she had previously met. Her only thought was, *they will despise me soon enough! Why, oh why, did I come?* Over dinner, the young gentleman at her side by name of Mr. Adsley, took it upon himself to procure a smile on the melancholy face of the Yorkshire beauty.

Previously he'd given her a wide berth on account of the captain, but today he made an effort to be amusing and solicitous. *When the cat's away…*he thought.

During the first course of soup a la reine, fillet of veal, breast of lamb, boiled fowl, tongue, and prawns, he tried amusing repartee, only to find Miss Tavistock was uncommon quiet and had an amazing small appetite. The second course, rump of beef, oyster sauce, two ducklings, French beans with sauce, gooseberry pie, an omelet, mushrooms, artichoke bottoms, and curry, was equally without success in both regards. Miss Tavistock was neither diverted nor given to much eating. The wittiest repartee of Mr. Audley notwithstanding, Margaret could offer only the merest smiles, and took the tiniest bites of the delectables, sweetbreads, apple and barberry pie, tartlets, orange jelly, even truffles. Mr. Adsley had witnessed modest appetites before, but to be so impervious to his brightest witticisms was beyond the pale. He was relieved when the ladies left the men to their port and snuff. But he watched Miss Tavistock exit the dining room for feminine conversation in the parlour, like Antony beholding the exotic mystery of Cleopatra.

The polite chatter of the ladies did nothing for Margaret, for nothing could wholly dispel the cloud of impending doom filling her. It hung in her mind like a ponderous graveyard knell, waiting only to toll its solemn and dreary sound for all ears. She had betrayed the captain by her dishonesty. Too soon, indeed, the mournful sound would go forth; her good standing and enjoyment of everyone she'd met in London would cease. Why, why, hadn't she come to her senses and dealt plainly with Captain Rempeare? She would be disgraced forever as the spreader of Canterbury tales, an imposter, a shamster. Worse, she would lose the good opinion of the man whose opinion, she now knew, she coveted above all.

His Grace, the Duke of Trent, lay down *The London Herald* before Her Grace, formerly Lady Frances, opened to the society columns. She stood beside him where he sat at his large mahogany desk in the duke's private study, leaned down and read the circled portion.

She looked knowingly at him. "Lady X is a widow with children! Just as you said, my love! Whoever is feeding the paper knows about me." She pursed her lips.

The duke smiled. "But evidently does not know all. It won't vex us much longer." He took pen, ink, and a sheet of fresh paper and dipped his pen. "We'll put an end to this directly." He began writing, and added, "Once the marriage is discovered, interest in our affair will die out rapidly. I've sent a letter to Feodora. As for your offspring, when they arrive for dinner, we will inform them the deed's done, the paper's signed, and you are my duchess."

"I am your duchess," she repeated lovingly. The ceremony had taken place in Toadingham's ancient stone chapel, witnessed only by the servants, each of whom received a guinea for their trouble and the remainder of the day off. The butler and a few other servants refused to leave their duties, however, feeling instead it was an honour to serve the newlyweds on their first day and night of wedlock. The duke and duchess smiled at each other.

"Let us hope George's animosity will dissipate once he knows there's no hope of preventing our union," said Her Grace. "Imagine it—my son advising me to enter upon the severest seclusion at his estate! His only aim was odious, to prevent my seeing you. But being the eldest, if he sets the example of acquiescence for the rest of my offspring—for they all know I was abused most horridly by their deceased papa—they must follow suit. My daughters, indeed, only put up a dust on his account, for he threatened to withhold aid to their sons seeking commissions, if they did not. I dare say none of my girls will wonder at my not having a longer mourning period. George wanted it only for propriety's sake, but who in this vicinity did not know of my husband's cruelty?" She looked lovingly at her bridegroom. "I warrant 'twill be a relief for them, for who, I ask you, could long resent their mama becoming a duchess?"

"Precisely my thought, my love," agreed the duke. "Depend upon it, they will come round." He folded the letter, which he'd directed to the *Herald* and then added his signet and seal. Her Grace went to the bell pull. When a footman arrived, the duke said, placing the missive in his hand, "To the London mail coach *directly!* It must go out this morning."

"Aye, sir," said the servant, who took the letter and exited swiftly.

Letters written, the new Duchess of Trent and her duke proceeded from the room holding hands, smiling, and staring at each other like mooncalves.

CHAPTER SEVENTEEN

Just when Margaret thought her woes could get no worse, the next afternoon's paper provided her with fresh despair. The society column declared, with all due triumph, that it had been vindicated. Despite the denial of the duke's ward and niece, Miss Tavistock, they were correct to print word of the Duke of Trent having an affair with a mysterious Lady X. The *coup d'etat* had occurred, they said, for which reason they could now announce with the utmost authority, for it came from His Grace himself that Lady X was none other than Lady Frances Hopewell, newly become the Duchess of Trent.

"Lady Frances!" Margaret couldn't have been more shocked. She wavered for a moment between horror and joy—horror that now the captain would know she wasn't Lady X—though, of course, his arrival at Toadingham would have assured him of it in any case, and joy that the duke had, indeed, got married! It was so unexpected and hardly to be credited, that she turned hurriedly to the "Married" notice, but saw it there as well. She read it aloud to Mrs. Filbert:

"Married. On Friday the 16th, instant, by special licence, at Toadingham Hall, Yorkshire, His Grace, the fifth Duke of Trent, to the Hon. Lady Frances Hopewell, daughter of Viscount Brest and widow of the late Lord Thom. Hopewell of Yorkshire."

"Lady Frances!" she said again, trying to comprehend it.

Mrs. Filbert expressed equal surprise, saying, "Good heavens! Who would have thought? Good heavens! The duke, married! And, to Lady Frances, his neighbour!"

Margaret passed the paper to Mrs. Filbert, saying, "She *was* our neighbour, though we seldom saw her. Now it seems she is my aunt." She sighed. "I can hardly fathom it." Looking up suddenly, she said, "Why did my uncle not say something to me of this lady? And do you know, Mrs. Filbert, this means that all along there really *was* a Lady X, and I have gone about killing her off." Bitterly she added, "I wonder how it is that a London newspaper knew more of her existence than I, who lived with the duke!"

"Someone knew—and leaked it," said Mrs. Filbert.

"But who..." Margaret began, then coloured. "You don't think my uncle—"

"I dare say, not he," said Mrs. Filbert. "He values his privacy too well for that."

"I wonder if... Do you think these vulgar reports in the paper hurried him to this wedding? Might it have forced his hand?" said Margaret, her mouth firming into a hard line. "I do not wonder if Lady Frances herself may have—"

"Recollect, dearest, we know nothing sinister of this lady. She may well be innocent."

Margaret reflected on it and had to allow that whenever she had seen her ladyship, such as at Sunday services, she had seemed a most amiable, sweet-natured creature.

Mrs. Filbert sat back and smiled. "The duke—married! I must think it can only be in his best interest. Especially as you will be leaving Toadingham when you marry the captain."

Margaret, who was already showing signs of great strain by a loss of her usual high colour and sparkle, edged her nuncheon plate of ham pie and strawberries in cream, away. "Marry the captain?" she asked tiredly. "I have no expectation of that. Neither have I an appetite." She paused and sighed heavily. "I know nothing at all. I saw nothing of the duke's interest in a lady though I lived beneath his roof. And I knew nothing of the captain when I vexed him in every possible way, for I thought I did."

She turned with large tortured eyes to her companion. "I have learned only one thing: that I am a Jezebel! Until the captain returns and the axe falls—I should call him Jehu, I suppose," she added tragically—"I must wait, but I will do so in utter starvation."

Mrs. Filbert frowned. "If you do not take nourishment, I will refuse to allow Mr. Turnbull to take you from home tomorrow, particularly to the prince's palace on such a day!"

Margaret cried, "But that is my last hope of pleasure in this life! To see the legendary luxury of the palace and grounds. I will be struck down, afterwards, Mrs. Filbert! You *will* allow it—"

"Not unless you eat your ham pie."

Margaret gave her an indignant look, considering whether to offer a set down, for really Mrs. Filbert did not have the right or station to tell her what to do. She was only a hired companion. But the thought withered; she couldn't reprimand the lady. Indeed, she much relied upon Mrs. Filbert's loving eye. If only she had listened to her from the start, when she tried to dissuade Margaret from hiding her identity! The dear companion was, indeed, older and wiser than she. Morosely, Margaret pulled her plate back and took one bite. Chewing it carefully, she swallowed and said, "But do grant me the luxury of languishing in misery at home today?" she asked wistfully. "'Tis only what I deserve."

Mrs. Filbert seemed to know intuitively when Margaret needed a stern hand. The girl's regrets were breaking like waves in a tempest upon the rocky shore of her conscience, but to no good purpose. She put on her severest maternal voice: "Mrs. Humphries's carriage has already been ordered, I dare say. 'Tis too late for you to cry off."

"Mrs. Humphries can change her order," returned Margaret stubbornly.

Mrs. Filbert raised her brows at the girl and tightened her lips. "I will not have you staying home to indulge this odious childish sense of self-reproach. It serves no purpose." She eyed Margaret with a steely gaze and then glanced at the rest of the pie. "Eat; when the captain does return, he must find you looking like Circe! He is already smitten with you. Don't protest, my dear; I know the look on a man, but still it cannot hurt for you to look your best, for your best is very fetching, indeed. Remember his words, 'Any man who weds Miss Tavistock must be blessed!'"

"He meant them not," Margaret moaned, with a woebegone look on her face. "His kindness made him say it."

"He meant them utterly," returned Mrs. Filbert. "Come, come, eat. We will not have him return to find an insipid miss waiting for reproval, but the beautiful and spirited Miss Tavistock." Mrs. Filbert hesitated, smiling. "It is she he fell in love with, after all."

When the captain saw the marriage announcement in the paper, he shook his head wonderingly. So Lady Frances was Lady X! He'd had time to consider what might have caused Miss Tavistock—the little firebrand—to deceive him by claiming that identity. The lack of letters reaching her was one infraction, though it was through no fault of his. His failure to keep an engagement at Toadingham with no good reason furnished was a severe lapse of judgment—that, on his part, a second infraction. Then, his honesty in calling her former self "homely." He recollected that might have displeased her—another infraction. The moment when she'd called him impotent, and he'd been provoked and served her a lesson with her own riding whip. Oh, heavy infraction! If he could go back, undo that fatal meeting, but still, despite his sins, she too had been at fault. And to think how long she'd kept up the ruse—'twas extraordinary.

It saddened him to think how grieved she must have been to take such a precarious course, but it put a twinkle in his eye, too. How sly she was in managing to keep him in the dark while going about with the use of her own name! He had to admire such spirit, such pluck, for how many women were that strong natured? It showed a kind of mettle that he—why, he *loved* it.

She would have received his note already, telling her he was en route for Toadingham, but that journey was now unnecessary. Roderick's flat disclosure of her identity, coupled with the marriage announcement, made Yorkshire the last place he would wish to be. Not only would a newly married couple cherish their privacy, but *she* was here in London.

He was tempted, in fact, to make directly for Berkeley Square and confront the lovely dissembler, but he thought better of it. He'd hold off a confrontation, though inevitably it must come, until he settled other business that was suddenly imperative.

For starters, he ordered Roderick to send for his trunks to deposit them at the captain's rooms on South Audley Street. It still irked him, the idea of Roderick seeing Miss Tavistock, staying with her, dining with her, enjoying the light of her countenance, the gracefulness of her person, which even now—when the newspaper's revelation of Lady X would inform her that her game was up—must be a pleasure to behold.

He turned his energies, as soon as his equipage had been fitted with a new wooden wheel and returned to him, to procuring a special licence from the archbishop. Since the duke had been married quietly by special licence, he saw no reason why he and Miss Tavistock, absurd girl, shouldn't be likewise wed. He'd been forced to spend the night at the inn while waiting for his curricle, but, no sooner than Glick put the money into the hand of the postilions, who would in turn pay the wheel smith for the repair, he set off back to the metropolis.

Finally, he had a wedding gift in mind, a thing that sent him to Rundell's—the supplier of jewellery for the *ton*, including the royal family—while Glick, meanwhile, would pick up the twin-tailed topcoat the captain had bespoken two weeks before. He meant to be married in full uniform, but new civilian attire would be needful in future if he continued without a commission.

He made one final stop with his man of business. And there, his hopes and plans came to a crashing abrupt halt. Instead of the comfortable fortune he'd accrued, he learned that saving Redmonton had cost him more than he realised. His brother's last unfortunate losses to Earl Winch had required selling a great many of the captain's bonds. Then, two of the prizes he'd already received monies for were rescinded by the prize board, requiring an immediate return of the funds.

"There are prizes that have not yet been decided," said the captain.

"There are, Captain, and if they end in your favour, your prospects are far from desperate."

"If they do not?"

"Sir, you must not cover any further losses of the earl's."

"Is the estate past salvaging?"

"No, sir: mortgaged and entailed, but still with an income." He paused and gave the captain a searching look. "I understand the earl is unwell."

"He's been unwell for many a year, sir," returned the captain.

"Forgive me, but I am acquainted with his physician." He eyed the captain with a question in his eyes. "A shrewd man, sir, might continue to back the earl—a man in line to inherit the earldom, that is."

Startled, the captain cried, "Great Joseph. You think he's dying!"

The man sat back and rested his hands across his stomach. "Not I, sir, his physician. Says it can't be long, now. The liver and spleen, sir, nearly useless. The lungs, sadly deteriorated."

Captain Rempeare swallowed. If Stafford died—heavens, he hadn't considered it—he'd be the new earl. The estate was let to nurse, a right mess, but he'd have a title to offer Miss Tavistock. He frowned and sniffed and said, "Speculation, sir. The earl's of amazing strong constitution, and I can hardly wish my own brother dead."

"I thought it worth a mention, sir. Before you give up the estate entirely."

"I'm afraid this raises another delicate subject for me," said the captain. "Considering my current state of affairs, I fear I am in no position to go forward with a betrothal to Miss Tavistock."

The man raised a brow. "Sir, on the contrary. It puts you in a position to welcome it better than before, not only for your own sake but for the lady's."

"For the lady's?" the captain asked, with a raised brow.

"Miss Tavistock's trust monies, you know, are contingent upon marriage to you."

The captain stared. He did not know.

"In all honesty, sir," continued the man, "there are legal means of trying to extricate the funds from such a stricture, but as things stand, she has use of them only on the duke's authority, due to an understanding that the wedding will go forth."

The captain sat forward. "She has use of them?" he asked. "Do you mean, she is drawing from the funds now?"

Primpley eyed him steadily but seemed almost as if smiling. "She is."

"Tell me," he said. "Is Miss Tavistock aware of that condition?"

"Yes, sir. She directs her bills here and receives a stipend from the account, with the understanding that she is to marry you."

CHAPTER EIGHTEEN

It was a mystery to Margaret why Earl Stafford hadn't lashed out at her yet, sprinkling the *ton* with word that she was an imposter, even though she wasn't, really. She looked haggard with worry the following day, not only because she expected that, but because she dreaded her next encounter with the captain. She shuddered to think of the scold she was bound to get, but even worse, the loss of his esteem and friendship.

She wondered at times, almost hoping, that he would have nothing more to do with her. In that case, there would be no excruciating confrontation. But her heart ached at the thought not to see him again! Not given a chance to express her sorrow and regret! No, one way or other, she must face him.

Nevertheless, today she would accompany Mr. Turnbull to see Carlton House. He was expected presently: much earlier than she or any member of the upper class usually left their homes, but they had agreed that an early start upon the expected long lines must be the best course. Mrs. Filbert was on hand to fuss and fret while Margaret's maid laced her stays and buttoned up her walking dress. There was no need of a spencer, for the day was warm and bright with the early summer sun. While she sat before a mirror as her maid undid her hair papers and pinned the curls just so about her head, Mrs. Filbert spouted a fountain of advice.

"Do not carry a reticule, as there will be nappers in abundance," she said. "Wear no jewellery. No, not in your hair, either. And wear your kid half-boots; half-boots are sturdier for much walking."

Margaret listened, nodding, but she did not think she would wear half-boots to the Prince Regent's palace.

"Do not wear a ponderous bonnet, on account of the crush."

To this she objected, "Recollect, this is Carlton House! I think you are coming it much too brown."

Mrs. Filbert didn't skip a beat, nodding gravely at Margaret. "Mind the exits—you may need to beat a hasty retreat. Do not allow yourself to be parted from Mr. Turnbull."

"I shall cling to his arm, I assure you," Margaret said with patient scepticism, meeting Mrs. Filbert's eyes from behind her in the looking glass.

Mrs. Filbert was not reassured. Margaret looked fagged to begin with, and ought not to be braving a situation that promised to be trying and fatiguing. But all too soon, Mr. Turnbull arrived. If he thought Miss Tavistock's appearance wanting, he hid it admirably, seeming inordinately pleased to leave Berkeley Square with her upon his arm. To Margaret's relief, he quite beamed with optimism about what awaited them on Pall Mall.

The papers assured them that the fête the day before had seen Carlton House, that "unrivalled bastion of splendour and luxury," completely thrown open to guests, including the basements, used for supper rooms. The grounds were canvassed for protection and laid with festooned marquees corded with gilt rope, for guests to dine beneath. Margaret rippled with excitement, almost forgetting the woes that lay so heavily upon her.

Despite their early departure, they arrived to join a long line of carriages the whole length of Pall Mall. Horse Guards attempting to keep order were at the entrance to the street, and on foot was a moving, excited, immense sea of people, crowding the pavements and overflowing into the road, all anxious for admittance into the gates of the palace. Mr. Turnbull, upon opening the carriage door to take a view of the situation, returned to his seat with the exclamation that he believed the line of equipages extended all the way to the top of St. James's Street! "This is a vast conglomeration of equipages," he added, with a note of gravity. "I believe our best course is to remain in the carriage until we can alight at the portico of the palace."

"I do not think," said Margaret, "that the front entrance will be opened for us—for anyone, that is. According to the papers, only the gates—"

"We are the upper class," he said, peering past her out the window, at the mobs. "The guards will grant us entrance; we shan't join this number."

For a good twenty minutes, while she hoped he was correct, they moved not at all, but watched with consternation as more and more ladies and gentlemen exited their carriages, which had been brought to a standstill, and made their way on foot, joining the throngs outside the gates.

Presently, Margaret could stand it no longer and cried, "Mr. Turnbull! If we do not join this crowd, we will never gain entrance!" With a fretful expression, he surveyed the personages now hurrying past the coach—many of whom looked perfectly respectable and well dressed—and gave his reluctant agreement. "I do not relish bringing you into such a close crowd," he said, but he helped her down, and in a minute, Margaret was in the street upon his arm. They joined the wave moving towards the palace and heard a great boisterous cry when the gates were suddenly opened. An instant surge of bodies moving as one great beast overwhelmed the entrance. The noise of the crowd increased.

Mr. Turnbull put a hand over Margaret's hand, which was upon his arm. "Pray, Miss Tavistock, are you certain you wish to proceed? Looks rather havey-cavey, I think."

"But I must!" she cried, nonplussed. "We are so close now!"

"Well, then," he said, though with a worried air. "Hold fast and hang tight!" They hurried to join the others heading to the great press, took up the line, and were soon engulfed in a large mass of humanity. The gate was closing again, as Horse Guards moved right into the press to make the unruly crowd stand back from the entrance. One horse, unnerved by the thronging complaining crowd, reared on its legs. The powerful front legs hung in the air for precarious seconds, while people unable to move aside stood in a heaving swarm below. "Good heavens!" cried Mr. Turnbull, as the horse fell to all fours, and another cry from the crowd rose. Margaret, fortunately, hadn't seen it. But she wouldn't have believed it possible. Not at Carlton House, the home of the "First Gentleman of Europe."

They had joined the throng—it couldn't rightly be called a "line,"— and were surrounded by eager visitors. Hardly moving beneath a warm sun, Margaret broke out in a sweat. Mr. Turnbull looked hot and uncomfortable as well. Women began removing bonnets. Bodies pressed against her; the crowd surged, and her hand lost Mr. Turnbull's arm. At that moment a woman's cries—she seemed to be trying to extricate herself from the stifling press—made Margaret shudder. A skirmish from within the mass of bodies ensued, and suddenly another surge of the crowd sent her forward, then back, tight against those around her. She caught sight of the unfortunate lady struggling to get past others—and saw her swoon! What became of her, Margaret didn't know. The Horse Guards were far too few to keep the crowd in check!

Another woman's face appeared briefly, contorted with a scream upon her lips, before she disappeared, slipping into the crest of bodies about her. Panic swept through Margaret. How quickly things got out of hand! Mr. Turnbull reappeared, thank heavens, and she entwined her arm into his. But every cry now sounded like that of one oppressed. She bethought her desire to tour the palace—but too late! Pushing and shoving sent her in first one direction and then another; she catapulted into Mr. Turnbull, who put an arm about her protectively.

"Shocking impertinence!" he cried, casting a severe eye about them. He tightened his hold on Margaret, saying, with their faces practically nose to nose, "I beg your pardon, Miss Tavistock! We must not lose each other!" Normally, it would have been unthinkable for him to hold her at all, much less so closely, but with bodies pressing against them, she was grateful for the security of his arms. When he turned his head to glare at the source of a sharp jab to his side, Margaret saw that his handsome side whiskers were false! It might have been comical under other circumstances, but he looked down at her, his eyes revealing that he was not impervious to the nearness of her face, and she looked away. Mrs. Filbert would chuckle when she heard.

But now the heat was becoming unbearable! All around her was a wall of humanity, perspiring and as uncomfortable as she. And then, after one particularly hard jostling sent her almost off her feet, Mr. Turnbull's arms were loosened, and in the next moment he was swallowed into the crowd. She cried out uselessly, for everyone was crying and shouting. And suddenly there was nothing but chaos, panic, and desperation. Hands pushed her, pummelled her—she couldn't breathe! Ladies screamed. Bonnets and sashes went flying. Margaret could neither control the direction she moved, nor the speed. She felt like a twig carried on a torrent towards a cascade. No palace grandeur was worth this!

The gates, she recalled from the paper, were only unlocked at intervals. When one suddenly swung open ahead, instead of bringing relief, the rush of the crowd—a sea of bodies—swept her forward in mortified helplessness. At some point her feet didn't touch the ground, and when they did, her slippers had vanished, and only her stockings remained. Mrs. Filbert was right; she should have worn half-boots! And the captain! *There's bound to be a terrible crush,* he'd said. Why did she never listen to those who tried to school her?

The frightful cries and sobs, the sound of tearing garments still surrounded her. Swept along, she stumbled over bonnets and shoes and then—*a body?* Oh, abominable day! Was it the lady who had swooned?

Her bonnet was caught—by what? She didn't know, but it tore, the ribbons chafing her chin as it left her head. She reached the gate—as it swung shut! She was instantly pressed against it by the crowd behind, and was beginning to suffocate. She heard the rip of her gown, felt it as it tore at the shoulder, and pain seemed to be everywhere. Her lungs were squeezed—she gasped for breath. And then, miraculously, the gate opened! She was pushed through it, and into the courtyard of the palace, where suddenly the crowd could disperse.

She stumbled out of the melee, and panting, tried to collect her shaken nerves. She shuddered at the sight of ladies on the ground, half-naked, who had not fared as well, who, for all she knew, were senseless. She looked about for help. There must be guards or servants. Seeing a footman, she started towards him, but he was off in a different direction. Oh! If she could only find Mr. Turnbull and leave this horrid anarchy! Indignation at the regent rose up in her. How could this happen at Carlton House!

And then she saw him—Mr. Turnbull! He was slowly coming to his feet, looking beaten and dishevelled. She started across the crowd towards him, slapped a hand that landed on her bare shoulder, and kept on. Someone stepped on her foot, not for the first time; she squelched a cry of pain and kept on. Finally, she reached Mr. Turnbull, only to behold the face of a stranger! She swallowed a cry of despair and moved on.

What should have been a lovely day had turned into a monstrous ordeal. She had lost Mr. Turnbull, her only protection; she had lost her shoes and bonnet, her gown was torn, and her hair, she realised, hung about her shoulders in sad disarray. Around her, other ladies looked equally undone, and she was not the only female staggering across the canvassed ground as if leaving a battlefield. Her whole body was smarting, it seemed. Holding tears in check, she stumbled forward. This was no time to get missish—she must be strong. She saw the much-praised and festooned marquees that the regent had placed on the property for his guests, but they no longer interested her. Their appearance of gaiety now seemed appalling.

She turned towards the gate, thinking only of escape. The guards had closed it. But beyond, she saw the same massive crowd of the kind that had imprisoned her. How to get out? And how, once she did, to make her way home?

Two young women came hurrying by sobbing, with torn muslin dragging behind them. Other women passed, covering their mouths with their hands, one with arms crossed over bare breasts. Something inside Margaret broke. "Dear God, help us!" she said aloud. "Where is civility?" She didn't dare brave those crowds to get out. Already her gown was torn. If she were crushed again so that the rest of her gown gave way—her stays and chemise like that poor woman. She shuddered at the thought.

Oh, why *hadn't* she heeded the captain's warnings? But the thought of Captain Rempeare sent her heart further into despair. Losing shoes and a bonnet were nothing—*he* was lost to her. An involuntary sob escaped her, and suddenly she felt faint. This was more frightening still—the thought of losing consciousness. She *must* keep going. She'd find Mr. Turnbull, or a way out, and then a hansom cab. *She must keep going!* But light-headedness made her stop, and for a moment she stood, swaying as the world around her spun. And then a pair of hands, gentle hands, took her by the arms.

"Here you are, thank God!" a firm voice said.

Margaret expected to see Mr. Turnbull. But just before everything went black, she saw the concerned face of Captain Rempeare looking down at her like an angel of light.

"I've got you now. You're safe," he said.

Was she dreaming? But she tottered against him, and then he swept her off her feet and into his arms.

CHAPTER NINETEEN

Margaret awoke almost at once and stayed semi-conscious while the captain carried her through the courtyard and into the palace. Her befogged brain struggled to make sense of his presence. How had he found her in the madness? How was he returned from Yorkshire so quickly? And did he not despise her? But, oh, thank God he came! And they kept moving.

Whether because of his naval uniform or the grave look on his face, an opening was made for them. She knew vaguely that he stopped to speak to a member of the guard, but what he said, she knew not. But they were now inside the palace. And then the murmur of the crowd touring the house fell away, and she was brought through wide corridors where the public was not allowed. A servant was leading them, she realised, a housemaid. Blinking, she caught glimpses of splendid paintings, gilt frames, ornate wallpaper and furniture. Even the ceilings were painted in gold leaf and designs. She came more awake, but it wasn't the palace that most interested her.

She looked up at the captain's face. Every line, every sea-tanned inch of his expression, though grim at the moment, looked now only like the epitome of kindness, of goodness. How had it taken her so long to realise Captain Rempeare was everything she could want? He'd warned her not to attempt the tour, said he wouldn't dream of going near it, yet he'd come and saved her. By now, he must know of her deception, which meant that he surely saw she was a shrew, an odious, stubborn, disagreeable woman—yet he'd saved her.

He glanced down at her. She blinked back tears, too ashamed to say anything.

"I'll soon have you safely home," he said gently.

This made Margaret bite her lip and resulted in more tears.

"There's a handkerchief in the pocket of my coat, if you can reach it," he said.

Shyly, Margaret did and blew her nose. But she was far from finished crying. She had, indeed, committed too many transgressions to be done with tears for the foreseeable future, she felt. They were conducted to the basement and then led to a service door that exited the palace onto St. James's Street. The captain thanked the maid, struggled to fish out a few shillings for her while holding Margaret, and then continued to the street, passing carriage after carriage until finally coming to one where a servant appeared and hurriedly let down the steps.

"Good man, Glick," he said. Still carrying Margaret, he mounted them, but when he went to deposit her gently upon a cushion, she was unable to release her grip about his neck.

"You're safe now," he said softly. But still she clung to him. He took a deep breath. With great resolve, he gently removed her arms from about his neck and put her down. He removed his jacket and put it about her shoulders. Margaret cried softly. He surveyed her a moment. He rummaged below one seat and pulled out a box. Inside it was a pistol—and a flask.

"Here," he said. "Sip this." Margaret took it cautiously. "Brandy," he said. She'd never tasted brandy but obediently took the tiniest sip possible. Her face puckered into a look of distaste, but he said, "No, no, take a good swig."

Grimacing, she forced it down. "That was loathsome," she said, clearing her throat afterwards.

"It will help restore you," he said softly. Then, surveying her, he murmured, "I'll be right back"—and exited the coach.

On the pavement, he turned to Glick. "Turn us about," he said, for his valet was today his coachman. "These carriages can make room for us to a hair. When we get about, turn into Cleveland Street and then head straight down into the Mall."

"Down *Cleveland* to the Mall, sir?" asked Glick, with a scrunched-up face.

"That's right."

"Past St. James's Palace? There's an avenue of trees there, sir," he said with surprise. "That ain't no proper road, sir," he warned.

"Right through it," the captain said firmly. "The proper roads about the palace are clogged. When you come out, turn onto Constitution Hill, then make a sharp right at Hyde Park Corner onto Piccadilly. From there, I dare say, you'll know how to reach Berkeley Square."

Glick nodded. "Aye, sir." But his eyes narrowed, looking about them. "It'll take some doing to get this lot to make way for us," he said.

"You must accomplish it, Glick," returned the captain, with a gleam of amusement in his eyes. "If anyone can, 'tis you. If we fail, Miss Tavistock will need smelling salts, if not a physician. We can't subject her to wait for this appalling traffic tangle to undo itself. We'd be here all day."

Glick nodded. "Aye, sir." But with sudden alacrity, he said, "A bit o' blunt won't hurt our cause, sir." He nodded at the double rows of carriages, all at a standstill equal to that on Pall Mall. "The whips'll find room more rightly if there's something in it for 'em, sir."

"Of course," said Captain Rempeare, rummaging in his pockets. "Good thinking, Glick." He handed him a pile of bank notes and coin. "Use what you must—and handsomely, now, eh?"

Glick nodded. 'Doing it handsomely,' was ship's jargon for *on the double*. He approached the carriage to their left, motioning that he must speak to the coachman at once.

When the captain returned, Margaret quickly blew her nose. Before he could take his seat she reached out and clutched his arm. "Please, Captain, sit beside me."

He did, studying her eyes. He took one of her hands.

Margaret blinked back tears, trying to get ahold of herself. Where should she start? What to say?

"I'm terribly sorry for what you've been through," he said.

She looked at him, all distraught. "Terribly sorry? You?" She shook her head, her eyes in a torment. She bit her lip, trying not to let a sob of anguish escape. She managed instead to only close her eyes as a silent tear made its way down her cheek.

The captain shifted uncomfortably on his seat. "My dear Miss Chrissendon—"

He hadn't called her Miss Tavistock! Did he not know her true identity? Or was it simply from habit? Either way, it brought forth more tears, making her shoulders shake. He stared for a moment and inched closer to her side.

"My dear Miss Chrissendon," he repeated. "I am utterly at a loss. How can I help you?"

Margaret glanced at him with an agonised expression, and then before she knew what she was about, she turned and cried into his chest. The captain put an arm about her and spoke soothingly. "It's over, now. You're perfectly safe and will soon be home. At peril of being charged with trespassing or disorderly conduct, I've ordered Glick to take a private lane, the fastest possible route to your home—"

"That isn't it at all, Captain!" she cried, keeping her head in his chest. She was too, too ashamed to so much as meet his eyes.

He hesitated, then said, "That isn't it?"

Margaret sniffed, trying to collect herself.

"That isn't it?" he asked again. Gently, he took her chin and lifted her head. "What, then? Have I distressed you?"

Margaret looked sorrowfully into his eyes. "I believe I have distressed *you.*"

Something passed over the captain's face—indecision? "How is that?" he asked softly.

Margaret sniffled. "I misjudged you," she said, tentatively. The time had come. She must work her way around to telling him the whole sordid truth.

"Misjudged me?" he asked, as if to prod her on.

"Yes, you must know—" She searched his eyes. "You've been to Toadingham?"

The coach started suddenly, and he glanced out the window. They were slowly making a turn-about. "Good ol' Glick," he murmured. Turning back to her, he said, staring at her strangely. "I have not. Other business kept me in Town, I'm afraid."

Margaret's whole face lightened. Suddenly, she felt that all was *not* lost. The captain must learn the truth—indeed, she wanted him to—but not at *this* minute. Not after all she'd just suffered at the palace.

"You may not have misjudged me," he said suddenly. "I'm afraid there is good reason for your disapprobation. I own I am fully deserving of it."

"Fully deserving?" she asked. "How is that, sir?"

He gave her a regretful look. "I am sadly to blame for a most monstrous injustice."

"Of what nature?" she asked, really curious.

"I am guilty, Miss Chrissendon. I am a blackguard." To her questioning look, he continued in a sorrowful tone. "I know myself to be betrothed, you see; you are aware, of course, that it is the case." He looked at her keenly.

She nodded earnestly. "Yes!"

He leaned into her. Their faces were close. Margaret swallowed. How handsome he was!

"But despite this knowledge and my every intention of being loyal to my future bride, I have, I am ashamed to say it—I have fallen in love with another woman."

Margaret gasped. It seemed almost like a smile flickered on his features for the merest second, then vanished. Her face was now dejected; she had the look of one who'd suffered a crushing blow. "Please, Captain, say no more!" She moved away from him and put a hand to her head. "I am utterly fatigued from this day." She looked over briefly to say, "Had I listened to you, I should never have had to suffer it."

"And I am exceedingly sorry you did."

"I can hardly express my gratitude at your coming. Considering what you confided to me just now, I mean, whatever made you do it?" Before he could answer, the coach finished its turn, and suddenly the horses took off. Clutching the edges of the cushion, she cried, "Fire and brimstone! I forgot Mr. Turnbull!"

"He will come through unscathed, I warrant. His greatest concern will be you. As soon as we reach Berkeley Square, we must send word of your safety."

"Yes, thank you," she said, nodding her agreement. She looked warily at him. "Sir, this woman you're in love with?"

"Yes?" His eyes looked piercingly at her.

She looked away. His coat was still about her shoulders, and her fingers played with the brocade as she asked, "Is she…very beautiful?"

He said evenly, "She is indeed, very beautiful."

Margaret grimaced. "Will you tell Miss Tavistock?"

"That depends," he answered slowly.

"Depends?" she asked. "Upon what?"

"Upon whether the woman I love shall have me."

She turned indignant eyes upon him. "Do you mean to say, that if she will have you, you will cry off from our—from your engagement?"

A flash of something sparkled in his eyes and vanished. In a serious tone he said, looking quite philosophical, "If she will have me, I will be the happiest of men. I couldn't possibly wed a different woman. And I will tell Miss Tavistock so." He paused, looking at her deeply. "I begin to think there isn't another woman in the world I could delight in by half."

"Oh!" The word came out in almost a moan. A thought hit Margaret. "And what if she will *not* have you?" There was unmitigated hope in the question.

"Then I should have to reconcile myself to marrying my cousin." He sighed long-sufferingly.

She searched his face unhappily. Her heart felt like lead. Every last bit of her had turned cold, and she was tired, so tired. She leaned her head back upon the cushion, but Glick, bent on "doing it handsomely," was running the horses as fast as the London street traffic would allow. There was nothing but jostling and bumping therefore in the coach.

"Lean against me," the captain said. Margaret turned large eyes to him, wondering that he should welcome her against him when he was in love with another woman, but his face revealed nothing. She slowly lowered her head, and he circled her with an arm comfortably. She sat there in perfect misery for the remainder of the ride. The captain hadn't gone to Toadingham, hadn't discovered the truth, but she'd lost him anyway! Lost him to some woman.

When they arrived at Berkeley Square, she was weak and feeling ill. He carried her to the house, for she had only torn stockings upon her feet. As he did, she looked up at the handsome face so close to her own. "Captain, if you please," she said forlornly, "what is the name of the woman you love?"

She did not *really* wish to know; she steeled her heart to ask it of him only because she could not stand to *not* know. He looked down at her with a little smile.

"Why, Miss Chrissendon," he said, now climbing the steps to the front door with her in his arms. "I thought surely you knew. You must know; there is only one woman I could love." She stared at him, dreading the worst.

"It is you, my darling."

CHAPTER TWENTY

Mrs. Filbert caught wind of the return of her dearest charge from Stevens, who scurried to fetch the companion after opening the door to a much dishevelled Miss Tavistock in stockinged feet, a naval coat, and in the arms of Captain Rempeare. Trained to maintain an impassive expression, he nevertheless balked at the sight of her and cried, "Miss Tavistock! Upon my soul!" The captain raised a brow at the expressive servant, but didn't slow a whit. Margaret was staring as if transfixed upon the face of her rescuer, but she swallowed and called out pitifully as the captain swept past her. "I'm all right, Stevens!"

Stevens found Mrs. Filbert in the kitchens giving her keenest opinion to cook, who wished to know whether Miss Tavistock preferred an additional teaspoon of double refined sugar to the egg custard *before* cooking, or simply to sprinkle it atop the custard during its final browning in a quick oven. When Stevens shared his remarkable news, Mrs. Filbert came hurriedly to her feet, telling cook she was sure Miss Tavistock would eat her egg custard whichever way the sugar was added, and then moved as fast as she was capable of, holding her skirts in one hand. She managed to catch the captain and Margaret in the first-floor corridor just in time to say, "Bring her to the blue saloon, sir!"

He stopped, not knowing precisely where the blue saloon was. But when Mrs. Filbert came abreast, he said politely, "I think her bedchamber is the best place for her, ma'am." Margaret was silent, transfixed in the peculiar position of experiencing both exquisite rapture and exquisite sorrow at the same time—on account of finding *she* was the loved woman of the captain's—and could only point wordlessly at the correct door.

Exquisite rapture was hers for knowing she was loved by him! *It is you, my darling.* The words rang in her head. But exquisite sorrow was on account of the same thing—he loved her: *Miss Chrissendon!* The tricky horrid showdown, in which she must set him straight about herself, was still impending. A change of heart on his part was still possible, therefore—a disastrous change of heart. When he learned the truth...oh, it seemed more horrible a prospect than ever.

Mrs. Filbert felt real concern when she saw, not only Margaret's tattered state, but the look on her face. With a great deal of clucking the tongue, and pulling the bell pull, and saying the doctor ought to come and sending cook for a calming tonic, hot water, a cloth, a mustard plaster, and a bracing libation, the captain merely stood aside and watched with almost a grin. He was certain the invalid was more shaken than injured, with no malady that some good kitchen physic couldn't cure—though, evidently, she'd been slightly mauled in the melee. Finally, Mrs. Filbert acknowledged him with many a thankful exclamation for his "undoubted heroism," which she was sure had saved Margaret from a much worse fate.

When Margaret's maid arrived, breathless and wide eyed, carrying a basin of steaming water and a cloth, Captain Rempeare recognised his cue to leave. He went to Margaret and found her hand, dangling languorously from the bed, for she was utterly distraught and overcome. He took it and kissed it softly. "If I can be of service," he said, "do not hesitate to ask it."

She stared at him with sorrowful eyes. "I *must* speak with you, Captain!" Whether she wished to reveal everything before he left, or simply longed to hear him say again that he loved her, Margaret hardly knew. She knew only that she did not want him to leave.

"Tomorrow," he said abruptly, turning to include Mrs. Filbert in the plan. "I dare say you need to rest."

"But I will *not* rest until I speak with you," she said. "What you told me earlier..."

He leaned in and spoke to her in a low tone. "But there's the devil in it. I can do nothing for it. I spoke out of turn—I must remember my betrothal." He stood back and nodded as he bowed lightly and then turned to leave.

"Mrs. Filbert!" Margaret cried, distressed. "He must not leave!"

Mrs. Filbert decided Margaret was on the verge of hysteria. Certainly it was only fitting that the captain take his leave. With a sad, worried look, she nodded at Captain Rempeare to depart and took the basin and cloth from Clarice, saying, "Has that doctor been sent for?" Margaret was in need of laudanum. She was overexcited: exhausted, too, no doubt.

While she gave Margaret a cloth bath, the story of what happened at Carlton House came out. Tears and self-recriminations, a startled realisation that she'd forgotten to send word to the Turnbulls that she was safely home, and a garbled explanation about the captain and how she would never, ever, be Mrs. Rempeare now! "*Tragically*," she said, "he loves me as Miss Chrissendon!"

"How is that a tragedy?" asked Mrs. Filbert. "Is it not precisely as I said? That he is in love with you? He will forgive all; I assure you!"

"But he loves Miss *Chrissendon!* Only think—we are a doomed love triangle when there are only *two* of us!"

Mrs. Filbert pursed her lips, but Margaret was oblivious.

"When he learns that I am Miss Tavistock, I fear 'twill be the *commencement de la fin*," she said, staring tragically into the air.

"Fustian," said Mrs. Filbert. "He loves *you* and shall love you by any name." She paused. "However, when he calls tomorrow—"

"Do you think he will?" Margaret asked, sitting up eagerly.

Mrs. Filbert smiled. "There is nothing known to man that will keep him away, dearest. He has declared his love. A man will not rest easy until he knows it to be returned."

Margaret settled back upon her pillow with a troubled expression. "And so I must tell him all," she said sadly. She closed her eyes. "My dear Mrs. Filbert. I fear my nerves are utterly shattered. I'm sure I'm not equal to it—telling him the truth."

Mrs. Filbert considered a moment. "If you are not better rested when he comes, I suppose I can do the deed—"

Margaret sat up abruptly, wide eyed. "Would you? Splendid idea!"

Mrs. Filbert nodded. "Of course. Though I should think he would prefer to hear it from your own lips."

Margaret waved a hand in the air. "Oh, what matters it? From me or from you, the thing is, he will be told." She sighed heavily. "I was mad to let it go on for so long. He must, indeed, be told as soon as possible! And then"—she stopped and heaved a soul-rending sigh—"he'll be done with me. And 'tis just what I deserve." She lay back despondently, frowning.

Late that afternoon, Mr. Turnbull appeared at the door. He , quickly ascertained from Mrs. Filbert that Margaret had arrived home safely, that a medical man had seen to her, and that she, poor invalid, was resting quietly. He gave his earnest, sincerest, and humblest apologies, for failing her during the crush and left only after assuring Mrs. Filbert that he had gone mad with worry when he was not able to locate her either on the grounds or inside the palace. Saying he would call again, with permission, the following day, he left for home with a great weight lifted. Indeed, it was vastly relieving to know Miss Tavistock was safe, but he felt sure he'd aged during the course of the many hours he'd spent searching for her. His only ambition was to get to his own home and bed. He, too, had been abused by the crush.

By the following morning, having received from the physician, Dr.

Carey, a very slight dose of laudanum mixed with tincture, followed by eleven hours of sleep, Margaret awoke with only minor aches from the prior day's tribulations. Her complexion was remarkably recovered, though there remained a heavy shadow over her heart, which somehow appeared about her eyes. Mrs. Filbert had Margaret's breakfast sent up on a tray and accompanied the housemaid who delivered it. Margaret was awake when they entered. She blinked sadly at her companion.

"Now, now," said Mrs. Filbert briskly. "Not in the blue devils again? I'll not have it, my dear. When all shall be brought to rights this very day: mark my words."

Margaret said, "Brought to rights? The criminal, rather, which is me, shall be brought to justice, you mean. She will lose the man she loves after having abused him monstrously since the day of their meeting!"

Mrs. Filbert clucked her tongue. "No such thing, you'll see."

"Where is Roddy?" asked Margaret. "Why have I not seen him?"

Mrs. Filbert said, "He sent for his trunks. I thought you knew."

Surprised, Margaret said, "Where is he stopping?"

Mrs. Filbert shrugged. "He did not send word of that." With an eye on the untouched breakfast tray, she added, "Take your breakfast, my dear. You are looking fagged. Good nourishment does wonders for the complexion, I own."

When Captain Rempeare left Berkeley Square the prior evening, he did so with the feeling of a man who had achieved his purpose. He'd found Miss Tavistock, thank God, and removed her from that bedlam at the palace. He'd been instantly concerned when word reached him of the terrible muddle along Pall Mall, and of the unprecedented crowds amassing outside the palace. Knowing Margaret, he did not expect that she would be deterred, and he'd been right.

He felt an amazing strong tenderness when he saw her, looking beleaguered and undone. It wasn't easy for him *not* to secure her hand and troth before leaving her afterwards. Nor was it without remorse that he allowed her to think he was still bamboozled about her identity. But he'd fought fire with fire, giving the lovely dissembler just a taste of what she'd been feeding him since they met. Yet it wasn't revenge he wanted. He hoped to bring her to the point of confession. She must trust him enough to tell him the truth—that was all he asked.

She hadn't been ready to do it. But he could wait.

However long it took, he'd wait.

In the middle of the night Glick awakened Captain Rempeare. "Sorry, sir, but there's trouble."

"What? What is it?" he asked, throwing off the bedcovers and blinking at the strange, ghostlike appearance of the valet in the light of a single taper. Glick turned and began lighting more candles, first the one on the bedside table, and then the sconces on the wall.

"I'm afraid it's the earl, sir. Doctor sent a messenger bidding you to Grosvenor Street with all haste. They say he 'asn't long, sir."

"Get the gig ready," the captain said, springing out of bed. *Great Joseph, if Primpley hadn't been right!* While Glick quickly laid out the rest of his articles—for he felt constrained to complete this service before leaving the bedchamber—the captain drew on stockings and pantaloons. "On second thought, saddle me a horse. That'll be fastest. But get the gig and bring Roderick to the house."

"Aye, sir," the little man said, before scurrying from the room.

A grim-faced footman emerged from the house and took the reins after the captain rode up. Despite his hurry, Gabriel did not think it could truly be a dire situation. The earl had tried to trick Miss Tavistock into marriage a mere week ago. How could he lay dying so soon after?

But he went past more dour-countenanced servants and saw a man in black sitting patiently, with his watch in hand, at the foot of the stairs, in a chair that must have been placed there specially for his use. He stopped in front of him, his face a silent question.

"I'm not the doctor, sir" he said.

"Who are you, then?"

"I'm the undertaker, sir." Gabriel grimaced and continued up the padded staircase and down a corridor to the stately bedchamber of his brother. To his surprise, the two seamen he'd instructed to keep Stafford occupied for a few days were in the room. They nodded a hasty greeting but looked away with speed. Their faces and manner puzzled him for a moment; they looked abashed—no, *ashamed*. But he passed them to speak to the doctor, who was leaning over the invalid in the bed, listening with a stethoscope. The physician's assistant hovered nearby.

At the bedside, Gabriel inhaled sharply at what he saw. The earl's face, gaunt as a skeleton and staring blank eyed at the ceiling, made the announcement even before the physician looked up at him regretfully and said, "He's gone, I'm afraid."

Gabriel stared at him.

"I'm sorry, sir. Are you his brother?"

"One of them, yes." He glanced at the earl. "I saw him not a week ago. No one would have supposed…"

"These things can seem very sudden," the man said, removing the apparatus from around his neck. "But I've been the earl's physician for two years and warned him for all that time, spirits would be his death if he weren't careful."

The captain must have continued to look stupefied, for he added sourly, "He was not careful." He motioned with his head to the seamen. "Ask these gentlemen. They brought him home and summoned me." The doctor took two coins from a waistcoat pocket and closed the earl's eyes, and then went to confer with his assistant.

The captain transferred his heavy gaze to the sailors, who shifted on their feet uncomfortably. He went to the men, who kept their gazes upon the floor. "Well?" he asked. "Let's have it." The two exchanged miserable looks.

"Well, sir," said one sheepishly, "we was only followin' your orders, sir. We didn't know as the earl was to lay off the spirits. He never said so."

"He did look an awful colour soon enough," put in the second, matter-of-factly, to which the first gave him a scandalised look. To the captain he said quickly, "I didn't take note of no colour, sir; we was intent on the cards. The earl worked up to a formidable stake, sir."

"What stake was that?" asked the captain.

"Said he'd confer his earldom on the winner, he did."

The captain's head rose. "And you believed him?"

They shared another look. "I *told* you, it warn't possible!" said the second severely.

The first looked at the captain hopefully, but Gabriel shook his head. The man's face dropped. "Well, sir, that's neither here nor there. On the second day, he took to coughing."

"Then he turned a *turrible* dark colour," said the second.

"We brought him 'ere and summoned the doctor, and that's the end of it, sir."

"Where were you when he took the turn for the worse? Were there no physicians about?"

Instantly, both men looked down, the first man clasping and unclasping his hands. "Well, sir, we had to convince 'is lordship we was worth his time. He didn't think we had the blunt, y'see."

"Yes?"

"So we took him to our ship by night, to the lower deck."

The captain's brows went skyward. "He agreed to that?"

Another quick exchange of a look. "Not in a word, sir. We had to ply him right good with rum, sir. Then he came most willin'!"

"Great Joseph! I've killed him," said the captain. He turned a severe eye on the men. "I said to keep him occupied at a club or a gaming parlour, not to get him in his altitudes and keep him prisoner!"

"Sorry, sir. We was doing your will, sir."

The doctor had apparently overheard at least the latter part of this conversation, and he approached Gabriel. "Not to fear, Captain. He was doomed in any case. Wouldn't have lasted but a week or two more, I dare say. The lungs, you see, were thoroughly decayed. If you would care to give the body to science—"

"I would not," said Gabriel sharply. There was a family cemetery with a mausoleum on the estate. Stafford would have a proper Christian burial with his body intact—even if he wasn't a proper Christian.

He took out a few bank notes and paid the sailors, thanked them, and bade them off just as a hazy sun was peeking over rooftops. The news wouldn't be in time for the morning paper. He took a last look at his elder brother, poor man. Meeting his maker now, he thought with a shudder. It couldn't be a happy meeting for one who had ever shirked his God.

Roderick arrived then and looked *almost* sorry as he surveyed the dead man. He stopped by the captain as he went back out. "Well, my lord," he said, with a flourish of his hands as he went into an exaggerated bow. He straightened up, smiling. "Seventh Earl Stafford, sir. How do ye like it?" Without awaiting a reply, he cried, "That puts me next in line, by Jove!"

The captain's mouth firmed into a line. "You should have your ears boxed for that. Your brother has just passed into eternity. Have a little respect." Roderick's face abruptly sobered and with a last worried glance, he left the room.

CHAPTER TWENTY-ONE

When the new earl was shown into the blue saloon later that day, only Mrs. Filbert sat to meet him. He bowed politely. "Is Miss Chrissendon not recovered from her shock?"

"She is recuperating, sir. Surely, you comprehend how delicate a female of her nature is."

His eyes narrowed as he considered how to politely answer such an idea, which he considered sheer fustian. Putting his hands behind his back and taking a few steps towards the front window to peer out at the street, he said, "I dare say her nature may be called delicate"—he turned to face Mrs. Filbert—"though I have never found it so. Miss Tavistock is the picture of a strong mind—and with a will to equal it."

Mrs. Filbert nodded appreciatively, comprehending that the captain understood Margaret too well to be fooled.

"Will she not receive me today?" he asked frankly.

Mrs. Filbert cleared her throat. "Captain, before you attempt an interview with her, there is something I must say to you."

The captain, with an assurance that he knew precisely what she wished to say, took a seat across from the companion with a knowing eye. The edges of his mouth were suspiciously curved. "Indeed?" he asked innocently. "Please do."

Mrs. Filbert shifted upon her seat. She sat forward and opened her mouth. The captain looked at her expectantly. She shut her mouth and sat back, looking perplexed. "My dear sir, there is no easy way to say it, so I will simply say it."

"Yes?" he asked, trying not to grin.

"You see, sir." She took a breath, blinking. "Well, that is—Miss Tavistock is quite young, sir."

He sat forward. "Is this what you wish to tell me?"

She frowned. "Not precisely. You see, she is...not schooled in...not *disciplined* in self-governance." Mrs. Filbert was amazed to find that she, like Margaret, felt muddled by the simple task of laying it all plain. Suddenly, it did not seem simple. Hurriedly, she added, "Her tutors and governesses failed to instill a sense of..."

"Honesty?" he supplied.

Mrs. Filbert studied the captain's eyes. Goodness! Her task was not necessary. "How long have you known?" she asked.

"Not long enough," he said reprovingly.

"I dare say," agreed Mrs. Filbert. "But sir, she thinks you are still in the dark."

"And so she must think, Mrs. Filbert, until she sees fit to enlighten me."

Mrs. Filbert stared. "I am charged with doing so."

"Tell her you couldn't." He gave a wry grin. "She will understand the difficulty of it, since she has not found it possible to accomplish herself."

Mrs. Filbert shifted upon her seat, her face suddenly sorrowful. "She has long wished, Captain—that is, she never had it in mind—to make a *lasting* deception." Mrs. Filbert hurried on. "She has a heart of gold, normally; she isn't a mean-minded creature." She wrung her hands. "When I think of the gossiping, disagreeable women in most drawing rooms and their petty mean ways, and compare them to Margaret. Oh, sir! If you knew her real goodness, you would forgive her all!"

Captain Rempeare nodded, smiling gently. "I understand Miss Tavistock, ma'am. I am fully prepared to forgive her all." His face sobered. "But *she* must desire it."

"Oh, she does! Most heartily!"

"She must heartily desire it of me, I'm afraid." He came to his feet.

"Since you have been her accomplice in it, may I ask you now to be mine?"

"You wish I shall not tell her that you know she is your betrothed?"

"That's it," he said. "May I have your word?"

Mrs. Filbert frowned, thinking. "Very well. But I pray you, Captain, not to let her suffer overlong. She hardly eats as it is."

He frowned and looked down. "Hmm. That is a concern." He looked up with a sudden smile. "I'll do my utmost to hasten the matter. May I see her?"

When Mrs. Filbert went to fetch Margaret, she found Clarice just putting the finishing touches to her headpiece. It wasn't the elaborate, diaphanous headdress that made Mrs. Filbert stop in surprise, however, but the rest of Margaret's attire. She wore a glorious evening ensemble of tight-fitting muslin that made her companion smile despite herself. It was not the hour to be seen in full evening dress, but the sheer loveliness of the air-light muslin draped with an equally gossamer overdress, both with columns of lace running the length of the gown, ending in triple-laced hems, made her such a picture of femininity that even Mrs. Filbert, who had seen Margaret in many an elegant ensemble, sighed and shook her head affectionately.

Clarice draped a delicate sheer veil over the cap, with its curled ostrich feather, settling the almost translucent fabric around Margaret's shoulders like a fairy shawl, and then tying the long ends in front to join the rest of the lacy fabric, in a soft cloud. Margaret met Mrs. Filbert's eyes in the mirror and smiled.

Mrs. Filbert was already smiling with equal parts pleasure and surprise. "You look much restored!" she cried happily.

Margaret thanked Clarice then turned on her seat to face her companion. "I am utterly restored, Mrs. Filbert. I have decided how to proceed."

A warning bell went off in Mrs. Filbert's head as she answered, with just the smallest trepidation. "Yes?"

"Since the captain loves Miss Chrissendon, then all I need do is convince him to marry *her*."

Mrs. Filbert stared. "Do you mean you are determined, still, not to tell him?"

Margaret stood up, surveyed herself in the mirror, and frowned. She adjusted her bodice just a degree, so the small white rise of her breasts was revealed further. Mrs. Filbert said, "My dear, what are you about? This is evening dress; you know full well."

"I am merely intent upon securing the captain as my husband. Tonight," she said, waving her hands expansively at her gown, "I am an *enchantress*, a *siren*."

Mrs. Filbert's face fell abruptly, and she moved stiffly to sit upon the bed, staring at her charge disconsolately. Margaret followed to sit beside her. "What perturbs you?" she asked.

"My dear," said the older lady, her expression pained. "You mustn't proceed in this. The captain is here, you must know, and—"

Margaret's eyes lit. "Is he? Famous! I'll see him privately in the...in the library. 'Tis such a *comfortable* room. We'll have a delightful cose there. I'll offer him a glass of...of"—her face scrunched in thought. "What shall I offer him?"

"You must offer him the truth!" she said emphatically. "No more of this dissembling! The longer you persist in it, the harder to undo it."

Margaret saw how despondent and earnest her dear, dear Mrs. Filbert was. She frowned. She put a soft hand upon her companion's arm and turned a heartfelt gaze of her sunlight-on-the-sea green eyes upon her. "I am at *point non plus*," she said softly. "I have determined upon this effort. If he refuses me, then I will reveal myself to him, for there is nothing else to be lost. But if he accepts me... Oh, that he may! I will secure his promise and then reveal myself. He is too honourable to cry off. But either way, he will soon know all."

Mrs. Filbert was happy to learn that it would all come out in the end, but she did not know how the captain would feel about Margaret the seductress, particularly when there was really no need for her to win him over. Her face must have revealed the doubtful nature of her thoughts, for Margaret patted her arm and said, "I give you my word. He will not leave this house unless we are betrothed, by whatever name it takes for me to secure him." But her face momentarily faltered, and she added, "Unless, of course, he wishes to be done with me. And I shall not blame him for *that*."

She put a hand to her headdress and rearranged it slightly and then met Mrs. Filbert's eyes. "I will receive him in the library. I expect, *of course*, that you will say nothing of my plan."

"Of course," Mrs. Filbert said stiffly, for she felt reluctant. She couldn't help but add, "My dear, 'tis an ill-advised plan; depend upon it."

"But I felt so much lighter and freer from the moment I conceived of it!" she cried. "I assure you, I was in the doldrums, but once I realised there was something I could do to bring about the happiness of both myself and the captain, I dare say, 'twas an epiphany!"

"My *dear!*" Mrs. Filbert's tone grew severe. "Why has no epiphany occurred to you that simply to own the truth is the way to settle this hobble? The captain will be swept away by humility. It becomes a woman to display a humble sweet nature," she added, to press her point.

"I fear I am neither humble nor sweet," Margaret replied frankly, with a frown. "But he is kept waiting!" She popped to her feet, and patted her lacy gown, and floated regally from the room. "Pray, send him to me, and then give us leave to be alone, Mrs. Filbert."

"The duke wouldn't approve—" the older lady said, grasping at straws.

But Margaret was not to be deterred. "I will keep you on when I am married, dearest," she said, over her shoulder. "Have no fear of the duke."

Mrs. Filbert went for the captain with a feeling of dread. Even Captain Rempeare must have his limits, she felt. How much flummery would he receive with equanimity? Especially now, when he knew it to be sheer fustian. She was quite dejected at the worry of it all. And how flummoxing it was, whether to support her dearest girl by giving her the secrecy she requested, or whether to tip the captain to what was afoot for the best interest of both. But if she told, and the captain revealed it, even unintentionally, Margaret would be irked. In the end, she must do as she was bade. She was a paid companion, not Margaret's mother or aunt.

When she reached the parlour, he was at the window with his hands behind his back, looking every bit the sea captain upon a quarterdeck surveying a tempestuous sea. When he turned at her entrance, there was no impatience on his features. Mrs. Filbert had lost patience, but she swallowed her misgivings and said, "My dear sir, she asks for your attendance in the library."

His brows rose, but he nodded with a slight bow. As Mrs. Filbert conducted him along the corridor, she said, "Pray, Captain, recollect yourself of Miss Tavistock's youth."

He looked at her for a moment searchingly, and then a smile curved his lips and understanding lit his eyes. He shook his head. "She's an original, by Jove!"

"I only mean—" the companion began.

"I know precisely what you mean, Mrs. Filbert. She has devised some scheme to avoid the inevitable *unmasking*," he said, with a knowing grin. "I am warned. I give you thanks."

Mrs. Filbert frowned. Somehow Captain Rempeare understood Margaret exceedingly well. She hadn't meant to reveal so much, but he'd instantly grasped that some scheme was afoot.

The library was indeed cosy with a fire going in the grate despite the warm weather, and a tray with two glasses at the ready on a table near a two-person settee, which had been moved up near the hearth. Margaret sat upon the settee, smiling, the image of sweet femininity in a cloud of gauzy lace surrounding a snug gown, with a daring décolletage. She motioned instantly to the captain to join her, patting the seat beside her. Mrs. Filbert gave Margaret a despairing look before retreating from the room, shaking her head.

The captain turned with surprise when the companion left the room, then surveying Margaret, he slowly approached the lovely form smiling sweetly at him. *This*, he decided, was going to be *exquisite*.

When he took his seat beside her, Margaret reached for a glass and offered it to him. He accepted it with polite thanks, took a sip and then held it out quickly, looking at the glass. "Is this...champagne?" he asked, startled.

She smiled. "Do you like it?"

He bit back a smile. "It's fine, fine."

Relieved, she took a sip from her glass, enjoying the tart bubbling sensation on her tongue. She had insisted that Stevens fetch it, despite his foolish fretting that it wasn't at all the thing to offer a gentleman in the middle of the day, for she recollected it was used on *celebratory* occasions. She was in a heady state of optimism, refusing to consider failure, and felt it was the most appropriate libation.

Glancing at her gown, he said, "I am much relieved to see you looking quite recovered. Are you going out tonight?"

Margaret shifted delicately on her seat. Looking at him coyly, she said, "If you must know, I thought only of your coming."

He put on a look of deep concern. "Do not say I have forgotten an engagement? Was I supposed to escort you to some entertainment? I fear I am frightfully forgetful at times."

"No, Captain," she said, with a slight frown. "I meant that I thought only of seeing *you* when I dressed." She shot a glance at him nervously and then straightened her gown.

He stood. "I thank you for that," he said. "But as you are well and recovered, I think the prudent course is for me to be off. You must recall my betrothal," he said softly, with a slight bow. "Under the circumstances"—he cleared his throat—"I'm afraid I find it unwise to linger."

Margaret looked bereft. "Surely, you don't have to leave so soon?" she asked, shrugging off the veil and shawl. He glanced at the shapely figure but remained staunchly unmoved.

"Only think of Miss Tavistock's sensibilities," he said. "I'm afraid I cannot forget them."

She gave him a reproachful look. "You did not mean what you said to me."

He looked as if he were trying to remember. His face cleared, and he said, "Are you referring to when I said that I loved you?"

She nodded stoically, her lips compressed. He took her hand and kissed it. Looking deeply into her eyes he said, "I meant it with all my heart." She stared at her hand a moment and then, looking up at him cried, "My dear sir! Is there any way I can prevail upon you to give up Miss Tavistock?"

The captain froze. A light went on in his eyes as he said, "Is that what you wish?"

Margaret looked away, flushing deeply. "Sir, I do." She nodded her head decisively. If he would only agree to *forget* about her, she reasoned, then he could *marry* her.

But he shook his head. "I am deeply sorry, my dear Miss Chrissendon, but I am bound, not only by duty and honour, but by everything that is good in the world, to stay true to my agreement." To her pained look, he added, "Would you have me cry off, throw honour to the wind? What could you respect in me should I have such a character as could do that?"

All this time he was looking down at her, still standing. Margaret came to her feet and searched his face. Desperately she said, "But...but...you do recall she is a pudding face?" The captain froze again, this time not so much from surprise but in order to prevent a bark of laughter from escaping. He took a sweet curl that hung about her head in one hand and gently pushed it off her face.

"'Tis a heavy blow, indeed," he said, looking utterly sensible of the weight of having an ugly bride. "But a cross I must bear."

She took his hand. "If I could only prevail upon you," she said miserably.

"What would be accomplished?" he asked, eyeing her keenly.

She looked at him with exasperation. "You would be free, then, Captain, to marry *me*!"

So that is your plan! He thought, finding it very hard not to grin.

But Margaret blinked back tears, and finally, he could control his reserve no longer. He took her chin in one hand. She held her breath. Lowering his face to hers, he hesitated tantalizingly, his lips near hers. Margaret closed her eyes. He said, causing her to open them again, "I have only just sworn my loyalty to Miss Tavistock!" He abruptly moved away.

Margaret felt crushed—utterly. Her plan had failed. "Sir," she said, her eyes storming with emotion. She hesitated, looking wretched. "But I *am* Miss Tavistock!" Tears brimmed in her eyes.

"No, but I mean the *real* Miss Tavistock," he said sadly, but with a gleam in his eye.

"I am the *real* Miss Tavistock!" she rejoined instantly. "I am the duke's ward and your cousin! It has all been a terrible mistake! I am heartily sorry—oh, if you *knew* how much!" She grabbed his hand again and clung to it, tears on her face. Pleadingly, she said, "I have been abominable! I have dishonoured you, and lied to you, and have been the most miserable creature that walks the earth! If you could but conceive of how heartily sorry I am." She shook her head reproachfully. "I do not deserve your consideration or to hold you to a promise which you could scarcely wish to uphold now...now that you know my villainy! But..."

His features had slowly changed as she spoke, from a look of regret and sorrow into a smiling, shining, *affectionate* look. He wiped away the tears on her cheeks.

Margaret grew bold and cried, "Captain...*Gabriel*...if you sincerely mean to stand by your agreement...to...to marry Miss Tavistock, then you, sir, though I deserve you not—you must marry *me!*"

"I have no other ambition than to do so," he said. He drew her up against him, and his lips came down upon hers. As the clouds cleared in Margaret's breast into a fountain of joy, he pulled her into his arms more closely and kissed her with all his will. After a minute, during which he held her tightly, kissing her deeply, their lips came apart. He sat down, putting her upon his lap.

Margaret stared at him, touched his hair, savoring every second of being in his arms, upon his lap, their kiss. The immense relief she felt was almost inconceivably freeing. Impulsively, she kissed his cheek, saying, "I *adore* you, sir! But how is it you do not despise me?"

"I despise *myself* for provoking you in the first place, and for not knowing you sooner," he said.

"Oh! You blessed man! You have not been at fault—not once! It was all my own folly, every bit of it!"

He kissed her again in a warm and welcome embrace. Afterwards, though she still clung to his neck, he asked teasingly, "What shall I call you now? I have called you Feodora, Feenie, Lady X, Miss Chrissendon, Miss Tavistock. I have called you a minx—"

"Rightfully so," she agreed sadly.

"A siren, a Juno, a Helen of Troy," he added softly.

A light came on in Margaret's eyes. She said, "But now there is only one thing you must call me, and it cannot be too soon. *Mrs. Gabriel Rempeare!*"

His eyes wrinkled into a frown, and he sighed. "I'm afraid that, I cannot call you."

Margaret gasped, crestfallen. She pulled back to search his eyes. He gave a wry grin. "For, as I find myself now the seventh earl, I must call you Lady Stafford."

She gasped again and then was transfixed, hung between both joy and sorrow, her pretty mouth hanging open. "The earl!"

"Last night, I'm afraid. I was called to Grosvenor Street."

"Your brother... I'm very sorry."

"I am sorry as well for his sake, but there was little love between us." He continued, "So you must be my Lady Stafford, unless"—he gave her a look of feigned doubt—"unless you are still of the mind that you could never be the Countess Stafford. I recall hearing you say those very words—"

"To your brother!" she cried, hitting his chest with her hands, smiling now. "I adore the thought of being *your* countess." This earned her another kiss. Afterwards, she said, "Though truly, I shall think of myself always as a captain's wife, Mrs. Gabriel Rempeare."

He smiled and drew her back to him, murmuring, before kissing her again, "I love you by any name, sweet, but I confess...I do like that one best."

The Fête at Carlton House

North Front of Carlton House, from, *The History of the Royal Residences*, WH Pyne, 1819, vol 3.

"…the fête given at Carlton House on June 19, 1811, being then the only experiment ever made to give a supper to 2,000 of the nobility and gentry…" --*The Mirror of Literature*

Miss Tavistock experiences a frightening crush at the Prince Regent's palace toward the end of the book which leads to a romantically pivotal scene. But many readers don't know that what happened that day at the palace *really* happened.

Here's the scoop:

The fête in June of 1811 was the Prince of Wales' first real chance to celebrate his becoming Regent earlier that year, in the lavish style he loved. The delay was an effort not to offend the public with a celebratory event, for he had become Regent on account of his father King George III's illness, thought to be madness. In a further bid for public approval, the Regent advertised the event as an entertainment for the French royal family who were in exile, and as a means of promoting British manufactory. More, he would hold it on the King's birthday on 4 June. Circumstances, however, prevented it, causing the further delay.

Like Miss Tavistock, many in the haut ton anxiously coveted invitations. At first reserved only for the peerage and their offspring, by the time of the event, more than 2,000 invitations had been issued to all classes. The details in the story regarding the enormous preparations really happened, and much, much, more.

Since our heroine was not able to garnish an invitation to the actual grand banquet, the extraordinary magnificence of the décor, food, and costume, of that night had to be excluded from the book. I'll touch upon a detail here, however, one of the most memorable decorations in history, which graced the main dining table (over 200 feet long) in the Conservatory, where the prince himself sat at the head.

"A large silver basin filled with water fed a stream [in a 'marble canal'] which meandered between banks of flowers and vegetation and was stocked with golden fish and silver gudgeons, reaching the whole length of the principal supper table." [1]

"At the head of the table was a large silver fountain" which released the flow of water, which ran trickling along its length and poured into "a series of cascades into a 'circular lake surrounded with architectural decorations, and small vases, burning perfumes."[2] It was an unprecedented display, and both amazed and perplexed the guests.

The prince was so happy with his lavish spectacle that he wished to share it with the public. The unruly crowd described in the book happened on the third day following the banquet. It was reported that more than 30,000 people tried to crowd their way in that day. Men and women lost hats, bonnets, coats, shawls, shoes, and even their clothing. London papers afterwards claimed there were great tubs at Carlton House filled with all the lost items.

Contemporaries both praised and harshly criticized the affair. It was described as "an assemblage of beauty, splendor and profuse magnificence," by admirers, but as one of the princes' "greatest follies and extravagances," by detractors.[3]

The Carlton House Conservatory, from *The History of the Royal Residences,* WH Pyne, 1819, vol.3.

Notes:
[1] *George IV*, E.A. Smith
[2] Ibid.
[3] Ibid
Images, public domain.

A free companion PDF, "Discussion Questions for Reading Groups," is available at Linore's website, along with other free resources for readers.

Get the Reading Group Questions here:

www.LinoreBurkard.com/resources

If you enjoyed this book…

Would you please take a minute to leave a review on Amazon, GoodReads, or BarnesandNoble?

Other places to let people know about it are Facebook, Twitter, BookBub, or Pinterest.

Authors really appreciate it when readers take a moment to spread the word about their books.

On behalf of Lilliput Press and Linore Rose Burkard,

Thank you!

Keep Reading:

Next, A Free Excerpt of Book Two of the Brides of Mayfair

Miss Fanshawe's Fortune

A young woman in search of her father and fortune…
A gentleman in line for a baronetcy wanting neither scandal,
nor love…
Can unexpected romance overtake even the staunchest
bachelor's heart?

EXCERPT
Miss Fanshawe's Fortune, Brides of Mayfair, Book Two

Edward Arundell suspected from the moment he almost ran her down on Monmouth Street, that Miss Fanshawe would be trouble. He had merely a few more corners to conquer before reaching his home on King Street, and had just rounded the bend to Monmouth when a young woman in a delicate sprigged muslin and a straw, beribboned hat, with a corded trunk at her feet, stepped lightly into the road. If he hadn't been such a sure hand at the ribbons, he'd never have managed to pull up the team in time to skirt around her. But with a hair's breadth to spare, he missed her and roared past.

He should have kept right on roaring. The curricle he commanded at top speed was not his own, first of all, and if he didn't reach home before his elder brother Sebastian awoke and discovered the theft (for surely he would call it that; Edward hadn't permission to borrow the carriage) he'd be in for a monstrous combing and quite possibly lose his monthly stipend. The combing he could take with fortitude. But losing his stipend was an unthinkable horror.

To complete his journey he needed only to bear left onto Grafton Street, angle quickly right onto Gerrard's, then make the razor-sharp turn onto Prince's in order to come up directly by the mews off King. He would have stabled the horses and got in the house before Sebastian would know the difference. Only he didn't keep on. The devil made him turn, he supposed, to spy the sweet vixen he'd missed by mere inches, and see her drop senseless in the street.

He was no saint, by Jove. But even he, a young sprig intent on making a wave among a set of wave cutters, had no choice but to slow the team, swallow an oath that flew to his lips, and return to the scene of the almost crime. At this early hour, only two passersby were on hand, and they hurried to surround the prostrate young woman. These lost no time in hailing Edward, begging him to be so kind as to take the poor thing in his chariot to the nearest inn or coffee house.

With a heavy heart, Edward allowed them to lift the young lady, and then her valise and trunk, into the curricle. She came to as he drove off, sinking his spirits yet further, for now he would have to apologize prettily, perhaps even take her somewhere across the metropolis—who knew? By the time he got back to King Street with Sebastian's curricle, his elder brother would be in rare form. And if he cut off Edward's stipend, which was by any standard already too meager to keep him looking all the crack, he'd be utterly dashed.

He slowed the team to a stop in front of The Boar's Head Inn and turned apologetically to his slim, dark-haired young victim. After craning her neck to get a good look at the establishment, Miss Fanshawe turned to him with large brown eyes infused with gratitude, eyes that would melt a sterner man's heart.

"Thank you, sir," she said quietly. Colouring, she added, "I—I believe I nearly swooned!" He looked past a riot of curls that had escaped her bonnet and met those luminous orbs with a suddenly gentle disposition.

"But you did swoon," he assured her. "And it was on my account. Please—please—allow me to—to—." He motioned with his head to the inn, but when the innkeeper emerged from the brick building dusting off an apron and followed by a porter, a sudden better thought occurred to Edward.

If he took this lovely creature into the inn to revive her with some refreshment, it would cost him something. More, he'd be detained and not get home before Sebastian—that starched shirt!—would discover his transgression. He'd been given set downs before on account of borrowing the curricle. With this infraction, he and his brother'd go to loggerheads and upset Mama. Or Edward would have to deliver a Canterbury story deep enough to satisfy the pope. In the few seconds it took for the servant to reach him, extending a hand for the ribbons to walk the horses to the mews, he'd made a decision.

"Allow me to offer you breakfast," he said magnanimously, turning only to dismiss the man with a curt nod. "My mother and elder brother are home, and there is no trouble at all in bringing a guest, I assure you." With an apologetic air, he added, bowing his head, "I beg your pardon. Edward Arundell, at your service."

"Miss Fanshawe," said Frannie with a nod of the head. "Pleased to meet you." Normally she would have left it at that. Normally she wasn't given to a display of emotions but the excitement and danger of her situation must have had her in its grip, for she added in a gush, "But oh, Mr. Arundell, you've no notion of my troubles! I have endured the most horrifying experience!"

Edward looked at her fairly amazed. "It's but nine o'clock. Have you already had the most horrifying experience?"

She nodded, with large, pained eyes. "Yesterday. I'm afraid I've been completely at sixes and sevens ever since, wandering in town like—like a nomad."

"Surely you didn't wander the streets all night," he said, half in disbelief and half in awe.

She shook her head, resulting in a ripple of curls that framed the bonnet. "I lodged at an inn. I was determined this morning to return to the house, but—."

"You haven't run from home!" Edward pronounced. Such an impropriety on the part of a proper looking young woman quite astonished him.

"No, indeed!" she said imploringly, turning to him. "My home is—was, in Lincolnshire. I meant to return to the home of my relations here in London. I have no other recourse. But it was they who only yesterday turned me away!"

"Why should they do that?" Edward asked, almost suspiciously. "Did they not expect you?"

Miss Fanshawe sighed heavily. "I daresay they did not. Oh! 'Tis such a tangle!" She turned troubled eyes to his. "I was brought up by my mother and Mrs. Baxter, but they are both gone now. I was directed to my relations here in London, but I have suffered the very worst sort of ill usage by—by my aunt! It is quite abominable."

"Bad luck," he said feelingly, regarding her now with a benign expression, his entire sympathies instantly on her part. Miss Fanshawe was certainly under the hatches. He'd found himself at the bottom end of deep scrapes for most of his eighteen years, so that a fellow sufferer he regarded as a military man would a fellow in arms. "Not to fret. My uncle's a baronet," he said importantly, "and my brother's his heir." Miss Fanshawe's eyes widened.

This satisfied Edward, who had yet to discover a commoner who wasn't impressed with a tie to nobility, whether high or low as to the scale of titles. Sir Hugo would scarcely know him by sight, but that was not to the point. The connexion was real, but tenuous because of an ancient feud between Sir Hugo Arundell and his mama; a mysterious affair that remained shrouded in reticence, with the result that Edward's family rarely saw the baronet. Nevertheless, claiming the blood-tie was social proof that Edward found uncommonly useful and irresistible, therefore, to make known.

He nodded toward King Street. "Whatever your troubles, Sebastian'll sort them out."

"Is that the brother you spoke of?"

Edward nodded. "My elder by nine years." In a disgruntled voice he added, "Thinks he's my father, I daresay."

Frannie's large eyes filled with hope. "Could it be—do you indeed think he will champion my cause? I find myself quite friendless. I own, it is a nasty kettle of fish, and I haven't the faintest idea how to proceed in it. But I prayed earnestly for divine assistance. I believe it was Providence that brought you to me!"

Edward would not have put it that way, but he gave her a wry glance while slapping the ribbons lightly to start off. "What sort of trouble is it?"

She swallowed, and said emphatically, "A mystery. Which I must get to the bottom of as soon as possible! My future, my entire fortune is at stake!"

Respectfully, and trying not to appear too curious, Edward asked, "And is that fortune very large?"

"Quite large, I am told." She paused and said philosophically, "Mrs. Baxter assured me that it must be in excess of £30,000 by now."

"Lud, that is a fortune," he acknowledged gravely, and rather in awe. "Mrs. Baxter?"

"The dear lady who raised me after my mama died." At this, Frannie blinked back tears. "She has only gone to her rest a fortnight ago."

"I say," Edward mumbled, sincerely. "Poor Miss Fanshawe."

Frannie stifled her tears with a handkerchief, turning to give him a look of gratitude for his understanding, her eyes large and dark and long-lashed. Edward sucked in his breath. Miss Fanshawe was first-rate, his friends would say. A pearl of the first water.

"But that is only part of my trouble. The worst of it is what happened since her passing!"

He turned the final corner onto King Street. With any luck they'd be in the house before Sebastian summoned his valet. Good thing his elder brother wouldn't countenance appearing at breakfast unshaved. But he turned to Frannie and said warningly, "Sebastian can be devilish unfriendly in the morning; he grows less formidable as the day wears on."

After a moment Frannie asked curiously and a little troubled, "Why would that be? If a gentleman is good-natured and amiable, he ought to be so always unless there has been provocation. He ought to be steady in his character, day or night."

"He don't sleep well," Edward explained matter of factly. He gave her a serious look. "Don't get in the vapours if he ain't amiable right off."

Frannie frowned. "I assure you, I am not in the habit of getting in the vapours."

"But you swooned earlier," pointed out Edward, "though you weren't injured by me."

Frannie sniffed again. "That's only because…because I haven't eaten for a whole day. And the fright of that close call— " She turned to him, her eyes dawning with recognition. "Injured by you? Was that you? Thunder and brimstone! It was this carriage that almost killed me?"

Edward's heart lurched. "Dash it, Miss Fanshawe, I meant no harm! Only I was—I am—in the deepest pickle; couldn't afford to lighten the pace! I daresay an apology will hardly answer, but I am sorry."

Frannie regarded him silently for a moment. "You did return to rescue me." In another moment her eyes brightened. "You are forgiven, Mr. Arundell. I maintain, it would have been worse for me had any other carriage nearly blown me down. Not many gentlemen would see their way to helping a stranger. That must compensate for one small moment of terror."

Edward swallowed, and hoped sincerely that his brother would indeed be able to untangle whatever ravel she was in. He owed her that.

He pulled up to the house. It was ungentlemanly not to assist her down, but he needed to get the curricle stowed and out of sight. Frowning, he explained he had only to get the horses in the mews himself—didn't wish to disturb a servant!—and would be right back with her valise, but was silenced by the arrival of a dour-faced Sykes, Sebastian's man. Glancing disapprovingly at Edward, Sykes assisted the lady from the carriage. After ordering a footman to lift down the woman's portmanteau, he looked back upon Edward with his peculiarly frigid gaze.

"Look here, Sykes," Edward said, "you needn't tell him."

"He knows, sir," said Sykes, in the deep, gloomy voice that always put Edward in mind of a mausoleum.

"Dash it!" Edward took a deep breath. "So be it."

Sykes took the ribbons and handed them to a groom who had emerged from the servants' entrance, while Frannie looked nervously at Edward. Edward climbed down and went around to the pavement where he offered her his arm. They walked, Sykes following with his singularly disapproving mien, to the door. Edward said bracingly, "Sebastian's a crusty fellow, but he won't dare comb me over in your presence." The words were more for his own assurance, it seemed, than Miss Fanshawe's. Escorting her inside, he hoped it was true.

CHAPTER TWO

"It must seem irregular to you," Frannie said apologetically, allowing him to usher her in ahead, "to accept such kindness, to come into your home on so short an acquaintance!"

A small, squat, but dignified little man hurried toward them and took Edward's things, and then Frannie's. He was not the usual butler to be found in an upper-class establishment, or most anywhere for that matter. In place of the long legs and fine calves that butlers and footmen were sometimes chosen for—because they showed off the breeches of livery to a turn—this man was thick set and muscular; not what you would call elegant by any standard. But he performed his office and was thanked by Edward as he bowed shortly to Frannie before Edward turned them toward the stairs.

Sykes, holding the valise, said, "Is your guest staying, sir?" His sepulchral monotone echoed in the hall. Edward could not understand for the life of him, how Sebastian could stand such a dull plate for a servant. Why, if he, Edward, had a gentleman's gentleman, it'd be a man with spirit, with conversation and suggestions. An energetic being, not a walking tomb like Sykes. Flustered at the unexpected question, however, he replied, "Yes, yes. Tell my mother. She'll direct you to which bedchamber she wants for Miss Fanshawe."

With both servants gone, Edward looked timorously at the young woman. "Are you stopping elsewhere? I suppose I should have asked you first, if you were wishing to stay."

But she answered, smiling, "It is exceedingly generous of you to put me up. Indeed, I have no lodgings in the city. You see, it was part—part of my troubles; that I ended up without a place to lay my head. And my purse was nabbed—and—and—" Her eyes watered at this, and Edward, alarmed, said, "None of that now. As I said, we'll get it sifted for you." He brought her to the morning room, which thankfully, neither his mama nor brother had as yet entered. Frannie looked with appreciation through its arched window at a small garden behind the house, a welcome spot of greenery in the city.

The sideboard, with delicious aromas wafting from an assortment of covers, beckoned, and lifted her spirits further. She'd been feeling the lack of nourishment, for she'd had nothing since her purse was snatched. Edward offered her a plate, and she chose what she wanted. When they were both seated with breakfast before them, *eggs en cocotte* and rolls, butter, a pot of chocolate and one of tea, he eagerly dug in but glanced her way, and stopped chewing.

"Is something amiss?" he asked.

"Do you not—" she hesitated. "That is, do you mind if I give thanks?"

Edward hurriedly put down his fork. "Forgive me. Not at all." *Sebastian must like this one*, he thought with satisfaction as Frannie said a heartfelt prayer of thanks. Indeed, it rather astonished him, for she gave thanks for the *mercy* of having *almost* been run down, for it led him to help her. Such a detailed prayer from the heart was not something he often heard. Must be a Methodist, he thought, instantly resolving to say nothing of it to Sebastian, a staunch Anglican.

When she'd done, he dug back in to his food, being famished. He'd been out half the night in pursuit of a fly-by-nighter, a man who'd promised to sell him a bang up equipage, a smart gig, just the thing for a whip-in-training, and for the smallest sum imaginable. All Edward had to do was convey said man from the low district club where they'd met to his home north of London. There, the transaction was to take place. But for this Edward was forced to borrow his brother's curricle, which meant waiting until the small hours of the night to do it undetected.

To Edward's chagrin, when he was presented with the supposed prize, he'd never seen a sorrier looking equipage. Outdated, outmoded, its sides peeling with strips of languishing wood, and the wheels uneven. The man was not eager to lose the sale and harped on most unpleasantly about a gentleman's word being his honour and other such drivel. By the time Edward got away (and only after pressing a few shillings into the man's hand) it was well past morning light. He pushed the team hard to make time and was cracking along nicely—until Miss Fanshawe stepped into his path.

Looking at her now, he wished he'd been less hasty in bringing her to the house, for it began to be borne in on him that it would be an uphill climb convincing Sebastian to take her case. He'd best learn all he could before facing him. The next half hour in the morning room was spent in earnest conversation as Frannie laid out her case for Edward. Many emphatic sighs with outstretched arms were heard and noted. Edward listened with a growing frown, rubbing his chin, nodding now and again. By the time he'd heard the whole sorry tale, he knew one thing.

Sebastian wasn't going to like it.

Frannie and Edward had removed to the parlour by the time Sebastian appeared in the morning room for coffee and toast, his usual fare. Mrs. Arundell stayed abed with the headache, but her eldest son, in fitted trousers, dark shoes, a white shirt with a lightly pointed collar and unremarkable, though spotless cravat, sat down content to have the room to himself. Over his shirt was a hunter green waistcoat patterned in black thread. It brought out the green in his eyes, though Sebastian would never have chosen it for such a frivolous purpose. Light sideburns and a sensible hair cut showed him to be more conscious of propriety than fashion.

His cutaway tailcoat in dark brown he began to remove, for he was alone, but he stopped at Syke's report of Edward's having brought a young woman home. Scowling, he allowed the servant to help him back into the coat. Edward, that fool pup, was an endless pest. The additional information, that said woman's portmanteau had been placed into a guest bedchamber—chosen by Sykes himself, in order not to wake the mistress during one of her attacks—only deepened the scowl.

He'd just opened his book to the page where he'd left off and taken one sip of coffee when Edward entered. "Beau, eat quickly! I've got a horrid scramble for you to untangle."

Sebastian eyed his brother dispassionately above a pair of narrow-rimmed spectacles, took a bite of toast, and chewing, returned to his book. "You *will* have a horrid scramble when I turn you out on the street for a thief."

"Oh, come, Beau! My entire object was to ensure that I never have to borrow your gig again!"

"Don't call me Beau," was the sole answer.

"It's what Mama calls you, and I own it puts you in a better mood!"

Sebastian lowered his book. "Nothing *you* say can alter my mood for the better. Stop blathering and explain to me why you stole my carriage, exhausted my horses, and brought home with you a street wench!"

"I don't associate with street wenches," Edward replied haughtily, with his nose in the air. "And Miss Fanshawe's genteel. She's an heiress!"

Sebastian's look lost some of its fierceness, though his eyes betrayed stark doubt. "Do go on," he said, wiping his mouth with a napkin. "Let us know the reason, for there must be some extraordinary circumstance, why this heiress is to be our guest?" He returned his eyes to the book.

"She's in a tangle, that's all."

Sebastian looked up with narrowed eyes. "How do you know her?"

"Let me tell you the trouble, then we'll get to that."

"What sort of tangle?"

Edward stared at his brother. "On second thought, I'll let her tell you."

Now hardness gleamed in his eyes. "You'll do no such thing. I've no idea how you stumble upon odd, low characters in your jaunts about town, rag-tag creatures from your gaming dens, no doubt—"

"Not at all!" interjected Edward hotly. "I've not been gaming, upon my word!"

But a gasp and a sob was heard in the corridor. Edward's eyes widened. Had he forgot to ask Miss Fanshawe to remain in the parlour?

Sebastian glared at his brother. "Is that her?"

Edward nodded guiltily. "Must be."

"You brought her? Without informing me!" He threw down his napkin, stood, and with a grim look on his face, still glaring at Edward, said, "I will make quick work of your heiress!" He intended upon doing it too, turning her out before she could say Jack Robinson. But only seconds after he'd left the room, he was back, preceded by Miss Fanshawe, who held a handkerchief to one eye and was sniffling. Edward gave her a weak smile, hoping it was bracing.

Sebastian had taken one look at her, instantly recognized a genteel looking creature, stifled the rebuke upon his lips, and, after a nodding short bow, said, "Please," and motioned for her to enter. Having expected to see a doxy (whom he would have unhesitatingly sent from the house) he instead was treated to the sight of a respectable, handsome, well dressed young woman. And when his eyes clasped her ridiculously large, intelligent but tear-rimmed orbs, a jolt of surprise ran through him. Without a word, she'd disarmed him. One sight of her was all it took. Was he a gudgeon? He'd almost offered his arm, by Jove, but checked himself.

"I beg your pardon," he said in the morning room, as he held out a chair, which she accepted. "I'm afraid I spoke rashly."

Edward breathed a sigh of relief. Sebastian was deuced particular, but never lacked manners in company, especially with the muslin set. It drove society belles near mad, as he never followed up his exquisite manners and courtesies with an offer. Edward wondered if his brother was waiting to come into the title before he'd wed. That would be Sebastian in a nutshell—doing everything strictly proper and in its time.

Sebastian cleared his throat as he resumed his seat. "Have you had breakfast, Miss—er—?"

"Miss Fanshawe," put in Edward, who hurriedly went on to complete the introductions.

"I have, thank you," she replied, watching Sebastian tragically. "I am very sorry to interrupt yours, sir."

To her sweet, expressive countenance of sheer misery, Sebastian visibly softened. The hard lines of his jaw relaxed, and his eyes, behind the round spectacles, looked almost large as he surveyed her with something approaching kindness. He had not quite decided whether to trust this young woman's account, whatever it might be, but he had lost the greater part of his suspicions.

He looked at Edward. "I'll deal with you and the matter of my curricle later." Turning his full attention to Frannie, he said, "Tell me your trouble, Miss Fanshawe."

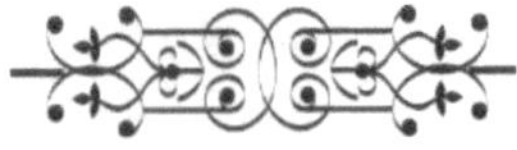

Frannie's heart was in a tumble, for she was sure Mr. Sebastian Arundell was predisposed against her. Had he not referred to her as a street wench? And how alarmed she'd felt at his countenance when he'd rounded the bend. With spectacles and a book in hand, he was studious looking but with the fierce mien of a stern schoolmaster. The look soon changed, becoming less formidable, but his was a cynical soul, she was certain. Behind those spectacles she sensed the strict, proper countenance of a barrister or a cold clergyman, one that would stand upon the letter of the law and be anything but helpful to a woman in her circumstances. Yet what recourse did she have? The younger Mr. Arundell had promised this man would help. With little hope of success, she breathed a silent prayer that God would grant her favour as she spoke.

"You will scarcely credit my history, sir," she began, "for 'tis most unusual. I was raised by my mama, who died, I am sad to say, a year and six months ago; and Mrs. Baxter, a wealthy widow—er, *at one time wealthy*, that is—the dearest friend of my mother's."

"Your father?" Sebastian asked.

Frannie blushed and swallowed. "Well, my father, sir, is a nobleman—."

"Who is he?"

The blush deepened. "As I said, I was raised by my mama, and given the assurance that my father guaranteed a trust fund for my use upon my majority."

"And what is his name?" Sebastian persisted.

Frannie looked apologetic and now the blush ran to the roots of her hair. She clasped her hands uncertainly. "My mother and father had a great falling out of some kind. She—refused to speak of him. She never so much as gave me his name, his full name, that is. She said my future was secure only so long as I stayed wide of his family. I assume his name was Fanshawe."

Only with careful control did Sebastian's face not reveal his instant appraisal of this admission. Miss Fanshawe was a blow by!

She continued on, having little choice but to lay out her circumstances as best she could. "I was given the name of Mr. Charles Fanshawe, of Cheapside. His identity was only just furnished to me by Mrs. Baxter."

"A nobleman? In Cheapside? By name of *mister*?"

Frannie shifted in her seat. "Mrs. Baxter said he must be my uncle; the case is puzzling, I own, but that the trust fund exists there can be no doubt. We received annual sums all my life, and they came, I was told, from the interest of the trust."

"Did you never ask to meet your father?"

She shifted again, her fingers gripping the edges of the seat. "My mother gave me to believe he had died, and so of course that is what I accepted as true. I never thought to question what I was told. But—a fortnight ago—Mrs. Baxter revealed that my father *lives!* Yet she had only the name of Mr. Fanshawe of Cheapside, which made me wonder whether it was he. Mrs.Baxter was inclined to think he must know all the particulars of my case. And if this is true, he will know the identity of my father."

She blinked back tears. "I—I know how irregular this must seem to you, sir. I assure you, I had rather not pursue the matter, for 'tis mortifying! Only Mrs. Baxter left debts, you see. Apparently, while Mama and Mrs. Baxter allowed me to dress fashionably and for us all to live in comfort, debts were accruing all along. Mama should have given all of our income to Mrs. Baxter, whatever was sent on my behalf. But instead they chose to allow me to believe we suffered no want. I am afraid I—I gave all my means to cover the debts." Frannie swallowed, valiantly not letting the lump in her throat that assailed her at every thought of her *dearest* Mama and Mrs. Baxter, get the better of her. Nor would she think about those horrible shopkeepers who descended upon the house and hounded her until she parted with nearly all she possessed.

"She left debts, you say. Has she absconded?"

"D-died, sir, a fortnight ago. Everything I've told you, she gave me to understand upon her deathbed." Frannie hated the waver in her voice. But she added, "She's in heaven now, God rest her soul."

His eyes pierced hers. "I am sorry for your loss. But you paid her debts? From your own means?"

"I paid all I could. I gave almost all I had, but it wasn't enough!"

"Great Scot!" he said. "You gave all you had?"

She stifled back a sob. "It wasn't enough. They have taken the house and all we owned. I had to dismiss cook, and our manservant and laundrymaid; and then last night—as if my troubles were too small—my purse was snatched! I now have only what is contained in my portmanteau and a single trunk!" She dabbed at her eyes.

"Had you no advisor? No one to counsel that you could not be held responsible for this Mrs. Baxter's debts?"

To his frowning look, she said, "Mrs. Baxter was ever, only, all kindness to me and my mother. How could I not endeavour to settle her accounts?"

To himself, he thought, *kind enough to leave you in debt!* But all he said was, "Was she a relation?"

"No, sir, a dear friend, the dearest of friends!" Again she blinked away wetness on her lashes and held a handkerchief to her nose until she'd conquered the moment.

To Sebastian, the case was now utterly clear. Miss Fanshawe was, in plain terms, an illegitimate brat that had managed to grow up in genteel circumstances. But wishing to know as much from curiosity as from necessity, he asked, "And how old are you?"

"I am but nineteen, sir."

"So, if there is a trust, you have no legal access to it yet." Gently he added, "No way to ascertain, even, that it exists, or that your father, if he lives, will acknowledge you."

Frannie's large eyes revealed the tumult in her heart. How foolish of her to suppose she could find help from a respectable gentleman of means! He had the disinterested mien of a magistrate and would of course find her case to be shocking. With a despairing heart, she said, eyes lowered, "Mr.—Mr. Fanshawe must be my connexion to the funds. That is what Mrs. Baxter tried to tell me. But sir, when I attempted to see him—as I told the younger Mr. Arundell—" here she gave a tearful glance to Edward, sitting silently in his seat; she swallowed, and finally conquering the urge to cry, finished, "This is the capstone of my misfortunes thus far—his wife turned me away! She—she said I was out to *grabble* what was not rightfully mine! So now it is quite impossible for me to discover more particulars of the case!"

He folded his hands upon the table, listening keenly. "So you are in dire straits, with no funds until this, er, trust is opened?"

Frannie nodded unhappily, her chocolate eyes pleading with him from their hopeless, troubled depths.

A sudden doubt crossed Sebastian's mind: that the whole presentation was a fabrication, a means of soliciting sympathy with an eye for financial gain. Everything about Miss Fanshawe *appeared* utterly earnest, herself a blend of innocence and sensibility, her grief for recent losses seemingly of the gravest nature; but he seemed to recall hearing of similar elaborate ruses done by such innocent looking actors as this woman, and perpetrated on those foolish enough to believe the lies.

Miss Fanshawe leaned forward earnestly, looking quite pretty with cheeks rosy with emotion, and her large eyes appearing larger than ever.

"Sir—despite the unhappy mystery of my heritage, which I *know* you can only despise—" she looked away. "Indeed, I despise it myself," she said, looking down at her hands. She looked up. "I beg of you: only point me to the proper authorities, someone who might help me gain an audience with Mr. Fanshawe, and I will trouble you no more. Believe me, sir, when I say I take no pleasure in asking! I am beyond mortification! I am painfully aware that I am, at this moment, very little different from a common—street urchin!" She bit her lip, blinked back tears, and refused to meet his eyes.

Sebastian, feeling his heart strings reluctantly moving toward this creature, said gently, "Normally such a dilemma could be easily resolved by applying to the benefactor of the trust; for he is the man, and the only man, with power to change the terms and relieve your current distress." His look hardened as he added, "But for that you must know his identity." He did not say the words that had flown to his mind, *if he indeed exists.*

Frannie's lips tightened as she fought to control a sense of panic or the urge to give way to tears. It was too, too, vexing! She didn't use to cry easily; it must be because of Mrs. Baxter's sudden death, and then, on its heels, the discovery that the inheritance she claimed to be leaving Frannie—enough to last until her trust could be obtained—was sadly dried up, according to the barrister who settled her affairs. It had all gone to long-standing debts that Frannie had known nothing about, the same debts that had swallowed up Frannie's funds. And now even their home had been taken from her on account of the arrears! She'd end up in the poor house, no doubt! How glad she was now that neither her mama nor Mrs. Baxter had lived to see this day. Mrs. Baxter's barrister had refused to take on Frannie's case, to try and locate her trust monies. She should have known then that it was hopeless.

Haltingly, she tried to explain this to Sebastian. Bits and pieces leaked out until he knew as much as she did regarding the trust. By the time she had done, he was certain he was dealing with an illegitimate pauper, but not a deceptive trickster. She was as genteel and well-spoken as any lady of his acquaintance, and still had not requested a shilling. The trust fund, sadly, was no doubt an invention of her mother's, a flight of fancy.

She went on to relate the details of how her reticule—her last remaining funds in it—had been napped the day before as she was jostled by a crowd on the street after she left the Fanshawes' house, reeling from the injustice of being turned away.

As he listened to Frannie, Sebastian found himself wishing her case was not so bedeviled. It was with something surprisingly close to regret that he had to accept his first deductions as true. Miss Fanshawe was a well-dressed, well-bred, blow-by orphan without a half-pence to her name. As such, she was the lowest of the low on the scale of gentility. He'd kept his countenance carefully neutral as he heard the sorry tale. But he took a breath now and asked, "Have you no other relations?"

"None I know of, sir," she said, hardly above a whisper, and with a sinking in her breast. *Why should he espouse her cause? Why would anyone?* "I have one friend, Mrs. Baxter's brother. But he is not a man of means. I did not wish to be a burden to him." In another second she hurriedly added, "Nor do I wish to burden you with my case, sir! Only I am come to such a pass—I know not what to do!"

Sebastian nodded, unsurprised. Only desperation would bring such a creature to this scene. "I understand you, Miss Fanshawe."

Edward had remained conspicuously silent until now, but at these words gave his brother a look of vast relief. "Well done, sir! I knew how it would be," he added, looking at Frannie. "When my brother isn't up to his nose in business or one of his books, he can be a vastly reasonable fellow."

Sebastian returned this dubious praise with a dour look. "Escort our guest to the parlour while I think upon what we can do for her."

Frannie's expressive eyes filled with hope. "Oh, Mr. Arundell! Sir! I hardly know how to thank you," she said in her earnest voice, coming to her feet.

"Don't thank me yet," Sebastian replied honestly. "I am in truth not at all certain that I can in any way relieve your distress." As Edward led the young woman out of the room, he turned back to give Sebastian a disapproving glare. He ought to have sounded more hopeful, Edward thought. At the very least he was sure his brother would never consign this lovely creature to the street! There must be *something* they could do for her.

The thought plagued him so much that he left Miss Fanshawe seated in the parlour by herself, begging to be excused, and with the assurance that he should return in a minute. He met Sebastian just leaving the morning room.

"You're a Job's comforter, an't you?" he cried, at sight of him. "You could have said something more kindly to her!"

"And you could have done me the honour of not bringing a penniless orphan to my door!"

Edward grimaced. "She's an heiress."

"If she's an heiress, I'm the Prince Regent," he returned smoothly. "You never did tell me how you know her."

Edward sighed. "I nearly ran 'er down."

Sebastian's eyes flared. "With *my* curricle, which you stole—again! We'd not have this young woman on our hands if you'd kept your paws off my property. I'm withholding your stipend."

A hearty argument ensued, and only because they were still on the ground floor did Frannie, in the first floor parlour, not hear a word of it. All of Edward's arguments fell upon deaf ears, that he'd be forced to take vowels at cards, he'd have the duns at his heels, he'd not be welcome at his favorite coffee house, nor able to obtain a newly bespoken jacket; but finally Sebastian cried, "No more of this!"

"That's fine for you, you're all flush in the pocket!"

"We have that unfortunate creature to deal with."

Edward paused, and then said slyly, "She's an amiable, attractive unfortunate, you must grant her that." Sebastian always displayed impeccable manners to the softer sex, and he hoped to play upon his brother's gallantry.

"That is not to the point," Sebastian replied without offering a syllable of disagreement. He was aware of Miss Fanshawe's feminine virtues, but determined, with the usual air of disinterest, to ignore them. "It won't answer. My suggestion is that you give her £10 and be done with her."

"I!" cried Edward.

"I shall provide the blunt. You may give it to her, though, with our best wishes for her future happiness."

Edward's jaw dropped. "You hen-hearted, cowardly cove! You won't face 'er yourself?"

Sebastian's features hardened. "*You* took her case the moment she entered the curricle. You must deal with her."

In a careless tone Edward said, "Well, then, as you're letting me deal with her as I see fit; haply I've already welcomed her as our guest."

"Which was a grave error and shall be immediately redressed." In case there was any remaining doubt as to his meaning, he added in a severe tone, "She *cannot* stay."

"That's your judgment, is it? The best you can do for a helpless female in distress?"

Sebastian scowled. "Even you, cork-brained as you are, should know there is nothing more I can do. We are not an alms-house."

"You can look into her claim. Locate the father. Interview the relation who turned her aside."

"Which may all but prove impossible and/or pointless and/or both!" he returned hotly.

"But it must be tried," insisted Edward, "Before we turn her out!"

Sebastian, looking grim, accompanied his brother to the staircase. He didn't wish to distress Miss Fanshawe further, but he must keep his wits about him. Had she been a young man, or a woman reeking of the street, he would have had no qualms about throwing her out. It wasn't right, was it, that a pretty face and gentility of manners should influence the case? With compressed lips, he resigned himself to facing the muslin threat that, to his mind, was most unwelcome and must be got rid of.

Before the brothers had climbed the top step, Mrs. Arundell met them with a delighted smile. She was a lithe figure though in her late forties, and exuded an air of surprising youthfulness.

"I've seen her," she said, with sparkling eyes.

The brothers exchanged a surprised glance. Sebastian quickly interjected, "Good morning to you, too, Mama, and may I assume you're recovered from the headache?"

"Oh, yes," she said airily. "Binnie gave me a tonic last night. I woke up with the headache, but now 'tis completely gone! Binnie is worth a hundred servants." With hardly a pause, she went on, "I must thank you, Beau, for heeding me for once and finding this girl upon so short notice! I own it is a great relief, for now I may attend the ball this Thursday evening. You know I do not like to go out without a companion, not with my woeful deformity."

"Dearest, tisn't a deformity, for the thousandth time!" Sebastian exclaimed.

"Oh, a defect, then. Ever since I took that horrid fall—you know what it did to my hearing." Her face took on a tragic look as she added, "As if being an *ace of spades* wasn't enough!"

"Mama, there is no shame in widowhood! I've said it before—"

"Oh, but everyone knows my income isn't what it was when your father was alive. In any case, I particularly do not want to miss this ball, not with Her Royal Highness attending. Mornay, too, you know, with his pretty new lady."

But Sebastian's face was a picture of concern. "Mama, a companion? Miss Fanshawe is—"

"Quite young, yes! I see that. Have no fear, Beau! I think, indeed, she is just the thing, I am sure we will suit. And the younger ones aren't nearly as particular as older dames, you know, who don't want to interpret conversations for me, because they cannot *remember* them! Which is the precise reason I need their service!"

Sebastian and Edward exchanged another glance, while she continued, "I was only just ready to decline the invitation—for this is not a public ball, as you know—so imagine my delight when I poked my head into the parlour to remind you, in case you were in that room because I didn't find you in the library or study, to find me a new companion. And there she was! A very genteel looking girl," she said, nodding with satisfaction.

"Did you approach her, Mama?"

"No. She didn't see me." Her features fell into a look of concern. "I'm sure she'll come around when she grows accustomed to it—being a companion, you know."

"Come around?" asked Sebastian, giving Edward a cautious look.

"Well, she looked rather blue-devilled. I believe she must be under some financial duress that forces her to take a situation? It is lowering, to be sure, but I've no doubt that once she is comfortable here, she will come around. I'm not such a drab that I'll keep her under lock and key! We'll go about town just as I used to. Perhaps, if she is truly as genteel as her appearance, and if she comes from good family, I may even introduce her as an acquaintance. Perhaps I can offer a lower wage if I promise this advantage!" Mama was always seeking ways to economize—at Sebastian's urging—though she wasn't usually successful in her attempts.

But at the words, "If she comes from good family," Sebastian made a sound in his throat. She had waved him to silence with a hand, but now he said, "Dearest," turning her so that they could complete their ascension of the stairs. "That is Miss Fanshawe in the parlour. And she is not at all suitable to your purpose."

Mrs. Arundell's face fell. "But whyever not? She is the picture of gentility, and I always like a pretty face. I'm too old to have pretensions for my own appearance—"

"Nonsense!" cried Sebastian.

"Not a whit!" echoed Edward. "Why all the swells say of you—"

"Pray, spare us from what all the swells say!" Sebastian interjected hotly. "'Tis perfectly plain that you, Mama, are still a handsome woman, and let that be the end of it." All this while, the brothers spoke in extra loud tones.

She smiled. "Thank you, my dears. In any case, I do prefer a pleasant face, and I daresay when Miss Fanshawe has got used to her new situation, she will be quite the pleasantest face in this establishment."

"Mama—" began Sebastian, but Edward took his arm.

"She is the perfect candidate to be your companion," finished Edward, giving his brother a look as though he were a scatter brain. "Hush!" he cried, beneath his breath.

"This won't answer!" returned Sebastian, in an equally low tone.

"Boys, boys, you must speak louder! You know my deformity!"

"Defect, mama!" pleaded Edward.

"Affliction," said Sebastian. "For goodness' sake, just call it an affliction," he begged.

"Call it what you like, I loathe it," she replied. "I am quite deaf and you must speak louder."

Nevertheless the brothers continued their conversation in hushed tones. "Don't you see?" hissed Edward. "This answers perfectly! She can stay as Mama's companion, no impropriety, no questions asked, while you look into her claims. If she is an heiress, you'll save her fortune, and in the meantime, Mama will have her social life back."

"I do not like it."

"Don't be a loggerhead!"

"Don't be a bottle-headed gudgeon!" Sebastian replied, in a heated whisper.

"Oh, I see how 'tis," said their mama. "You don't wish me to hear. Well, take me into your Miss Fanshawe and let us have our introduction. I shall see what her terms are."

"Mama," said Edward. "Don't trouble your head. Sebastian will take care of all that."

"Will I?" Sebastian intoned. "Am I the housekeeper now?"

Mrs. Spencer was of course the usual personage to interview and secure new help, but Edward merely shrugged. "You've always been the tactful one in the family. Miss Fanshawe didn't come on a recommendation or with papers. You'll have to secure her; and we'll inform Spence that she needn't take the trouble of any further interviews." Edward's ears had been boxed as a youngster for dubbing the nickname on their housekeeper, but over time it had stuck. He fancied the stout woman employed for two decades as their housekeeper had even grown to enjoy the designation.

All this time Mrs. Arundell had been watching them with perplexity, for her skill at lip reading left much to be desired, and all efforts at it failed her now. "What are you boys disagreeing on?" she asked.

"Nothing of import, Mama," Edward said. "Go and have an early nuncheon, and we'll see to getting your new companion settled." After kissing her hand and bowing her off, they approached the parlour. Sebastian had one more objection. "If Miss Fanshawe is very genteel, she will shrink from hiring herself out."

Edward said, "When her alternative is poverty and the street? I think not!"

Sebastian ground out between tight lips, "You had ought to have brought her to a clergyman!"

"To send her to the poorhouse? I didn't even think of it, if you must know. I heard of her fortune and thought my elder brother, an intelligent and enterprising man—for even I can acknowledge you are considered as decent a buck as anyone—would do the pretties by her. Take care of the tangle."

"That's what solicitors and barristers are for," Sebastian replied.

But Edward turned to look behind him at his brother and said, "She can little afford either! And you are more than capable of untangling this hobble, I've no doubt."

Sebastian eyed him with his usual dispassion. "She will refuse. No properly bred young woman will accept a servant's situation."

"A companion ain't like a servant!" hissed Edward. "All the old cathedrals these days have companions, they don't attend a ball or rout without 'em, and they're as respectable as you please."

"Are you referring to our mother as an old cathedral? She'd swoon if she heard!"

"O' course not," cried Edward. "I only meant that a companion is just the thing, these days. Miss Fanshawe won't be insulted."

"I suspect she will," said Sebastian. "And then I'll send her packing."

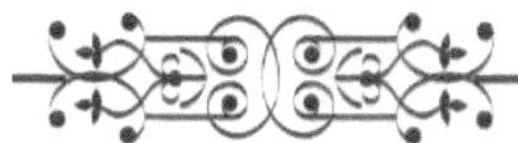

It took only a few minutes for the gentlemen to ascertain that Miss Fanshawe was more than equal to serving as a companion for Mrs. Arundell. It had never occurred to Frannie that she might be of some service to the household, but the thought filled her with relief and gratitude. She wasn't merely a pauper relying on their charity; now she would be of use to them. At the first mention of the situation, she closed her eyes and exclaimed, "Oh, thank God! I can be useful to you!" She looked up with eyes alight. "My prayer was, if you would be a blessing to me in my distress, that I would also bless this family in turn!"

Sebastian seemed at a loss by this reaction, for he hadn't expected anything of the sort. He explained her duties, expecting objections to erupt, but she remained calm, eager to please, nodding sagely. Chief among her responsibilities, she was assured, was to listen to conversations and help their mama understand the gist so that she might participate, answer questions correctly, and hopefully without appearing as deaf as she was. They explained the terrible fall on the stairs six months prior which had resulted in utter unconsciousness and such injury that they feared the worst. Mrs. Arundell had finally come awake and seemed no worse for the episode, save that her hearing suffered lasting harm.

Frannie felt uncommonly suited for the role of companion. Indeed, it filled her heart with oddly familiar warmth, for Mrs. Baxter had been much older than she, and their relationship was almost the same. For most of her life, Mrs. Baxter had been the superior and Frannie, younger, the inferior. Both understood that upon her majority Frannie would assume the superior rank on account of her wealth, but as she was not in possession of that wealth at present, it seemed entirely fitting that she ought to be in subservience to Mrs. Arundell.

By the end of the interview, Sebastian felt almost satisfied with the day's events. Miss Fanshawe's presence, which at first seemed a vexation, did indeed answer the purpose for Mama, and saved the household the trouble of finding a better applicant. Whether or not he would exert himself to study her affairs was another matter. He'd never let a pretty face sway his better judgment. Indeed, he might have succumbed to the charms of countless ineligible young women and found himself ill-married but for a determination never to allow a female to turn his head for frivolous reasons. When he needed a wife, he would of course approach the softer sex in that light, searching for a possible future mate. But he wasn't looking for just a pretty face. If and when he became the next baronet of Bartlett Hall, he would want a sensible, intelligent woman by his side. Until then, he wouldn't think of displacing his mother as mistress of their home. There was no need for it. It was not to be thought of.

But Edward was a concern. Miss Fanshawe, with her ridiculously large, chocolate eyes, was just the sort of female his younger brother would be smitten by. That she was utterly without consequence would mean nothing to the pup. Had she known the name of her supposed noble father, it might have helped her case. But without his identity, the idea of a trust could only appear as a desperate hope, a wish, a longing, a prayer. She'd referred to her parents "tragic marriage," but he doubted there had been a marriage. Miss Fanshawe might be an orphan or her natural father might be alive; but either way, she was a blow-by. Exactly the sort of woman no Arundell could possibly align themselves with. He'd have to keep a weather eye upon Edward, to be sure.

Despite her determination to embrace life as a companion and all it must entail, Frannie was abashed at how much energy was required to make herself heard by her new mistress. She realized now why it was that Mrs. Arundell had a difficult time keeping a companion. Because of this, she was not enraptured later that day when the lady instructed that she must take meals with the family. She would almost have preferred to be consigned to the servants' hall, shrinking at the thought of raising her voice at table. Too, she was conscious of her new status. Ladies' companions weren't always welcome at upper class tables. What if either of the Arundell men did not think her worthy of sitting at table with them?

She took courage when the younger Mr. Arundell gave her a bracing smile as she settled in her seat. She hardly glanced at Sebastian, for his stern countenance could easily unsettle her, but one chance peek made her stare. She had never seen Sebastian without his spectacles before. His entire demeanor underwent a transformation. The studious looking bookworm was a Byron! Mama called such men 'handsome devils' Frannie thought, though she saw nothing devilish about Sebastian. A strong nose and noble brow revealed keen, clear eyes that made you want to hold their attention just to look into their depths. He caught her startled gaze and she looked away, but with a sudden flutter in her stomach. What a handsome gentleman! Amazing how she had missed it, earlier.

A rich, three course meal followed, replete with lively conversation among the Arundells, to Frannie's surprise. She and Mrs. Baxter had been companionable dinner partners, but meals were mostly quiet. Here, it was quite the opposite. But both men were forced to speak every bit as loudly to their mama as she, however, so that any discomfort on that head soon dissipated.

Mrs. Arundell's favorite topic was town news, who was getting married, who had been declared a bankrupt, or who was moving into the apartments recently vacated by the French Ambassador. Edward's aim seemed to be to say as little as possible about his pursuits in the metropolis, while Sebastian plied him with questions about whether he'd been active at gaming dens, or laying bets at cock fights, or getting into fisticuff matches. About this last low pursuit he went on for some time, admonishing his brother that, if he wished seriously to comport himself as a gentleman, he must assiduously avoid street brawls. "Shows of physical strength are required only by the weak to prove themselves," he said. "Good men hunt, fish, or fence for a contest, but physical matches are repugnant to them." With a glimpse toward his mama and Frannie he added, "And even more so to ladies."

"I daresay you've forgot I'm studied in pugilism," Edward replied hotly.

"Keep your boxing to Gentleman Jim's establishment along with other young sprigs in training, and you'll do well. But I'll not hear of another street brawl. Striking a man for a provocation is the meanest sort of response I daresay a gentleman can display."

Frannie surmised that apparently Edward had been guilty of participating in a fight that had not occurred within the bastion of Gentleman Jim's, that most famous of fisticuff instructors. Even she had read snippets about the famous boxer and his rooms on Bond Street, where he taught upper class males his art. Edward looked with supreme disinterest at his brother, as if further objections were not worth the effort. Sebastian finished his admonishments with a warning that Edward not fall into the duns again.

"I little see how I shall avoid *that*," Edward replied, "if you withhold the blunt!"

"Dearest," said their mama to her elder son, "Are you indeed allowing dear Edward's pockets to be turned out? That looks shabby for an Arundell, my dear."

"He has only himself to thank," Sebastian returned. "I've warned him more times than I care to recall, not to conscript my carriage to carry out his cork-brained schemes without my consent."

"If I hadn't borrowed your curricle, Mama would lack a companion, for Miss Fanshawe wouldn't be here!"

"What was that?" asked the mama. "About Miss Fanshawe?"

"*I* brought her!" cried Edward gloatingly. "Not Sebastian. And for this, he persecutes me!" Sebastian eyed his brother with cool disdain. He wasn't about to attempt an explanation of the whole situation to their mama, and only nodded, with a congratulatory smirk at Edward when Mrs. Arundell went into a rapture of his defense, exclaiming that Sebastian was too hard on him and must not exact the slightest punishment, for she was *that* grateful to have Miss Fanshawe.

Frannie sat guiltily by, blushing, and would not meet Sebastian's eyes. But he declared he would come to a compromise with Edward, a settlement that seemed to satisfy Mrs. Arundell. Conversation then turned to the matter of a coming ball on Thursday evening.

"Since I will now accept the invitation, Beau, because I have a companion to help me,"—she   stopped and smiled benignly upon Frannie—"you will, of course, accompany me."

Sebastian glanced at Frannie, who hurriedly looked away. She'd been admiring him furtively, still rather in awe of the high good looks that a simple pair of spectacles hid so well. His manner of dress was not meticulously fashionable like Edward's, but he exuded a far greater air of consequence and masculine presence, surprising for one she at first took for a bookish scholar.

He cleared his throat, returning his attention to his mother. "This reminds me. I've had a letter from Sir Hugo." He paused, giving his mama the opportunity to exclaim her utter astonishment that Sir Hugo had sent a communiqué of any sort to his heir, but she merely regarded him with curious expectation. Casting a keen look her way, he said, "He has accepted the invitation to that ball; he will shortly arrive in town; and begs the honour of giving *you* his escort."

Now Mrs. Arundell reacted as expected. Looking fairly amazed she cried, "Sir Hugo in London? What is that man about? He never comes to town!"

"The passing of his father must have something to do with it," offered Sebastian. "Perhaps Sir Malcolm required his presence until now; he would not be the first son to suffer an overbearing sire. Now that he's the baronet of Bartlett Hall, and his own man—."

"Sir Malcolm was overbearing, indeed; and crotchety, to be sure, or we might be more familiar with Bartlett Hall. He was more severe upon poor Hugo, his eldest, than your father; but he never cared a fig to know you boys. I daresay he thought of us as poor relations—"

"Mama! We are nothing of the sort!" replied Sebastian.

"No, of course not; but I never felt the slightest compulsion to encourage a better understanding between our families for I did not wish to subject you to his temperamental ways." She gave Sebastian a wide-eyed look. "It is all very well if Sir Hugo now wishes to become part of society. But to *presume* that I have not already accepted an escort! He is quite disagreeable in it!"

"He no doubt assumed what is most often true: that *I* would escort you. And he knows I should willingly allow him the honour in my place as he is rightly entitled to it, Mama. He is my elder in the family, my superior, not to mention, your cousin-in-law."

"How could he possibly know that *you* would accompany me!" she said scornfully.

Sebastian gave a little smile. "I am sure he reads the society columns."

But she shook her head dismissively. "In any case, really, Beau, you know better than to ask."

Sebastian placed his fork down and gave his mother a piercing look. "I am his heir; he is my uncle."

"He isn't your uncle really; he is your father's cousin, which makes him your first cousin once removed."

"True," said Sebastian, "But have we not always referred to him as my uncle?"

"Because he is older, dearest. And who wants to keep saying *your cousin once removed*?"

"There is no need for that," Sebastian said with a little smile, "but we are no children here, and for now on, I shall call him my cousin, and leave it at that."

"Call him whatever you like," his mama replied, waving a hand at him. "The important thing is, there are no other male heirs beside you and Edward."

Sebastian said, "Precisely, and for which case if he comes to town, by rights we ought to offer him hospitality. Isn't it time you let bygones be bygones—whatever it is that makes you refuse to see him? With Sir Malcolm gone, there is one less ogre for you to fear. In my past correspondence with Sir Hugo, he has always seemed very gentlemanlike and proper." He paused and gave her a penetrating look. "We had ought to be on good terms with the man who leaves his title and estate to me."

"He has no choice!" replied his mama, delicately dabbing her mouth with a cloth.

She took a sip from her glass, but put it down decisively, her eyes widened. "So *that* is why he wrote to you!"

Sebastian's brows rose. "You knew?"

"Binnie saw the letter and told me of it," she explained, while moving aside just enough to allow a footman to give her a serving of cauliflower in sauce. "I daresay I thought it would be some such fiddle faddle."

Sebastian rubbed his chin, as though deliberating on what to reveal. "Actually, Mama, the biggest surprise in Sir Hugo's letter is that he wished to advise me of his intention to find a wife."

Mrs. Arundell froze. Her eyes widened. Quickly she put her fork down and sat there blinking.

"Have no fear, dearest," Sebastian hurried to say. "If he sires an heir and disinherits me, we shall do well enough with my investments. We'd not suffer the slightest lowering in our current lifestyle, and you, I suppose, can grow accustomed to your son *not* being next in line to inherit. There is nothing you cannot countenance in it." Seeing her stricken face he added, "Perhaps I needn't have mentioned it. Perchance it may come to nothing."

"But—Hugo has ever been utterly *averse* to marriage, which I always thought nonsensical for a titled gentleman. But to change his mind now! So *that* is why he comes! He wishes to find a wife from the best circles, does he?" She stabbed her fork into a mound of boiled turnip. "Who would *wish* to marry that old clodpate!" Then, looking up as struck she said, "May I read his letter? I must hear his tone, the manner of his speech. I must determine if he is in earnest or if he seeks merely to vex me—"

"To vex *you*?" asked Sebastian. "I am sure my cousin has no wish to marry simply to vex you, dearest. 'Tis only natural a man wants an heir from his own loins, I daresay."

But Mrs. Arundell's face scrunched in distaste. "You don't know him as I do. He wishes to marry! Either his estate is out at the heels and he needs a wealthy bride, or 'tis *only* to vex me, I assure you!"

"If anyone has reason to be vexed, it is I; but I believe I can say with equal parts equanimity and honesty, that I wish him well. I wish him success. The few times I have met and spoken with my cousin—and I will continue to call him that, if it's all the same to you—I have found him nothing but amiable and good-natured. I never understood why you refused invitations from Bartlett Hall and denied us the society of our relations for most all our lives."

Mrs. Arundell hadn't heard this very well and looked to Frannie. She startled to attention, but then echoed loudly, "Mr. Arundell is *not* vexed by Sir Hugo, ma'am!"

"Yes, I caught that much," the lady said, nodding. "Refer to him as Beau for me, Frannie. That's what I call him, so you must also."

Frannie blushed, keeping her eyes on her plate.

"What else did he say?"

Frannie took a deep breath and replied with admirable volume, "He doesn't understand the difficulty between you and Sir—"

"Pray, Miss Fanshawe, do not trouble yourself," Sebastian interrupted. "My mother and I have trod this path before. She refuses to disclose the cause of their ancient argument. But more to the point, there is one other reason for his writing me, which I will inform her of." He turned to his mama and said vigorously, "Sir Hugo invites us to his home for the Christmas holidays; and I mean to accept!"

"For Christmas? So we may admire his new, simpering wife?" she said acidly.

"He hasn't found a wife yet, Mama. He wrote only to warn me that he is on the hunt." Sebastian could hardly repress a grin. "It does seem irregular for him to warn us."

Edward said, "You smile. Don't you feel the least sorry for it? To be disinherited when all your life you've been set up as the next baronet of Bartlett Hall after Sir Hugo? I daresay it disappoints *me*, and I'm not as close to it as you are."

"He's not married *yet*," replied Sebastian. "And baronetcies bring headaches and obligations as well as honours." But he returned his attention to his mother. "I shall reply by special messenger that you do not require his escort for Thursday night's ball; and that we will be happy to descend upon Bartlett Hall for the Christmas holidays."

"Wait, wait, sir!" cried his mama, as color rushed to her face. "I have not decided about Christmas! I must think on it."

Sebastian said, leaning forward gently, but speaking slowly so she might have the benefit of reading his lips, "As the head of the family, I have made the decision. I've supported your ancient grudge far too long by indulging your dislike of him; but I have no such aversion to the man; he is my elder relation. We will go, Mama."

Mrs. Arundell looked dejected. She swallowed. "If he has a new wife, I shall *not* go, no, by no means. You cannot force me, Beau."

Sebastian's mouth twisted, stifling a grin. "Mama, if I did not know better, I should say you were jealous!"

Edward too regarded his mother with a face that looked mildly embarrassed. "Indeed, Mama," he said gently—and thereby went wholly unheard.

Frannie shifted in her seat, feeling as though she were eavesdropping on private family affairs. She wished she could excuse herself. But if Mrs. Arundell didn't send her from the room, she was not at liberty to take leave. She looked imploringly at Sebastian.

Receptive green-grey eyes surveyed her and seemed to instantly comprehend her discomfort. "You must excuse our conversation, Miss Fanshawe. I'm afraid that as Mama's companion, you are fated to be included in all the familial, eh, *niceties,* otherwise known as dirt."

The matriarch apparently heard that. "Do not exaggerate, Beau! You'll give the poor girl frights! We aren't ogres; and as for being jealous, don't be absurd! I am not in the least jealous except on your account, for you are the rightful heir to the title!"

"Only if Sir Hugo has no son of his own, dearest!"

Mrs. Arundell pursed her lips, and nodding at Frannie to follow, rose from the table. The men instantly came to their feet and bowed. But their mother stopped, her head turned in thought. She leveled a defiant stare upon Sebastian. "You may reply to his letter," she said imperiously, her small nose in the air, "with the information that I will *accept* Sir Hugo's escort!"

While her sons stared in amazement, she turned on her heel and took a step but then turned back and added forcefully, "But I will not put him up, for there are inns and posting houses all over London where he may stay, or he can let rooms anywhere he likes!"

"Very *good*, Mama," said Sebastian approvingly and with no small surprise. He might have wished to open their home, but he knew a concession when he saw it and accepted it graciously. "I may count myself excused then, from the ball?"

"I suppose you may," she said, "though everyone shall ask why you aren't in attendance. You are talked of as almost a recluse, Beau." She paused, frowning. "Do you not care to see the princess?"

He gave her a patient look. "I am not averse to it, but I had my fill of balls during the season. Why there should be one now, when all the best families are at their country estates, I cannot fathom."

"Word was put out long ago," she returned. "Many of those 'best families' have harkened back to town for this event. There may be some special announcement from Her Royal Highness, I daresay."

She glanced at Frannie, whose face was frozen in amazement. Imagine it, passing up a chance to meet Princess Charlotte! Frannie had often daydreamed of meeting the Regent's daughter, who seemed to genuinely care for her subjects. She'd never known anyone who could enjoy that opportunity and now this family, the Arundells, her only benefactors in the world, had the social standing to meet her—and Sebastian wasn't interested!

Seeing Frannie's countenance, Mrs. Arundell cried, "Oh, dear, I have it! You must come, Beau, and take Frannie upon your arm. We can style her a long-lost cousin or some such thing."

Frannie's heart swelled at the thought, both of meeting the princess *and* of being upon Mr. Arundell's arm! But Sebastian's countenance darkened. "Mama, that is quite impossible. Be sure there will be some who go home and search Debrett's, or otherwise discover the falsehood. The Arundell name has never been associated with a scandal, and I wish it to remain so." Frannie's hope plummeted as quickly as it had risen. Shame brought a blush to her features. Sebastian feared her dubious background would provide fodder for gossips, occasion scandal-broth gatherings to the detriment of the family name.

Mrs. Arundell gave him quite the oddest look

"What, do you know of a scandal?" he asked, though in a tone that made his disbelief evident.

She merely said in a fallen voice, "If I have not Frannie, then I may not accept Sir Hugo's escort. For he will discover my deformity."

"*Defect*, Mama!" Sebastian and Edward cried together.

"I have a notion about that," ventured Frannie, getting everyone's instant attention. She said the words with a sinking heart, for her only means of subsistence and best hope was to stay on with the Arundells. If Mrs. Arundell's hearing defect was redressed, she would be out of a situation. But her heart refused to remain silent. The poor woman was clearly tormented by the problem. Frannie knew of a solution and must speak. She looked at Sebastian. "If I may have use of a carriage to call upon Mrs. Baxter's brother—he resides in the warehouse district—I believe he has an instrument that will help your mother's affliction." With all eyes still upon her, Frannie felt a blush steal across her cheeks.

Mrs. Arundell said, "Thank you, Frannie dear, but I could never use that monstrous hearing trumpet, such as the one Earl Brent goes about with. I have a horror of such a device!"

Frannie said, "No, ma'am, the one I have in mind is quite small."

"You know of a small instrument that can help a hearing defect?" Sebastian inquired.

She nodded. "I do, sir. I have seen it work for someone who is similarly afflicted with the impairment. Mrs. Baxter's brother, one Mr. Withers, is something of an inventor, sir. If he is still making the devices, your mama can safely keep her engagement...." In a low tone, she added, "without me."

Sebastian eyed her keenly, but Edward cried, "Impairment! I dare say, that answers better than *defect*! We must only call it only an impairment, Mama!"

But Sebastian's attention was still on Frannie. "You know where to find Mr. Withers?"

She nodded. "I know the street name."

He surveyed her with cautious optimism. "Very well. I think we must acquire this marvel."

"Mama," put in Edward, "you could allow *me* the honour of taking you to the ball. I can translate conversation for you. Sebastian cares nothing for society, for it always welcomes him. He can rub shoulders with anyone he likes, all the *ton*, any blue blood, whilst I am completely ignored and overlooked. A younger son must have *some* right to society, and if you will go upon my arm it will raise my consequence, I daresay."

"You have no consequence," said Sebastian, with an arched brow, "None to begin with, and you will not prevent my mother from extending this olive leaf to Sir Hugo. It hasn't come betimes!"

Frannie's brows rose. The lack of accord between the brothers surprised her, though she had no experience of siblings other than in the families of her acquaintance from the village where she'd grown up.

Mrs. Arundell smiled fondly at Edward. "Do not take it to heart, dear. Your brother is to inherit a baronetcy. He is of course good *ton* on that account." All this while the four adults had been standing at the table, ever since Mrs. Arundell had risen to leave. She now turned once more to go but stopped and said to Frannie, "In the morning, Beau will take you to town." To Sebastian's knit brows, she added, "Your curricle is open, my love; there's no need for a chaperon. And if Miss Fanshawe knows of anything that can ameliorate this dreadful deformity"— Sebastian ground his teeth—"then we must have it!" she finished, smiling upon first Frannie and then her son.

"I could take her," muttered Edward, giving his brother a look of some resentment.

"I wouldn't dream of putting Miss Fanshawe's life in such danger as that," returned Sebastian instantly. Frannie's heart went out for the younger brother, but she said nothing. It was not her place; and she could not dislike the thought of Mr. Sebastian Arundell accompanying her.

Read the rest of *Miss Fanshawe's Fortune.*
Available September 2020
online or at a bookstore near you!

ABOUT THE AUTHOR

Linore Rose Burkard is a serious watcher of period films, a Janeite, and hopeless romantic. An award winning author best known for Inspirational Regency Romance, her first book (*Before the Season Ends*) opened the genre for the CBA. Besides historical romance, Linore writes contemporary suspense (The Pulse Effex Series, as L.R. Burkard), contemporary romance, and romantic short stories. Linore has a *magna cum laude* English Lit. degree from CUNY which she earned while taking herself far too seriously. She now resides in Ohio with her husband and family, where she turns her youthful angst into character or humor-driven plots.

Other Historical Romance Novels
by Linore Rose Burkard

Before the Season Ends

Heartwarming, Inspirational, Romantic!

"A Tasty Confection"
Publishers Weekly

Miss Ariana Forsythe is sent to her wealthy aunt's London townhouse and thrust into the world of the upper crust. Trouble finds her with an instant enemy in Lady Covington, an aging beauty. Ariana must team up with the Paragon, the darkly handsome and powerful Phillip Mornay, to quench the scandal. She can trust God's hand in her life, but can she resist Mr. Mornay's increasing claim on her heart? When she finds herself betrothed to him, she is faced with a terrible choice-- and she must make it soon, before the season ends!

Available online and wherever books are sold

The House in Grosvenor Square

Sequel to *Before the Season Ends*

Award-winning heartwarming romance with rollicking humor!

With only two weeks until Ariana Forsythe is to marry the Paragon, Phillip Mornay, what can possibly go wrong? *Everything!*

From a disgruntled aristocrat seeking revenge to an irate servant, Ariana encounters one threat after another. Mr. Mornay is determined to protect his irrepressible adventuress, even if it means keeping her under lock and key! Readers will hold onto their bonnets while enjoying Ariana's breathtakingly convoluted march to the altar.

Available online and wherever books are sold

The Country House Courtship

Ariana's sister Beatrice is ready for a romance of her own!

More of the characters you love from previous books with a new romance!

What are wealthy sisters for, if not to help younger sisters marry well?

The Mornays are happily embedded in domestic life at their elegant country estate when Ariana's sister Beatrice visits. She soon despairs of ever getting her own come-out into society. When two eligible men appear on the scene, she thinks one of them is the answer to all her hopes--but is he? Two handsome gentlemen, one dark secret, one pretty girl and a huge country estate--can a country house courtship like no other be far behind?

Available online and wherever books are sold

FREE OFFER!

Three French Hens:
A Romance Novella of England during
The French Revolution

Young Mademoiselle Christine D'Ornay and her family are exiles in England, seeking safety from the Revolution and *Madame La Guillotine.* At her first Assembly ball, Christine meets the dashing and elegant Lord Russell. But the lives of French aristocrats are cheap in an age of betrayal, and Jacobites are on the prowl. Can Christine and her family trust this new friend? Or is Lord Russell the enemy they fear most?

Receive this novella FREE when you sign up for Linore's Newsletter at
https://www.LinoreBurkard.com

A Short Glossary of Regency Terms

A

abigail: a lady's maid; any female maid (servant).
Ex. "I see you've hired a new abigail."

ape leader: an old maid; based on a strange myth that single women who never bore children would end up leading apes in hell.

ague: (Pronounced ah-gyoo) Originally, malaria and the chills that went with it. Later, any respiratory infection such as a cold, fever or chills.

assembly, assemblies: Large gatherings held in the evening for gentry or the aristocracy, usually including a ball and supper. Almack's in London was the ultimate Assembly in the early part of the 19th century. A handful of high-standing society hostesses had autocratic power of attendance as they alone could issue the highly prized vouchers, or tickets. . Competition to get in was fierce. The Duke of Welling-ton was once famously turned away—for being late.

B

ball: A large dance requiring full dress. Refreshments were available, and sometimes a supper. Public balls required tickets; private ones, an invitation.

Banbury tale: A story with no basis in fact; A rumour; Nonsense.

banns: Banns of marriage were a public announcement in a parish church that two people intended to get married. They had to be read three consecutive weeks in a row, and in the home church of both parties. After each reading, (and this was their purpose) the audience was asked to give knowledge of any legal impediment to the marriage. If there was none, after three weeks, the couple were legally able to wed. To bypass the banns, a couple could try to get a marriage license instead. Without banns or a license, the marriage would be illegal. (null)

beau monde, the: The aristocracy and the rich upper class. The fashionable elite. In practice, anyone accepted into their circle, ie., a celebrity or an "original.".

blunt: (slang) Cash; ready money.

C

Carlton House: Given to the Prince of Wales by George III upon reaching his majority, Carlton House was in a state of disrepair (for a royal, at any rate). The house consequently underwent enormous alterations and changes, and was the London palace for the Regent. He spent a great deal of time there but eventually came to favour the palace at Brighton—an even larger extravagance. The Brighton "Pavilion" is today a museum, but Carlton House, unfortunately, no longer exists.

chamber: A private room in a house, such as a bedroom, as opposed to the parlour or dining room.

chaperon: The servant, mother, or married female relative or family friend who supervised eligible young girls in public.

chemise: A woman's long undergarment which served as a slip beneath her gown. Also, a nightdress. (Previously, the chemise was called a 'shift'.)

chintz: Patterned cloth, usually floral, with a pleasant satiny "shine" for texture.

chit: A young girl.

clubs: The great refuge of the middle and upper-class man in 18th and 19th century London. Originating as coffeehouses in the 17th century, clubs became more exclusive, acquiring prime real estate on Pall Mall and St. James's Street. Membership was often by invitation only. Among the more prominent were Boodle's, White's and Brooke's. Crockford's began to dominate in the very late Regency.

consumption: Pulmonary tuberculosis (TB)

corset: A precursor of the modern bra, usually meant to constrict the waist to a fashionable measurement, as well

as support the high bust required for a Regency gown.
It consisted of two parts, re-
inforced with whalebone that
got hooked together in front
and then laced up in the back.
The garment could also be
referred to as 'the stays.'

countess: The wife of an
earl in England. When
'shires' were changed to
'counties,' an earl retained
the Norman title of earl; his
wife, however, became a
countess.

cravat: (pronounced as kruh-
vaht, with the accent on the
second syllable). A loose
cloth that was tied around the
neck in a bow. Throughout
the Regency, a fashionable
gentleman might labour
much over this one detail of
his appearance, hoping to
achieve a number of different, much-coveted effects.

curricle: Two-wheeled carriage that was popular in the
early 1800s. It was pulled by
two horses, and deemed rather sporty by the younger
set.

curtsey: The acceptable
mode of greeting or showing
respect by a female. By mid-
century the curtsey was less
in evidence except for social
inferiors like maids to their
betters, or by any woman
presented at court.

cut: An effective means of
social discouragement that
involved pretending not to
know or see a person who
was trying to be acknowl-
edged. A woman might use
this technique to discourage
unwelcome attentions from a
gentleman; but many others
'cut' people, too. Getting the
'cut direct' from a social superior was vastly humiliating.

D

Debrett's: A published
guide to the peerage, often
called simply, "the Society
Book."

dowager: The name given to
a widow of rank. Ie., if you
were a duchess and your husband died, and your oldest
son was married, his wife
would become the duchess,
and you would be dowager
duchess.

draper (linen draper): Merchant who sold cloth.

drawing room: A formal
parlour used in polite society
to receive visitors who came
to pay calls during the afternoon.

F

first floor: The second floor in the US. The English called the floor level on which one entered from the street the "ground floor." Entertaining was never done on the ground floor.

foolscap: A paper of certain dimensions, some varieties of which originally bore a watermark of a fool's cap and bells.

footman: A liveried male servant beneath the butler but above the boy or page. He had many duties ranging from errands to lamp-trimming to waiting table, or accompanying the lady of the house to carry packages when she shopped, or to deliver calling cards when making calls.

fortnight: Two weeks.

fustian!: "Nonsense!" "Don't be absurd!"

G

gaming: Gambling. Nothing to do with 'game' in the sense of hunting, or innocent playing of games.

gig: A one-horse carriage. Light, two-wheeled, and popular in the early century.

groom: The servant who looked after the horses.

Grosvenor Square: (pronounced "Grove-nuh") A part of Mayfair, considered the most fashionable square in London. Mr. Mornay's town house is in the Square.

H

hack: A hack was a general purpose riding horse, but the term might also refer to a "Hackney Coach" which was a coach-for-hire like a taxi-cab today.

have a pet: a tirade; a burst of temper .(to "freak out" in today's lingo.)

L

Ladies' Mile: A (horseback) riding road in Hyde Park for women.

lady's maid: The servant who cared for her mistress's wardrobe and grooming. A French lady's maid was preferred, and she was particularly valued if she could do hair in all the fashionable styles. A lady's maid was an "upper servant," and could not be fired by the housekeeper; she might also be better educated than the lower servants.

lorgnette: Used by ladies, the lorgnette was eyeglasses (or a monocle), held to the eyes with a long handle, or could be worn on a chain around the neck. The monocle used by a man was called a "quizzing glass."

laudanum: A mixture of opium in a solution of alcohol, it was used for pain relief and as an anesthetic.

livery: A distinctive uniform worn by the male servants in a household. No two liveries, ideally, were exactly alike. Knowing the colour of the livery of someone could enable you to spot their carriage in a crowd. The uniform itself was an old-fashioned style, including such things as a frock coat, knee breeches, powdered wigs, and a waistcoat.

M

ma*ma*: Always pronounced by the upper class with the accent on the second syllable.

Mayfair: The ritziest residential area of London, in the West End, and only about a half mile square in size.

mews, the: Any lane or open area where a group of stables was situated. The townhouses of the rich often had a mews behind them, or close by, where they kept their horses and equipages when not in use.

modiste: (French) seamstress.

muslin: One of the finest cottons, muslin was semi-transparent and very popular for gowns; (beneath which a chemise would be worn).

O

on-dit: (French; literally, "It is said.") During the Regency it was slang for a bit of gossip.

P

Pall Mall: A fancy street in the West End of London, notable for housing some of the most fashionable men'sclubs. Carlton House faced Pall Mall.

pantaloons: Tight-fitting pants that were worn, beginning in the early 1800s, and which pushed breeches out of fashion except for formal occasions. They had a "stirrup" at the bottom to keep them in place.

parlour: The formal or best room in a modest home. Grand houses often had more than one; a "first" or "best," and a "second parlour."

peer: A nobleman, that is, a titled gentleman with the rank of either duke, marquis, (mar-kwiss), viscount (vy-count) or baron. The titles were hereditary, and the owners were entitled to a seat in the House of Lords.

pelisse: An outdoor garment for women, reaching to the ankle or mid-calf; and often hooded.

pianoforte: The piano. Genteel young women were practically required to learn the instrument.

pin money: A colloquialism for a woman's spending money. The allowance agreed upon in her marriage settlement, to be used on small household or personal (vanity) items.

R

regent: A person who reigns on behalf of a monarch who is incapable of filling the requirements of the crown. When George III's relapse of porphyria (most scholars agree this was his malady) rendered him incapable of meeting his duties, his son, the Prince of Wales, became the Prince Regent. The actual regency lasted from 1811-1820.

reticule: A fabric bag, gathered at the top and held by a ribbon or strap; a lady's purse. Reticules became necessary when the thin muslin dresses of the day made it impossible to carry any personal effects in a pocket without it seeming bulky or unsightly. The earliest reticules (apparently called 'ridicules,' as it seemed ridiculous to carry one's valuables outside of one's clothing) were, in effect, outside pockets.

rubber: In games like whist, a rubber was a set of three or more games. To win the rubber, one had to win two out of three or three out of five.

S

season: The London social season, in which the fashionable elite descended upon the city in droves. It coincided, not unnaturally, with the sitting of Parliament, though the height of the season was only March through June.

smelling salts (smelling bottle): A small vial filled with a compound that usually contained ammonia, to be used in case of fainting.

spencer: For women, a short jacket that reached only to the high "empire" waist. For men, an overcoat without tails, also on the short side.

squire: 19th century term of courtesy (like "esquire") for a member of the landed gentry.

T

tendre: (French adj. *soft, tender;*) Regency slang for "a soft spot"; an attraction to.

***ton,* the:** (pronounced 'tawn') High society; the elite; the "in" crowd; Those of rank, with royalty at the top. To be "good ton" meant acceptance with the upper crust, and opened most any door in fashionable society. Occasionally, those without fortune or pedigree could enter the *ton*—if they were an Original, for instance, having something either sensational or highly attractive about their person or reputation; or could amuse or entertain the rich to a high degree.

V

valet: The "gentleman's gentle- man." The male equivalent of a lady's maid, his job was to keep the wardrobe in good repair and order, help dressing his master, stand behind him at dinner if required, and accompany him on his travels.

Vauxhall: A famous pleasure garden, across the Thames from London, especially popular in the Georgian era.

W

wainscoting: Wainscot was a fancy, imported oak. The term 'wainscoting' came to mean any wooden panels that lined generally the top or bottom half of the walls in a room.

waistcoat: Vest.

www.ingramcontent.com/pod-product-compliance
Lightning Source LLC
Chambersburg PA
CBHW051140190726

48290CB00006B/1932